RAVE REVIEWS FOR
A DEEPER HUNGER!

"An intense and compelling tale of lovers whose undying devotion has been forbidden and doomed throughout countless centuries. *A Deeper Hunger* is a marvelous read!"

—*Romantic Times*

"*A Deeper Hunger* sweeps the reader into a sensual, deeply exotic world of eternal passion. Powerfully poignant...definitely an auspicious debut for Sabine Kells."

—Kathleen Morgan, author of *Firestar*

"All the drama, mysticism, and haunting poignancy of a writer entering Rice world. Every bite of *A Deeper Hunger* definitely satisfies those deep cravings for a fantastic but different love story."

—*Affaire de Coeur*

D0816325

A LOVE BEYOND TIME

"Be still, Cailie."

Alexander's arms came around her gently, drawing her into the harbor of his embrace. She held still for endless, raw heartbeats, gathering strength from him, then pushed away.

"No. I...I can't...you have to...." She sucked in a ragged breath, steeled herself to meet his gaze. "Please, go. Now."

"Don't talk, Cailie," he whispered against her mouth. "Not of time, nor of parting."

His black eyes half lidded, he kissed her cheek, her forehead and eyes, traced the line of her throat with liquid fire. "This night is for you. It is forever. There will be no tomorrow."

His husky words struck her to the core, beating with cruel irony at what little strength remained. She clung to him, because alone she would have fallen.

With a low sound, Alec swept her up into his arms and carried her out onto the balcony, into the warm night and soft moonlight.

A DEEPER HUNGER

SABINE KELLS

LEISURE BOOKS   NEW YORK CITY

A LEISURE BOOK®

March 1994

Published by

Dorchester Publishing Co., Inc.
276 Fifth Avenue
New York, NY 10001

Printed in the United States of America.

To Hermi, for her constant support and understanding and generosity, for putting up with the quirks and unpredictable working hours of a writer, for the years of freedom and the gift of a home—my love, always. I couldn't have done this without you.

To Günter, who let me find my way into the wonderful worlds of science fiction and fantasy at a very young age, but probably never guessed I'd end up in front of a computer rather than inside a cockpit—I wish you could have seen this. But then, perhaps, you can.

To Margaret, for her encouragement and patience, her smile, and all those years of wild, high-bounce aerobics classes; to Charlotte, who can't read this, but will keep it all the same; to Oskar and Minchen, for their long-distance Spenden; and to the local ladies of the RWA—you know who you are. Thank you all!

A Deeper Hunger

Prologue

The darkness of his grave was impenetrable. Yet Tresand was at home in the silent, all-encompassing night. He had lived in darkness forever and he did not need the light now to know that he was dying.

Even in his dreamlike, deathlike state, he was aware of the truth. His injuries had been too severe; after all this time, he was at last fated to die. Trapped in an avalanche of cold, hard rock, he knew immortality was his no longer. Now it was only a matter of time . . .

Yet time had no meaning. It flowed, as did the faint currents he felt in the stone, slowed as did the blood in his broken body . . . until his cocoon was ruptured from a violent tremor of the ground.

He was aware of the change, became increasingly aware of it as the veils of deathlike sleep scattered from his mind, freeing the unrelenting will to survive . . . awakening the racking agony of hunger.

The sharp rocks of his grave had shifted in several places, allowing wan shadows of a dying day to soften the ebony cloak of darkness. Tresand blinked as tears flooded eyes that had seen no light for . . . How long? Years? Decades? Centuries, or more?

He did not know. Nor did he care. *He was alive.* That was all that mattered. He had survived the rock slide meant to kill him so long ago, had survived the imprisonment in cold, dead stone.

Yet he was weak almost to starvation, and with the new fissure in the stone, easy prey to those who would hunt him.

Tresand let the hunger of his blood flood through him in a wave of raw agony, channeling it into a summons stronger than the pull of the moon on the restless sea.

It was a call that would be answered. And later, when he was stronger, he would break free of this prison. He would heal. And he would walk the Earth once again, undaunted, untouchable, immortal.

Before the darkness of night was complete, the bulk of his grave shifted again in another, more violent tremor. Tresand's world spun crazily as he tumbled alongside the rocks. And for one hellish moment he relived that stormy day, the day he'd been buried alive under a mountain of stone. . . .

Then the movement ceased. Reaching out with senses sluggish from disuse, Tresand felt first and foremost the crushing weight on his legs, yet another injury to add to the cacophony of pain in his body. But nearly as overwhelming was the gradual realization that he lay in shadowed twilight under an open sky, on lush, green grass. He could feel the dark, rich soil beneath his body, could feel the life all around him, trees and insects and little animals scurrying through the thickening darkness.

His triumphant cry was no more than a voiceless breath, yet that mattered not at all. He gloried in the sight of shadowed pine branches swaying lazily above him, the touch of the cool evening breeze, the multitude of earthy, verdant scents drifting on the mountain air; exulted in the gentle welcome of the pale, silvery orb hovering above the wall of trees surrounding the small clearing. Not only had he been freed, he'd been spared the fire of the sun.

With the strength of a man given a reprieve from death, Tresand sent out his call once more. Then he was spent, and his eyes closed. Now he need only wait. The creatures of the forest would respond, for this was not the first time that he lay near death from injury and starvation, and it might not be the last.

Hunger raced through him with devastating violence, wringing a moan from a throat long silent. The pain of it was worse than that of his broken, battered body, flaying his very soul to the core. But acceptance of death was only a faint memory now, lost in the passage of time.

Tresand smiled grimly, ignoring the sharp protest of the torn flesh of his cheek, almost reveling in the pain. No mortal could have survived this. But he was stronger than any mortal. He would heal quickly, once his hunger was met.

He glanced around, anticipating the response to his summons. Soon, soon . . . He could feel one creature already, a still elusive presence in his mind, like the memory of a sunbeam warming the skin on a winter's day. Only a short while now, infinitesimal compared to his deathly sleep . . .

He did not mark the passage of time; there was little point in it. The clamor of pain in his body distracted him, made him shift weakly in a futile effort to assuage it. Then his physical discomfort became utterly insignificant, forgotten in an instant, as all his senses came alive, focusing on the presence approaching from the forest.

There was the faint rustle of branches, of leaves; a hesitation, only momentary, then renewed steps, growing closer . . . A thump, as of something falling on the ground . . . and suddenly quickening motion, coming toward him, the heat and aura of the living enveloping him, silent breaths and surging blood, so very close, within his reach, only a single step away.

14

A Deeper Hunger

Hunger exploded through him with shattering force. His eyes snapped open, filled with the snaring, compelling power of the Blood, seeing all too clearly in the full darkness of night. And yet, his eyes had deceived him. He was dreaming, surely, was perhaps dying after all, because his kind never dreamed.

He was staring not into the mild eyes of a doe or some other creature of the wild bound to answer his call, but into those of a young woman, kneeling by his side as though in prayer. Her braided dark hair was disheveled and adorned with pieces of tree moss and branches, her moon-kissed features dreamy, entranced. Familiar eyes.

Recognition seared his mind like lightning. No dream this, after all . . .

With willpower he'd not thought at his command, Tresand forced his eyes shut. Merciful God. This, he had not expected. This was too cruel to contemplate, yet only too fitting considering the fickle dance fate had led him through these past centuries.

She was still there, beside him. He could feel her unsteady heartbeat, quickened with fear perhaps, like a drum pounding through his brain, painful, luring, beckoning. He could hear the soft sound of dismay rising like a sigh from her throat, could almost feel the touch of her gaze flowing over his broken body. And yet he forced himself into utter stillness, utter control over the hunger that surged like a storm within him, driving him toward the source of life so near.

15

He felt the warmth of her body near his shoulder, and he viciously suppressed the instinctive shift of his body toward her.

"Just stay still, mister. I'm going for help."

It was the sound of her voice that first penetrated his mind, soft words, rich with a faint tremor and foreign accent, husky with underlying fear. Then the reluctant distancing of her warmth struck him like a blow. Only then did the meaning of her words sink in. She would get help.

"No! Must—not—!" His words ended in a harsh cough that shook his body even as he reached out, blindly, to the memory of her presence.

She was there again, suddenly, taking his hand in both of hers, innocently, reassuringly, muttering something about a stubborn horse that wouldn't come up the mountain, and a cabin in the valley, and her father being able to help.

"Mister, I have to—"

"Don't." His voice was growing stronger, becoming accustomed to use again. She was still holding on to his hand, squeezing it gently as though about to let go. Yet before she could move, Tresand opened his eyes again, struggling to force the hypnotic pull of hunger from his gaze.

He did not succeed, not fully; he could see the shock in her face as she saw the inhuman color of his eyes, shock he'd seen before, centuries ago, in those familiar eyes. . . .

Tresand groaned softly with the pain of remembrance, the soul-shattering agony of loss. Aye, it was her. Again. After all this time . . . No difference. He could not touch her, could not lose her again . . . kill again.

He jerked his hand from hers, mourning the loss of her touch. She had to go, now, and not come back. No matter how much he craved even to look upon her for just another precious moment, and glory in the sight of her as a damned man might in the radiance of an angel. She wasn't safe. The hunger surging red-hot through every fiber of his body knew no conscience.

God, if only he could hold on to his last shreds of control until she was gone, keep from reaching for her, from thinking about the life so vibrant within her . . .

"Who are you?"

The whispered words penetrated his mind like living fire. Realizing that his eyes had drifted shut, not daring to open them again lest he could not guard the power of his gaze against the hunger of his blood, Tresand curved his bruised lips into a mocking smile. "I am Death."

He had been so often in the past millennium. Always, he'd brought death to her. . . .

He heard her faint scoff, realized how melodramatic his words must sound to her. Gruffly he added, "It matters not. Not anymore. But you must leave. And not return."

"Don't you talk like that," her gentle voice argued shakily, and with it came a feather-soft touch on his unmarred cheek, an innocent caress that burned hotter than any iron of the Inquisition. Tresand's eyes snapped open to focus on her face, carefully avoiding her gaze, drinking in the nearness of her soul like a man dying in the desert. One last moment, to sear her presence into his heart, to know that she lived again in this time, that she was well, safe.

He turned his head away, fixed his gaze on the black wall of interwoven trees that bordered the clearing. No more. His raging hunger, his weakness, threatened to betray him.

"You must go—*now*," he repeated hoarsely, feeling his control slipping as another wave of need and pain swept over him. Oh, it would be so easy, so easy. . . .

"I won't leave."

Her stubborn refusal, in a voice thick with unshed tears, cut across his whirling thoughts. Tears for him.

The realization stole his breath. When, a moment later, she smoothed back a strand of matted hair from his forehead, he could not still the traitorous tremor of his body. She snatched her hand away guiltily.

"You do not understand." His voice was raspy. Still, he would not look at her, did not dare it. "It is not safe here for you."

"Don't worry about that." She was quick with her reassurance, stroking his brow again with aching gentleness. "I've got Pa's new Winchester with me."

The word meant nothing to Tresand. A weapon,

he thought. A pistol, a rifle perhaps. He felt like laughing, or weeping. As if a bullet could save her from him.

She shifted closer, cradled his head in her lap, and his instincts went berserk. The power of his blood lashed at him, commanding *life*, no matter the cost to his conscience and soul. With a last remnant of control, he jerked back.

"Damn you, you will listen to me! Get away from here if you value your life!"

He snarled the words at her viciously, his lips drawn back like the rabid animal he was so close to becoming, shocking her with the unspeakable truth in one last effort to save her.

She inhaled sharply. Her eyes grew huge and dilated in the wan moonlight as she stared at the slender, dagger-sharp canines.

"I know you." Her voice was soft, trembling. Yet there was no terror, no revulsion in it, only certainty.

Silently, she rose to her feet and backed away into the night. With a half-forgotten prayer, Tresand let his head fall back into the soft grass. He retreated into the silent darkness behind his closed lids even as his canines retracted. He dared not call out again, for she would hear, would return. So perhaps he would die after all. At least then she would be safe from him.

The crushing weight on his legs shifted abruptly, unexpectedly, and he stiffened with a groan as agony flared anew. He looked up and saw she was using her rifle as a lever to move the boulder pinning his legs. Then the rock was gone, and the pain subsided slowly. Still caught in the much hotter flame of hunger, Tresand turned his face away from her, a soundless cry of anguish tearing at his throat, a curse and a prayer in one. Still, she was here!

He heard the rifle fall to the ground, recognized the sound from when she'd first entered the clearing. As before, she sank to her knees beside him. Softly, so very softly, she touched his shoulder.

"You're free now, mister."

The words hung in the air around them, on the night wind, barely louder than the song of the crickets. He felt her uncertainty, then poured a single command into her mind: *Run!*

Tresand felt her shrug off his unspoken command, felt her there, beside him, so close, so warm and alive. Burning with life. Too close . . .

A shudder wracked his body as he fought himself, fought the hunger to live—to feed. His body, his mind, his very soul were ruled by the searing lash of hunger. He was running out of time . . . out of life, and the power of his blood, the curse of it, was survival.

With a strength he'd known would be there, Tresand twisted around to capture the woman's shoulders, bringing her down beside him. A small cry escaped her throat, more a sound of surprise than one of protest, yet it had the power to turn his body to stone.

"For the love of God—" Tresand's voice

deserted him as her sky blue eyes burned into his. Though his grip had loosened, she did not move away, did not even attempt to escape.

Tremors wracked him. It was but a matter of heartbeats before he'd take what he so desperately needed. Yet he couldn't—*not from her*, not like this, not when he would kill her in his need. But he would, and he no longer had the strength to push her away.

She lay perfectly still in his arms. He could sense each pounding beat of her heart, each ragged quest for breath. Her gaze traveled from his exposed canines to his eyes, remained locked to them, searching and, God help him, under-standing, accepting. Slowly, yet unhesitatingly, she reached out and touched the unmarred, beard-roughened plane of his cheek, then his jaw, then, shockingly, lightly traced his cracked lower lip with her fingertips.

A shudder tore through his broken body as he pulled her closer and touched his lips, his tongue, against the pulse racing in her throat. Her skin was cool from the chill of the night, a drugging contrast to the hot blood surging just beneath. As his canines broke the skin, a soft sound of surprise, pain, and pleasure escaped her, and she arched against him, closer, mindless. Then all he knew was the ecstasy of life, renewed, surging into him with each beat of her heart, a tornado tearing through his blood, his mind, until only darkness remained.

* * *

His consciousness returned slowly, reluctantly, and Tresand knew what he had done even before he opened his eyes. The intoxicating vitality rushing through his veins, the absence of pain and hunger, and the supple power of muscle and bone unmarred by injury were proof of it.

The analytical part of his mind reported that he had taken half the night to recover. The body in his arms had already lost its warmth.

Not a trace of humanity remained in Tresand's features as he stared at the still form of the young woman. He touched the dark strands of hair tousled about her face, a face so very still and tranquil in the fading silver of the moonlight.

Again. Again, again, *again!* His silent cry shattered what reason yet remained, drove to near madness his soul watching life through his violet eyes.

Again she had died because of him, had died so he could live.

With a stony countenance, Tresand buried her in the soft, rich earth of the clearing, by the light of the waning moon. Had there been a way, he would have taken his own life in retribution for what he had done. Yet the life of an immortal was no easy thing to end.

Tresand stared up into the velvety sky studded with the stars flickering like diamonds. It could not—*must not* happen again, not ever again.

Slowly, he sank to his knees, his hands knotted into fists on his thighs, his head falling back, his eyes tightly shut against the gentle lingering beams of light. Like a wolf howling at the moon, he called to another of his kind, in voice and thought, a desperate cry drifting to the heavens. "Aramond. Merciful God, Aramond, find me quickly and do what must be done!"

Part 1

– PARADISE –

Chapter One

Sunday, May 4

Such a beautiful place to spend eternity, Cailie thought with a wistful smile as she stepped out of the shade of the airport walkway and into the bright Honolulu sun. She'd left behind her the Boeing 747's air-conditioned climate and the arrival gate's still, humid warmth, and ahead of her, in the brilliant mid-morning sun, was the rest of the sprawling Honolulu airport complex.

It was quite incredible, really. With only a handful of steps, she had crossed some invisible, intangible boundary from cold, harsh reality into the gentle, welcoming world of a fairy tale. She had left behind the past and entered a realm where time would stand still for 14 beautiful days.

People milled around her, eagerly rushing into the engulfing warmth of the tropical day with wide-eyed wonder. Seattle had lain buried under a shroud of fog and drizzle only six hours ago. Now, warm winds fragrant with hibiscus blossoms were stirring distant palm fronds under a brilliant sky.

Glancing down the busy arrivals strip, Cailie caught sight of a blue-and-white bus departing 40 yards away. Several people she recognized from her flight ceased trotting down the sidewalk as the bus rounded a corner and disappeared from sight.

Cailie smiled crookedly. *Just catch a* wikiwiki, *it'll take you to your departure gate*, the portly woman at the information desk had said. Right. Catch it, if you can.

With a shrug, she shouldered her carry-on bag and started down the sidewalk among a number of other Maui-bound passengers. There would be another bus, of course, to take her to her connecting flight. And even though she hated waiting, technically this was her first chance to go for a walk on a tropical island.

Her crooked smile broadened, becoming genuine. It was as if the sunshine pouring down on her, and the soft wind's gentle embrace, could purge from her soul the darkness of her endless nightmares, of the dreams she'd been so utterly defenseless against since fate had stolen her family away.

Cailie released a slow breath, not wanting to

think of the past, a past which, as of today, no longer existed for her. But it was hard—still, even after all these years—to think of her family without feeling that pang of loss. She supposed that one never completely got over it, though one certainly learned to live with it. But the bitterness at life's unfairness remained. If her sister Beth hadn't chosen that particular Saturday for her wedding, if they'd all left just one minute later, or earlier, if Dad had turned down 42nd Avenue instead of 45th, if someone had stopped that idiot from getting behind the wheel after spending the morning with a bottle . . .

Cailie's smile faded and her gaze sank to the concrete sidewalk's squares.

If, if, if. Useless word! They'd done what they'd done, and now they were dead, Mom, Dad, and Beth, long gone, buried in the cold ground.

But *Cailie* had survived, with no more than a slight concussion and some scrapes and bruises. Beth, who'd had everything to live for—beauty, charm, wit, and a wonderful man who adored her—had died. But Cailie, shy, quiet, plain Cailie, who had always preferred curling up with a good history book to dressing up and going out, had survived. Had survived to make arrangements for the funeral, to sell the mortgaged house in the small town of Duvall that had been the family home for as long as she could remember, to dispose of Mom's wheelchair and all of her family's belongings and memories of their lives.

Had survived only to become lost in the world of her nightmares.

Over the last five years, reality had progressively faded from her life, until it was but an interlude between one dream and the next, until life itself was hardly worth living.

"God, look at this! Isn't this *gorgeous!*"

Cailie's gaze flew up from the ground to the young woman exuberantly striding along in front of her, delighted by the hedges of hibiscus, the rustling palm fronds, the beauty of the tropical day. Shelly, Cailie recalled her name; one of the college students heading to a beach camp on Maui to study marine biology.

That's what *she* should be like, Cailie mused, a wry twist to her mouth. Happy, exuberant, full of excitement and energy. After all, she was here to have the time of her life. But sitting near that lively group of students on the plane, right next to Shelly, had only left her battling more demons. She might have been one of them once, if she'd gone to a university instead of the small-town college, if she'd moved out instead of staying at home, if Mom's multiple sclerosis hadn't gotten so much worse in those last years. . . .

Ifs again, Cailie thought sourly. But again, they were irrelevant. She'd been content at home and had been doubly glad, after the accident, for every day she'd spent with her family. Besides, she'd always been too timid and too much of a loner to go on a group-anything, too unremarkable to go on something as exotic as a class trip to Hawaii.

Yes, that was the one word that described her perfectly: unremarkable. Nothing about Cailie's appearance had ever caught anyone's attention, from her mousy-brown, straight long hair to the ten pounds she never could manage to lose. Her face, though not ugly, was plain, ordinary, like a passerby's in the background of a movie scene.

She was exactly the sort of person whom nobody would miss when she was gone.

But Cailie had spent months preparing for this trip. Spare pounds had not been a problem since the car accident, yet she'd still exercised diligently so she wouldn't feel self-conscious among all the beautiful people on the sun-drenched beaches. Her abominably straight hair had been fashionably cut and highlighted, though she'd nearly broken into tears when the hairdresser had chopped off a good eight inches, leaving her with strands that barely fell past her shoulders. But the feathered bangs made her face look softer, her blue eyes bigger. And her nails, for the first time carefully grown and manicured to perfection, gave her hands an unexpectedly slender, delicate appearance. She'd even spent time in tanning beds, so she wouldn't have to worry about burning her fair skin under the tropical sun.

All in all, she was as ready as she'd ever be to enjoy the vacation of a lifetime: two weeks without a single thing she *had* to do, two weeks without the constraints of a schedule. She didn't even know where she'd be spending the night. All she had was a rental car waiting at one of the agencies at the airport on Maui.

For a woman who had had her every waking hour planned days in advance to cram as much productive time into each day as possible, it was a frightening prospect. But it was an exhilarating one too, despite the abyss of shadows lurking in the back of her mind.

Cailie shook her head mildly to dispel her rambling thoughts that always tended to slip into the past, and picked up her pace toward her departure gate. She had to get away from her past. After all, as of this morning, her past had ceased to exist.

The connecting flight to Kahului was scheduled for takeoff in one hour. Cailie claimed a seat in the waiting area and stowed her only piece of luggage—the worn, plain carry-on bag—between her feet. In that old canvas bag rested all her worldly possessions: basic toiletries, a book, a few miscellaneous items, a pair of comfortable low white heels, and her purse containing travelers checks in an amount that had made the bank clerk's eyes bulge and prompted him to ask if she was sure, *really* sure she wanted that much.

The corners of Cailie's lips tugged up in remembrance. No, it probably wasn't every day that someone cleaned out her entire account . . . or got rid of all her belongings, including a well-worn English saddle, at the Salvation Army. Perhaps if she'd been allowed to keep that cranky old mare, she wouldn't have come to this.

A Deeper Hunger

Her smile turning wistful, Cailie shook her head, then checked her watch. She did not dig the novel out of her purse, or stare into the distance, letting the past creep up on her again. She got up and roamed.

Fifty minutes later, she was the last passenger to hustle onto the scorching tarmac and board the white Aloha 737-200. For the first time in her life, Cailie had almost been late.

As the jet rolled down to the runway, she watched the taxi strips zoom by from an aisle seat, her stomach churning. God, how she hated flying—feared it, really. It was unsafe. There were too many airplanes being hijacked, bombed, and just plain falling apart these days.

The utter absurdity of her thoughts tightened her lips into a wry line. Preposterous, for her to be afraid of anything now! That would be like . . . Cailie violently shoved the train of thought away from her as the jet, leaving the runway, conquered gravity and rose nose-first into the azure sky on its climb to over 30,000 feet for the 20-minute flight.

Her friend Janey had wanted to come to Hawaii again for her honeymoon, Cailie recalled as she stared across the portly man beside her into the crystal blue of the Pacific Ocean. She remembered Janey's phone call, just three weeks ago, remembered Janey boasting about the fact that Don had been determined to take her on a Caribbean luxury cruise instead.

Just as well. The last thing Cailie wanted was

to run into her friend whom she'd known since high school and her new husband. She'd never understood how someone could treat love so casually as Janey had. She was a year younger than Cailie, and on husband number *two*, for God's sake.

But perhaps it was not Janey, but *she* who was abnormal. Perhaps she simply wanted too much, wanted a perfection that did not exist in the real world, wanted to find in real life the kind of love she'd found only in her haunting dreams.

She shook her head. None of that mattered anymore. And Janey wouldn't miss her anyway, not with Don to keep her living the high life.

Oh, hell, there she went again. Cailie clenched her hands into fists until the unfamiliar pain of her long nails digging into her flesh penetrated her mind. She uncurled her fingers, and stared at the crescent marks on her palms.

This was going to be *her* time. Two weeks in paradise, with no questions asked, and not one single thing to mar the good time she was going to have, especially not her own cowardice and self-pity. Otherwise she might as well forget the whole thing, go back to her quiet job in the library and her lonely sparsely furnished apartment in Fremont, and hope like hell that her travelers checks wouldn't disappear.

No. She would not break the pact she had made with herself. It was too easy to rationalize her way out of it, by far. Then she'd be right back where she'd been before, lost in a world of dreams that were slowly driving her out of her mind.

No. She would banish the past. She would have her time in paradise, and live one perfect dream of life.

An hour later, a lei of purple orchids and white plumeria around her neck, Cailie stood on the hot asphalt of the rental lot with the keys to her new mode of transport. Awed, she tossed her bag and purse into the passenger side and swung herself into the plush bucket seat behind the wheel.

The Probe was everything she could have hoped for. Blindingly white in the midday sun, with blood-red velour interior, air-conditioning (of course), stereo AM/FM radio, cassette deck, sunroof, and power-absolutely-everything, it was every vacationer's dream.

For a bus-riding Seattleite, it was the next best thing to a private spaceship.

With a brilliant smile, Cailie maneuvered out of the parking lot onto the access road. Except for a few excursions in Janey's car, she hadn't driven since the accident. It felt good to be behind the wheel of a car again, exhilarating.

Cailie refused to turn on the air-conditioning. By the time she was on the main road from the airport, she had the radio on and both windows down. Hot wind surged through the car's interior, tousling her hair and swirling the delicious scent of her lei all around her. Smiling, she reached up to open the sunroof, struggling briefly with the too-tight lock. She yelped in pain and dismay as it suddenly gave, breaking four of her fingernails.

Nursing the abused digits, and indulging in a few choice, silent oaths, Cailie pulled off the road to dig through her purse. Ruefully she quickly filed down the ruined nails, then clipped the remaining perfectly manicured ones to match. No sense in doing things halfway.

With a philosophical shrug, she joined the traffic heading for Lahaina. Burning cane fields in the verdant isthmus impaired visibility, causing cars to crawl at a snail's pace. Cailie had the windows up in a flash, but didn't touch the sunroof.

Then, from one second to the next, the smoke was gone. She lowered the windows again, and moments later turned off on the Honoapiilani highway that followed the coastline to Lahaina.

It was definitely a route with a split personality, Cailie decided as the miles of winding road passed. To her right, hillsides of arid, reddish ground studded with stunted trees and occasional black cattle rose into the West Maui Mountains; on her left, far below, the ocean stretched toward the horizon in breathtaking shades of blue and turquoise. Waves crashed in billows of white foam against the foot of black lava cliffs, the edges of which too often came shockingly close to the highway. Now and then, the road cut through a steep, rugged lava hill, or tunneled through one in blinding darkness. After a while the highway dropped to sea level again. Patches of dense vegetation alternated with dry, bleached grass and clumps of pale-leaved trees, and on the foothills, fields of dark green sugar cane billowed in the wind.

Two minutes into the sea-level stretch, Cailie understood the minimum speed limits posted along the highway. Anyone not used to the sight of endless blue-green breakers glowing with sunlight the instant before they exploded into white foam and plunged onto a sandy or rocky shore might have difficulty keeping from staring, and end up slowing down traffic. She certainly did.

Then the tall, branching trees that looked as though they belonged on some windswept African plain lined the road again, blocking the ocean view but casting welcome shade. With a sigh, Cailie fluffed her long cotton skirt; she was definitely overdressed for this climate. But that would be remedied quickly enough.

Another ten minutes brought her to the far side of Lahaina, where the tree-sprinkled parking lot of the Cannery Mall lay in the early-afternoon sunlight. Cailie wrapped her lei around the car's mirror, and went shopping.

Two hours and an obscenely thick wad of travelers checks later, Cailie was the proud owner of one designer white cover-up and swimsuit, a daring string bikini which she never, absolutely *never* would have dared wear within ten miles of anyone who knew her, a Crazy Gecko T-shirt to sleep in, and a Maui beach towel. She'd also purchased an anklet and matching thongs, a baby-blue silk dress, and Royal Hawaiian

Sabine Kells

suntan lotion and after-sun lotion. She'd found that she couldn't resist a gauzy, Greek-looking aquamarine sun dress, two boxes of caramel-covered macadamia-nut chocolates, a six-pack of POG, a scorching paperback romance, a book on Hawaiian history, an old ABBA tape, and a tiny bottle of White Hawaiian ginger perfume. There'd be more time later to shop for anything else she might need or fancy, she reasoned.

With some of her newfound treasures contained in an equally new, bright blossom-print beach bag, Cailie headed for the ladies' room to complete the first part of her plan.

She came out looking—and feeling—unlike anybody she'd ever known. Certainly not herself. Certainly not the unremarkable, ordinary Catherine Linette Wellington, who had more often shopped at Thrifty's than a designer store.

The woman in the mirror had been almost beautiful: a fair-haired, blue-eyed, exotic vision in vivid, flowing aquamarine over her bikini, with a shell anklet showing off her small feet, which were a touch too pale in the delicate leather-and-shell thongs.

The woman in the mirror had looked more carefree, more alive than Catherine Wellington could ever have laid claim to being.

Cailie's mouth twisted at the supreme irony of it all. Somewhere, Janus was surely laughing at her. She shoved the dark thoughts from her mind, shouldered her new bag and purse, and headed

A Deeper Hunger

for the parking lot. She'd broken more of her own shackles in the last twenty-four hours than she had in all her life.

And she wasn't done with breaking them yet. Not nearly.

Chapter Two

The heat came as a physical shock as Cailie exited the air-conditioned mall. By the time she found her Probe among the scores of other white rental cars, she was hot, somewhat less elated, exhausted—and without her keys.

She searched her purse three times in vain, then rummaged through her beach bag and the pockets of her old skirt, which had been stuffed into it. She peered in at the car's ignition. Nothing.

Slinging both bags across her shoulder again, she strode back into the mall to check the lost and found. But no luck.

Forty-five minutes later, even hotter and utterly embarrassed, she again had her car keys, delivered by the clerk from the rental agency, who undoubtedly did not relish the thought of repeating this performance several times over the next two weeks. He'd been infallibly courteous, of course, but Cailie had seen his kind before, and knew what he'd been thinking.

No. This was her vacation. Her *perfect* vacation, and nothing, absolutely nothing—especially not a clerk with a condescending smirk—was going to ruin it.

Summoning her brightest, most defiant smile, Cailie settled herself into the plush seat of the scorchingly hot Probe, and made a mental note to park in the shade next time. She opened all the windows, turned up the volume on her new tape, and with a vengeance, she tore into the first box of candy.

More calories than she'd usually allow herself for a whole day at least, Cailie reflected smugly as she finished the last chocolate in the box, a can of juice mix, and stuffed both remains into the plastic garbage bag. She looped the handles over the gearshift so the bag wouldn't upend, and started the car.

While eating the chocolates, she'd leafed through several tourist brochures, found exact layouts of the streets and shops in Lahaina, and promptly trashed all of them. After all, this was her time of living dangerously.

She drove aimlessly for half an hour, up and down the busy, touristy streets, before snatching up a parking spot by the ruins of the old fort behind a banyan tree.

Now *there* was an invitation to climb if she'd ever seen one. Awed, Cailie studied the ancient tree as she crossed the block it covered, mindless of the round, red seed pods and bird droppings on the walkways. The banyan looked like a gigantic, hovering green jellyfish, as its mass of aerial roots trailed from branches and turned into stems. Benches stood in the sun-dappled shade, and tiny doves scooted along the square cement tiles, unflustered by the presence of numerous ambling tourists.

Cailie paused by an arm-thick vine that hung just past her shoulders, and stared up into the green canopy speculatively. Then she shrugged, walked on. Climbing the tree was probably frowned upon, if not prohibited, and certainly out of the question in broad daylight. But perhaps one night . . .

Smiling, Cailie headed down Front Street.

People were everywhere—pale, tanned, old, young, tall, short, rotund, and slender. Some were dressed tastefully, others in ridiculously bright polyester print shirts, shorts, and dresses, strolling along the colorful shop-lined street, shopping, window-shopping, or sitting in the shade on the rock wall by the old missionary home, enjoying ice cream cones. On the side-walk at the corner of the historical Pioneer Inn, a young man with nine—Cailie counted them twice—parrots was taking pictures of tourists after loading them up with as many of the colorful birds as they could hold, and then some.

A Deeper Hunger

What a tourist trap! But she was smiling as she thought it, the kind of amused smile she saw on several other faces watching the parrot man at work.

For over an hour, Cailie wandered along the sun-bright strip, delighting in the soft, warm air, drifting through the multitude of tourist shops and art galleries, and successfully distracting herself from the festering darkness that was never more than a thought away. After indulging in a huge Kauai Pie and mango ice cream cone at Lappert's, Cailie extricated her car from between two other rentals—their drivers had obviously never learned how to park—and headed out toward Kaanapali.

This was paradise: the glorious tropical sun, the delicious scents of suntan lotions carried on the warm, shifting currents of wind, the soothing, lulling rhythm of the waves rushing against the shore.

Cailie stretched out on her new beach towel, absorbing golden sunshine into each pore of her body not covered by her bikini. She could almost pretend that nothing was wrong with her world, that she was simply taking a bit of time off from, say, a demanding job, leaving a loving husband to look after the house and the cats. It was getting easier by the minute to forget that the few men she'd ever dated had fallen pathetically short in her inevitable comparison to the phantom of her dreams, and that she was about to do the unspeakable, and live the kind of love she'd found only in her nightmares. . . .

Willing the rising tension away, she sighed, yawned. Practice. That's what she needed. Just a bit more practice in spinning this waking dream, a bit more practice to truly believe in the illusion she was about to weave for herself. In the meantime, she could risk a nap. Just a brief nap here, in the bright light of day, where the haunting dreams would not be so overwhelming.

Turning onto her stomach, she pillowed her cheek on her folded hands, and let the rhythm of the waves carry her into sleep.

Pain. It was all she knew, all she was. Endless, throbbing pain in every pore, every bone, every sinew and muscle, every hair. Around her still, hot air, thick with the stench of burning flesh, of excrement and fear and sweat, and the nightmarish concert of howls and groans and screams, undistinguishable as to sex, speaking in the universal language of agony.

" . . . must tell us, Erlina. Where is the one who calls himself Fernando Esteban de Bautista? We have told you what he is. We do not want to hurt you. But you must tell us where his lair is, so that we may seek out the demon and consecrate him to the flames!"

Such gentle voices, such concern, such compassion. Liars! Devil's spawn! She'd never betray him. . . .

The pain in her shoulders was a living thing,

snaking up her arms to her bound wrists that had borne her weight forever, flowing down her body into her ribs and belly. Still the voice went on, insinuating itself into her mind, twisting what she knew, what she believed in.

"Doña Erlina, we know the devil has seduced you to his ways. Why will you not confess this to us, so that you may be forgiven?"

She would not open her eyes. The iron was so close its heat bathed her naked belly. It moved down to her thigh, up again, past her breasts, to her cheek. Jesu, no, she'd not open her eyes.

"But tell us what we wish to know, Doña Erlina, and you may return to your family. Think of how they will rejoice to have you restored to them. Now tell us. Where is de Bautista?"

She shook her head. Ah, to be back in her cold, black cell, where she could dream of Fernando, could wrap herself into the memory of his love, drown in the unearthly fire of his eyes . . . If only she could see him one more time, be held by him . . . But perhaps a merciful God would bring them together again in Paradise.

"Please, Erlina. You have seen what the iron can do. We do not wish to hurt you. If you tell us where he is, your sins will be forgiven. You will be free to return home. Tell us, Doña Erlina. Where is the devil's lair?"

The heat of the iron was singeing the fine hairs of her cheek, glowing through her closed lids. They'd never let her go. She'd heard them talk. They'd burn her as a witch, a bride of the devil . . . just as they'd *burn Fernando. But she'd not betray him.*

"I am a citizen of Castile." Her voice was a whisper, dry, lifeless, hopeless. *"I have done no wrong. I know nothing of a man who is the devil in disguise. You have no right—"*

Fire . . .

Cailie woke with a start, her heart pounding in her chest and a scream lodged in her throat. She sat up, wrapping her arms around her knees, breathing deeply until her frantic heart beats slowed. A shiver coursed down her stiffened spine despite the streaming sunshine, despite the glittering ocean and golden sand and the gentle wind in her hair. Yet already, the images were fading, losing their power, releasing her.

Shaken, she tried to smile. It was always easier to free herself from the dreams during the day. At night, she was too vulnerable to the horrors, and to the love—the heartbreaking love for her phantom, who chased away her fear.

But he wasn't always there in her dreams, was never there in the real world. And with each night, her dream world, no matter how horrifying at times, became preferable to her waking one. Her mother had always understood, had helped her retain her hold on reality. After the accident, her friends had offered comfort, but over time they'd drifted away, alienated by her remoteness and withdrawal. They'd never understood her dreams, never understood that she'd *wanted* to lose herself in them—because in her dreams, *he* was there. In those rare, brief interludes there was bliss, the purest love that existed only in fairy tales, leaving her to wake up crying from its loss.

But she would find a love like that. It was one of her reasons for coming here, after all. She would live her beautiful, perfect dream of love and it would last her into eternity.

Resolute, Cailie pushed to her feet. She took the aquamarine dress and slipped it over her head, then vigorously shook out the towel. The second part of her plan awaited her, and she was wasting precious time.

The thongs were scorchingly hot on her feet, but she ignored that minor imperfection and turned to stare up at the towering luxury hotels lining the busy cream-of-wheat beach. She took a deep breath, straightening her spine in grim determination. Nobody had said this was going to be easy, least of all herself.

Cailie didn't quite feel like smiling as she started toward the hotel, her beach bag and purse slung over one shoulder, but she curved her lips upward anyway. After all, she was here to have the time of her life, and every moment counted.

Her step a bit faster, she headed along a cement-tiled, hibiscus-hedged walkway that led up from the beach and through an inner garden to the hotel lobby. Fountains and fish ponds, flowering shrubs and trees, even full-sized palms were incorporated into the architectural design of the ten-story high rise, flanking her progress and monopolizing her attention. Twice Cailie stubbed her toes, limping on only to stare some more.

God, she must look like the textbook tourist, gaping at everything around her! But Cailie couldn't help it. The grandeur of the place so awed her that she had almost forgotten her goal by the time she finally reached the top of two flights of steps and entered the hotel lobby.

Counters and tiny shops, ranging from a receptionist's desk to a miniature florist and jeweler, lined the polished marble walls in the shade of numerous, second-story awnings. Yet the orchid garden, the small pool with sparkling blue tiles and fountains, the tropical greenery, and the bored-looking green parrot on a bamboo stand left no doubt that this wasn't a posh West Coast hotel.

Only a handful of people were drifting through the stylish atrium, browsing. Cailie spotted the pay phones at the front entrance and made a beeline for one. Then she slowed, staring incredulously. No telephone books. Her smile disappeared, and was replaced by a frown. Jewelry stores but no phone books?

Not to be foiled, she squared her shoulders and approached the man behind the front desk with her most personable smile. The dark-skinned young Hawaiian in the flower-print shirt and plumeria lei smiled back just as cheerfully as he produced the requested telephone book.

Thirty seconds later, Cailie carried her prize back to the wall phones. In their questionable privacy she leafed through the Yellow Pages until she found the ads.

Quickly now, before her determination could fall prey to common sense and years of rational living, she picked up the receiver and sunk a quarter.

It took all her courage to dial the number she'd picked. She pushed a two instead of a five, broke the connection, retrieved her quarter, and tried again. Biting her lip, she held her breath as the phone on the other side rang—too long. Her sanity was starting to come round from its stunned disbelief, was screaming inside her head in outrage.

Good God, what did she think she was doing, calling up an . . .

"Aloha, Starlight Escorts, how may I help you?"

The voice was purely feminine, modulated perfectly, soft and sultry and casual all at once. Despite never having seen the woman's face, Cailie still felt utterly outclassed, awkward and ridiculous.

"Ah—hi, I—um—" Her squeak broke off. She should have thought about how in the world she was going to say this!

Cailie closed her eyes, struggled for a breath. Her heart was probably beating loud enough for The Perfect Voice on the other end of the line to hear.

"Hello?" the voice said.

"Ah—yes, good afternoon!" Cailie found her

voice again, and the deep breath came out in a shaky rush of words. "I was wondering if you could help me. I'm looking for an escort for this evening to show me around the town."

There, it was out! She sucked in another breath. God, she still couldn't believe it, but she'd done it, had taken the leap, and now there was no going back.

"I'm sorry, ma'am, we're all booked up tonight. Would you care to make a reservation for tomorrow? Hello?"

"Uh—no, thank you, that won't be necessary. Bye."

"Have a nice day. Aloha."

Have a nice day indeed.

Cailie hung up, her head spinning. Her pounding heart seemed to have ground to a complete stop inside her chest. She sucked in another deep breath of tropical air, then slowly turned.

Rational thought had reasserted itself by the time she'd crossed the lobby. How could she have been crazy enough to try this anyway? It was probably for the best that it hadn't worked out. God only knew what might have happened.

"Hello? Miss? Excuse me, miss?"

Cailie jerked around, startled half out of her wits by the unexpected voice, to find the young man from the front desk coming after her.

God, he was probably ticked off that she'd forgotten to return the telephone book. But no, he was smiling and he was holding out a paper.

"This fell out of your purse."

"Oh. Thank you." She took the proffered local flyer, caught between a flustered smile for the nice hotel clerk and a frown for her scatterbrained self. She really must check more often to make sure the zippers on her purse were closed, especially considering the amount of travelers checks in the purse.

"You're welcome. Have a nice day now." And he was off, leaving her with that flashing smile.

Cailie turned and continued down to the walkway, making a mental note to sock the next person wishing her a nice day. Though really, it wasn't their fault that her perfect vacation wasn't turning out quite that perfectly.

Banning that thought, she began to stuff the flyer back into her oversized purse . . . and stopped dead when the word "escort" caught her eye.

She straightened, inhaled deeply, then closed her eyes for a moment. She was being stupid undoubtedly. It just wasn't meant to be. She could have just as much fun on her own, if not more, and it was much safer anyway if she didn't get involved with a perfect stranger. But she hadn't come here to be safe.

Cailie sat down on the rim of one of the concrete planters by the stairs, and flattened the paper out on her lap. It was one of the weekly directories/calendars-of-events/fliers that she'd picked up . . . where? In one of the shops in town, no doubt.

That the small ad had caught her attention

Sabine Kells

amazed her. It was in the personals section, and read:

SOPHISTICATED, MATURE MALE ESCORT.
BUSINESS OR PLEASURE.
HOURS AFTER DARK.

Other than the mug shot, there was nothing remarkable about the ad, nothing particularly flashy or riveting. And yet there was something. Something compelling, magnetic . . . Probably it was only her desperation that made her think that.

Frowning severely, Cailie stared at the ad a moment longer. "Hours after dark." Her frown dissolved into something too much like relief. Oh, it would be perfect—in more than one way. She'd stay up all night, and sleep in the daytime, when the light of the sun could wash away her dreams.

Determined, she fished through her change purse for another quarter, and found none.

Not meant to be, the rational part of her affirmed gleefully.

She rummaged deeper, into the bottom of her purse. On one side, she encountered a chapstick, crumpled tissue, her wallet, a nail file, the paperback—mangled by now—car keys, a barrette, and more flyers. No change.

The other side revealed an equally diverse assortment of items, including the spare keys she'd had made in town, a pocketknife—and, at the very bottom, several coins. Three pennies, a nickel, and a quarter.

A triumph over fate. The coin clutched in one hand, Cailie resolutely headed back to the lobby phones.

She got the number right on the first try. After the fourth ring, the unmistakable, dreaded click of an answering machine opened the line. Cailie's hand flashed out to break the connection before she could check her habitual response. She never, *ever* talked to those horrible inventions. They were . . . intimidating.

Cailie waited two seconds, three, then sighed. Her quarter obviously wasn't going to be regurgitated. She replaced the receiver, stared mutinously at the telephone, and considered her options.

Then she drew herself up to her full five feet four inches, and strode out of the lobby into the parking lot. Ten minutes later, she was back with her carry-on at the front desk of the hotel.

"I'd like a room for the night. With a view, please."

The jovial receptionist she'd encountered earlier checked the computer screen in front of him, then nodded, still smiling. Cailie wondered uncharitably if the man ever *not* smiled.

"You're in luck. We have two suites left on the ocean front. For how many?"

"One."

"Certainly."

While he proceeded with his paperwork, Cailie fished the travelers checks out of her purse. She was not going to ask about the room rate. From the looks of this place, if one had to ask, one probably shouldn't bother.

But it was a place to stay for the night, a place such as she had never even dreamed of staying at before. And it would have a telephone in the room. Depositing her purse and the flyer beside the bowl of fragrant plumeria blossoms on the counter, she started signing checks.

The clerk's gaze was fixed on the open page of the ad paper when Cailie looked up. He met her eyes instantly and took her book of checks with a *"Mahalo."* Cailie managed not to gape at the number of 50-dollar checks he appropriated before handing her a paltry amount of change and the card to her room—with a smile.

"Sixth floor." He pointed toward the far wall of the lobby. "Closest elevator is right over there. If you need anything else, just dial 9 for the front desk and ask for Kimo."

"Thank you." Cailie forced her lips to curve upward, cleared the counter of her belongings, and headed for the elevator. Its doors opened immediately, revealing a mirror-paneled interior.

Cailie entered and pressed the button for the sixth floor, momentarily captivated by her own reflection. Purely by chance, her gaze captured the curiously intent stare of the receptionist. Yet before she could more than raise her brows in surprise at his attention, the mirrored doors slid closed and the elevator surged upward.

Chapter Three

Her room was perfect.

Cailie plopped her bags onto the king-size bed and stared in wide-eyed wonder at the impeccable interior decorating. She'd never even seen a home furnished so lavishly before, not to mention a hotel room.

Her admiring gaze found the high-tech entertainment center inside its painted wooden cabinet, and quickly changed to disapproval. Why anybody would want to watch TV in a place like this simply eluded her. Good God, she'd be entertained enough just by looking at the water-color seascape and floral paintings on the walls!

Shaking her head, Cailie strode across the thick gray carpet and stepped out through the open balcony door. The magnificent view of the golden, sunny beach, sparkling ocean, and a distant, hazy island instantly dispelled any and all traces of annoyance.

Ah. Paradise.

Cailie sighed, then straightened and sauntered back inside. Snatching up the paper, she bounced onto the bed.

As with the front-desk counter of the hotel, a glass bowl with water and floating white blossoms decorated her bedside table. Cailie tucked one of the fragrant flowers behind her ear, then hauled the telephone onto the mauve comforter.

With slightly unsteady hands, she dialed and listened to four rings, a click, and static. Then the recording came on.

"You have reached the Alexander Creighton residence. Please leave your name and number, and your call will be returned as soon as possible."

The message was utterly ordinary. The voice was anything but. A shiver danced all the way down her spine and into the pit of her stomach at the rich, smooth, mellow timbre. It was impossible to fall instantly, head-over-heels in love with a voice. . . .

Beeep.

Cailie pulled her scattered wits together, took a deep breath, and proceeded to do one of the things she hated most in life: Leave a message on an answering machine.

Despite the fact that the only parking spot she could find was halfway across town, Cailie arrived at the Hard Rock Café a full 20 minutes early.

It was a good thing she hadn't planned on dinner, Cailie mused as she squeezed past the line of people waiting to be seated, and headed for the row of tiny, round bar tables lining the huge waterfront windows.

Hiking up the skirt of her new blue silk dress, she scaled a bar stool at an empty table, and watched the last glow of deep red disappear from the sky above a distant island. The sea was already black, lashing out above the rock wall on the far side of the street in geysers of white foam. The wall had crumbled at one place; it looked, Cailie thought, as though something had crawled up out of the ocean and had taken two big chomps out of the mortared rock.

It wasn't until some minutes after she had paid for her drink and had started sipping the tall glass of coconut and pineapple juice that Cailie realized there was only mosquito mesh between her and Front Street.

She smiled wryly. That certainly explained the soft, pleasantly humid night wind which had begun to blow in from the sea, ruffling her hair and dress, carrying the occasional whiff of exotic fragrance from lei-bedecked tourists passing by on the sidewalk outside.

Cailie shook her head. Anxiety had never done much for her powers of perception. And she certainly felt anxiety.

Valiantly trying to shrug off the whole concept of anxiety, she glanced at her watch, then turned her attention to the crowded, lively interior of the Hard Rock Café. At the table in front of her, two young black men were discussing the merits of surfing at Hookipa; she could hear them quite clearly over the strains of "Don't Let the Sun Go Down on Me" echoing out of numerous speakers. Letting her gaze wander, she realized with something of a shock that there was a burgundy antique T-Bird sitting some ten feet above the rectangular bar, sporting several surf boards. Below it, back on floor level, a black-haired, deeply tanned woman with a drop-dead-gorgeous body and a skintight, short white dress was flirting with one of the handsome bartenders.

Cailie checked her watch again and sighed. She compared London and Maui time on the neon clocks above the "Save the Planet" logo on the far wall, and read the story of the Hard Rock Café on the back of the drink menu twice before, inevitably, she began to fidget.

This had been a bad idea, and being early only gave her more time to worry. Too much time to worry.

God, why hadn't there been a picture with the ad? Cailie's gaze settled on a blue-and-white police car cruising slowly down Front Street, and her overactive imagination kicked into high gear. Maybe the man was some escaped criminal, snaring his victims with an escort-service ad!

She shook her head impatiently, frowning at that outlandish thought. But what exactly did *mature* mean anyway? What if her escort was five feet tall, nearly as wide, grandfatherly, and bald?

Worse yet, what if whoever he was didn't show up at all? What if he'd listened to her squeaky voice on his tape, asking him to meet her here, and had indulged in a good laugh before erasing it? What if . . . Cailie stopped the thought. There was that useless word again. *If.*

But God, she knew she shouldn't have done this . . . Cailie's thoughts stopped as she realized one of her heels was stuck. She'd twined her legs around those of her bar stool, and couldn't get loose with her right foot. Since her feet couldn't reach the floor, Cailie ended up contorting her body into a position a yoga instructor would have been proud of before finally extricating her stuck heel.

Righting herself, her face flushed from bending down, Cailie nearly knocked over her drink as she caught sight of a man standing just inside the door.

He was watching her, she realized with a jolt of nerves. Then she did some most impolite staring of her own. It wouldn't have surprised her in the least had her heart stopped right then and there.

The man was wearing a short-sleeved, off-white dress shirt and slacks, casual but elegant. His black hair curled slightly, just short of touching the tops of his shoulders. And his face . . . Cailie caught her breath sharply. She felt dizzy, as though the floor had slipped out from under her, leaving her in free fall.

Heavens above, he was the phantom from her

dreams in flesh and blood. Except his eyes, of course. She couldn't tell what color they were yet, but no man alive could have eyes like the one in her dreams.

He was coming directly toward her now, easily making his way through the crowd. Cailie would have given anything if time would only freeze dead in its tracks, give her the opportunity to stare some more and then beat a hasty, unseen retreat. But Cronus granted no such special dispensation, did not stop the flow of time for a mere mortal such as herself.

"Miss Wellington?"

That voice. Cailie snapped her mouth shut, because her thoughts had scattered into oblivion and anything she said was bound to be idiotic. His eyes were midnight blue, she noted with the mesmerized stare of a deer watching twin headlights rushing toward it.

One dark, arched brow rose higher. "You are Miss Wellington?"

His voice was smoother, warmer than she remembered it from the answering machine. Sensual. Seductive. A tiny muscle in her cheek twitched nervously as she tried to smile.

"Um—yes. And you would be . . ."

He inclined his head politely, one corner of his mouth curving up in faint amusement. "Alexander Creighton."

As if there were any doubt. Cailie tried to draw a deep, inconspicuous breath, because her chest suddenly felt constricted.

Good Lord, what a voice. It held a soft, barely discernible accent, and a thousand unspoken promises. She glanced toward the bustling room, at the ponytail-sporting bartender half hidden behind a crowd of people, out through the mesh window into the street—where two Harley Davidson riders had just caught the spray from another wave—*anywhere* but at the shockingly attractive man standing in front of her.

She'd seen his face as he had stood watching her from the entrance. He'd looked stricken, until he'd found her staring at him and had smoothed his features.

Mortified by the realization, Cailie blushed to the roots of her hair. He was probably having a hard time keeping from laughing at *her*, unremarkable, ordinary Cailie, having the audacity to hire *him*.

"You wished to see me, I believe."

Her gaze flew to his. Her face was flaming, radiating enough heat to warm an igloo on an arctic winter's night.

"I . . ." She exhaled, then swallowed hard. "Actually, I think . . ."

A slow smile softened his chiseled features as he eased onto the barstool across from her and casually rested his forearms on the table. Cailie automatically straightened; the table had become minuscule with the presence of this man on the other side of it. His smile was a warm, sincere gesture, one that was meant to put her at ease, not show amusement at her sudden attack of nerves.

It didn't work. Not by a mile.

Cailie bit her lip. No wonder the man hadn't included a picture with his ad. He'd have to hire bodyguards, for God's sake, to keep potential clients from breaking down his door!

She couldn't seem to do more than stare at him, noting the way his blue-black eyes glinted in the lights, the way those full, sensual lips kicked up at one corner. The way his shirt—it was silk, she noted—shifted gently in the breeze, outlining broad shoulders, leaving bare the definition of lean, muscled arms.

Cailie tore her gaze away, stared self-consciously out into the night, while her benumbed brain found another "what if" that hadn't occurred to her before. What if the man who showed up was so stunningly handsome that he left her tongue-tied like an idiot? Not that it took much to make her look the fool.

The thought suddenly occurred to Cailie that, if she was going to be this timid in even asking for his . . . services, she might as well throw her whole plan to the winds and catch the next flight to Seattle.

Resolutely, she looked back at him. He hadn't moved a muscle while she had indulged in her bout with shy little Catherine Linette Wellington. Cailie took a deep breath, and straightened faintly.

"I wish to hire you for the next two weeks, Mr. Creighton," she blurted out, a little too loudly. Her voice didn't shake, not quite. Perhaps it should have.

His features darkening ominously, the man across from her abruptly pushed to his feet. "Perhaps we had better continue this conversation outside."

Cailie gulped at the chill in his voice, but got no chance to protest or apologize for whatever she had done wrong. Alexander Creighton was already striding toward the door, heedless of whether she followed.

Worrying her bottom lip with her teeth, Cailie rushed out into the busy street, nearly tripping over the black-and-white dog sprawled across the entrance to the Hard Rock Café, a pink lei for a collar.

Alexander Creighton waited for her to catch up to him at the corner of the building, then started across Papalaua Street toward the Seawall. Live music from the Lahaina Broiler drifted off behind them.

"I—I'm sorry if I misunderstood the ad," Cailie finally squeaked. "I thought—" She stepped into the street to dodge an oblivious couple hogging the center of the narrow sidewalk, then joined him again once past them. "I thought that—"

"Just precisely what kind of services did you have in mind for the next two weeks, Miss Wellington?"

Cailie gulped. She could taste his anger, savagely leashed into control, though she did not understand it. Her face was flaming even hotter than before, and the well-lit street probably did little to hide her embarrassment. It was a good thing he was staring straight ahead, not looking at her.

"Your ad said that—that you—uh, had an escort service. I've never been here before, and I would like to be shown around the island."

There. It wasn't quite what her original plan had called for, true. But at the moment, she would have bitten off her tongue before admitting that unspeakable truth.

He eyed her noncommittally, his brows slightly furrowed, his square jaw taut. "If you read the ad, you surely read my hours."

After dark. Oh, yes, she was quite aware of that. She shrugged, quickening her step to keep pace with him. "Well, there is a lot of nightlife even in this city. I should like—"

Her voice broke off as Alexander Creighton ground to a halt without warning and spun to face her. She almost ran into him, and stumbled back a step. People milled past them. The night wind feathered strands of ebony hair across his eyes and sculpted cheekbones, and played enticingly with the silk of his shirt. Cailie had the absurd notion that he should be standing on the deck of a pirate ship, cutlass in hand, ordering the red flag raised.

"Should like what, Miss Wellington?"

She cringed under his unwavering regard. No mercy indeed. His piercing midnight eyes seemed to see right through her, to the very heart of her, to her very soul. With something of a shock, Cailie realized that she wasn't going to lie again. She was going to live this one dream. It was all she had left.

Drawing a deep breath, she stiffened her spine and raised her chin. Then, mindless of the passers-by, she blasted him with the truth.

"I want to hire you for the next two weeks—whatever hours you keep. I want you to show me the island, take me out to dinner, dancing, whatever there is to do. I want you to enchant me, romance me, cherish me as though I were the most precious thing you ever found. Make me believe in love, Mr. Creighton. That is what I should like."

Chapter Four

Cailie held his gaze an instant longer, then stared at the sidewalk when he showed no reaction. If he was shocked or repulsed by her words, he hid the fact masterfully.

She waited in silence for another 20 long, pounding heartbeats, before turning and slowly heading for her car at the other end of town.

Two seconds later, soft footsteps matched her own.

"You don't ask much."

His tone was dry, ironic, but strangely, no longer angry. Cailie bit her lip and kept on walking, refusing to look up at him for fear that he would see her blinking away stupid, ridiculous tears.

"If you're not up to it, I'm sorry to have bothered you," she snapped defensively. "If you are, you'll find your time well paid for."

She could see his mouth tighten out of the corner of her eye, his taut skin highlighted by the glow from shop windows and street lights. She shouldn't have pushed it, should have just shut up.

"My time does not come cheaply, Miss Wellington."

Callie shot him an astonished sideways glance, but bit back the retort on the tip of her tongue. She had almost 15 grand for this vacation—money that remained from the sale of the family house after the bank had taken its share, for she'd spent little enough of it over the past five years. Since Alexander Creighton would probably end up with the better part of that tidy sum, his time and expenses should be generously covered. If not, he could sue her.

"I don't think it's necessary to discuss your fee now," she replied evenly. The fact that she *was* paying him was bad enough; having a price tag attached to her fairy tale would be unbearable. "I'd prefer to settle our account at the end of the two weeks. Cash, if you like."

Alexander Creighton seemed to consider her words. His cool gaze flickered over her pensively. Then he nodded. "Very well."

Even as Cailie smiled tenuously, he pivoted and faced her once again. "Where are you staying?"

She blinked at him owlishly, finding only a blank in her mind where the name of her hotel should be. "At—Kaanapali."

He inclined his head slightly. "I will pick you up tomorrow night at eight. In front of the eagle sculpture in Whalers Village."

Before Cailie could reply, Alexander Creighton added, "One more thing. No pictures."

Cailie nodded coolly, she hoped. "That's all right. I—didn't bring a camera, anyway . . ."

She doubted that he heard her. He had already turned again, and was disappearing into the darkness of one of the side streets with quick strides.

Cailie stared after him for another ten seconds, then shrugged, an unsettling mixture of emotions churning in her stomach.

Perhaps he really was some escaped criminal, this mirror image of her phantom. But whatever he was or wasn't, Alexander Creighton was also the most stunning man she'd ever laid eyes on—and he had agreed to her proposal.

The second part of her plan was accomplished.

Tresand drove too fast on the highway and the back roads leading to his estate, where fewer spectators were likely to witness his loss of control.

Control! The word was a curse, burning sarcastically in his mind. Hell, he'd lost half his sanity the second he'd seen her. All gold and sunshine, fragile and hopeful, looking so much like the first time he'd met her—God, nearly a thousand years ago.

A Deeper Hunger

Memory washed over him like the effect of a poison, unwanted yet unstoppable. He'd been only a lad then, in body, though nearly a hundred years had passed since he'd become of the Blood, and she'd been hardly more than a child, willful and spirited. Her hair had been longer, falling far past her waist in a single braid, and crowned with a wreath of wildflowers. She'd run too far from the village, chasing a kitten, had gotten lost in the hills after darkness fell, and had sought shelter in the same cave Tresand had chosen to pass the hours of daylight. He'd found her there, sitting by the empty fire pit, her thin arms wrapped around herself, telling herself stories of dragons and legendary battles and Valkyries in an innocent mixture of Norse and Gaelic.

He'd wrapped his *brat* around her, and had told her tales of the *sidhe* in her native tongue, the language of his own mortal youth. He had told her of fairy castles deep under the hills, while walking her back down to the fortified earthen walls of her village, all the way to the doorway of her family's home, before fleeing like a thief in the night.

But the next night, he'd found her there again, claiming to be lost, a stubborn tilt to her chin. And the night after that, and after that, and for a score of nights after that. She hadn't always come, and on those nights Tresand had felt all too keenly the twisting blade of loneliness. He'd no longer thought of her as a child, though she could have been no more than 13, for she'd told him of her upcoming marriage to one of Ivar's jarls, and of the dreams and hopes and fears she harbored for the future.

He'd taught her Gaelic, told her of other times, of peoples far away, of treasures and journeys and distant lands, feeling as young as his body looked, carefree and joyful and mischievous.

They would speak of silly things, of sad things, of legends and myths and eternal things, would sit together round the fire, time and again, talking for endless hours. Until one night, she'd begged him to let her stay—stay with him, and live in the hills as he did. She had not wanted to return to her parents' dwelling and marry the man she no longer wished to wed, who had likely been killed in the raid he had gone on some time ago anyway.

That was the night Tresand had taken her back to the village for the final time, knowing it had gone too far, knowing now why Aramond had warned him not to associate casually with mortals. She'd had no idea what he was, that the hunger of the Blood still controlled him, that if he'd not fed for too long, he might kill her if she came near. In the darkness out of sight of the village walls, he'd forbidden her ever to return to him again, had told her he would be gone by morning light and she'd not find him, no matter where she searched. And she, boldly meeting his gaze, had sworn by the gods of her people and those of the land that she *would* find him again, no matter where he went.

A Deeper Hunger

The next night, he'd woken from restless slumber in the hour after nightfall to find a smudge of red staining the horizon where no sun would ever set. Like a man possessed, he'd rushed down from the hillside to find Limerick a sea of flames. Its narrow streets were filled with pandemonium, women and children fleeing, solitary Northmen trying futilely to stem the wave of the Irish warriors bent, once and for all, on avenging with equal ferocity the innumerable attacks on their own villages.

Dodging spears and axes and swords from both sides, Tresand had searched the streets with mounting desperation after finding her family's home a pyre of flames reaching into the night sky. A Munsterman's sword had caught him high in the shoulder once, and he'd stumbled to the ground with the blow, near blinded by smoke and blood and roaring flames as the roof and walls of the house beside him collapsed.

Then suddenly she'd been there beside him, crying his name, struggling to drag him out from under the burning timbers, flames licking at her own hair and clothing. He'd pulled free, at that moment thanking God for the superhuman strength of the Blood, but in the next instant hands had torn her from him, fire reflecting like blood on raised blades.

A blow to his head had sent him staggering. A second blow had driven him to his knees, even as he'd screamed with blinding rage at the sight of the tip of a sword protruding from her rib cage. Her beautiful blue eyes were empty and glazed. Thrown to the bloodstained ground like a discarded, broken doll, she had had her precious life stolen from her because he'd forbidden her to come to him again, because he'd not been there when she'd needed him. . . .

Tires squealed as Tresand roughly spun the steering wheel, sending the 4 × 4 skidding around a corner of the narrow road. A cloud of dust from the dirt shoulder rose in the darkness behind him.

He'd built a circle of stones around her grave that time, on a hillside overlooking the Shannon. Just like he'd buried her in the soft earth of another clearing, only a hundred years ago.

Aye, control. What a joke.

It was his loss of control that had killed her last time. His loss of control that had made him nod casually at her proposal tonight—and *accept it*, by God, when he should have bolted the instant he'd seen her eyes, should have turned on his heels and gotten the hell out of that place. Even left the island, for good measure, until he could be certain she was gone. Then live the next sixty-odd years of her lifetime torturing himself with the uncertainty of where she was, with whom . . .

Tresand cursed viciously. But no, he hadn't done any of those things. He'd stayed, and talked to her as though she were a stranger to him, no more than another prospective "employer." Not a woman he had known time and again in the centuries gone by, had killed . . .

A Deeper Hunger

Damn you, Aramond! Why did you forsake me?

Tresand squeezed his eyes shut for a heartbeat, then shifted down and slammed the gas pedal to the floor.

The engine roared in protest, and the tires left black streaks on the pavement. Tresand held the wheel steady in his clenched fists though the road curved sharply right just up ahead.

The 4Runner shot off the blacktop, hit the gravel of the shoulder, and skidded violently out of control as he jerked the wheel around an instant before it was too late. The truck rammed up against a telephone pole on the far side of the road at a 45-degree angle, twisting metal, shattering dark glass. The force of the impact hurled Tresand forward, against the wheel, dashboard, and tinted windshield.

He regained consciousness almost at once. The night was black and silent, except for the rushing of waves against the rocky shore below. Blood trickled hotly across his forehead, down the left side of his face, congealing quickly.

Tresand stared up through the shattered windshield, and felt his ribs grate with fiery pain as he tried to breathe. With a hoarse cry, he slammed his fist against the dashboard. Through it.

Cursing hurt his cut face. He stopped, backed the truck onto the road again, and slowly drove toward home.

It had been worth a try. Anything would have been worth it, to save her from the monster he was, whose very nature would not even allow him to die by his own hand.

Tresand slept that night, to escape his condemning conscience. But sleep brought no reprieve.

Buffeted by guilt, pain, and bitterness, his mind traveled back to a tiny village high in the mountains of a distant land, where a desolate boy ran through muddy streets at night, hungry, lonely, and terrified. Watching from above, Tresand saw him collapse in the corner of two houses, trembling with cold and exhaustion, huddling in the shadows, hoping against all hope that they wouldn't find him even as the sounds of his pursuers rang through the night . . . when suddenly the door of one of the houses opened, and a young woman held out her hand to him and drew him inside. . . .

Tresand watched the scene change to that dark, fetid cell branded indelibly in his mind. He felt again the blinding rage that all but shattered the man who tore the door from its hinges and stormed into the cell, only to find the slender form in the penitent's robe crumpled on the floor, bruises and burn marks covering her skin, twin streams of crimson spilling from her raw wrists. Like the countless times before, he drowned in the horror and agony of that day, cursing Torquemada and the fanatics of the Church, cursing himself for coming too late—cursing her too for her stubborn loyalty, her unconditional love, for taking her own life rather than facing further interrogation and risk betraying him to them. . . .

And Tresand saw a youthful aristocrat and his lady on horseback, riding along the windswept shore after dusk, stopping and dismounting on the cliff to look out over the foam-tipped black ocean. He could almost feel the warmth of the lithe, young body in the man's embrace, hear their softly whispered words of love, her insistent question, and finally, his reluctant confession. . . . And the shock, revulsion, the horror in her eyes as she drew back in mindless panic, stumbling away too fast for him to catch her when suddenly the only ground beneath her was the surf far below . . .

Tresand jerked upright among the twisted sheets, shaking, his body slick with sweat. After a single heartbeat of suspended motion, he slowly let his head fall back and expelled a sharp breath, overwhelmed by the agony of too many memories, memories that would never lie buried in the dust of the past.

He slowed his breathing, deepened it, fighting for dominance over ancient emotions. There was no pain from his ribs, or the gash in his forehead. He touched the hairline over his left eyebrow, found the skin unmarred . . . and cursed, long and thoroughly, in a language forgotten by most of the world, in a voice barely above a whisper.

Disentangling himself from the clammy sheets, Tresand rose and silently walked out onto the wood-planked terrace, closer to the sound of the rushing waves.

Moonlight bathed the rippled sea, reflecting off it in a river of unearthly radiance. He drew the cool, moist sea air into his lungs in deep draughts, felt the wind surround him, drying his sweat and raising gooseflesh on his skin. For long moments, he remained unmoving, a statue silvered by moonlight, held fast in a web of memories.

Recent memories now. These were vivid images of that plain, timid creature who had hardly been able to meet his eyes as she'd "talked business" with him. How he had gotten through that hellish hour, he'd never know. Her proposal had nearly driven him to his knees, right there on the sidewalk, not only from utter shock and disbelief at her words, but from the pain and desperation and shame in her voice. And from the fragile hope.

He didn't dare think on what could have driven her to this, what loneliness and heartache, because if he dwelled on it, he would lose those last shreds of control still grasped in his hands. And God help them both if he did.

Tresand clenched his hands into fists, and slammed them down on the railing of the terrace. Four-inch-thick wood splintered in half. He barely noticed.

Damn. Damn, damn, *damn!*

Catherine Linette Wellington. A new name, a new face, but a familiar soul shining through guileless blue eyes. Bashful, hopeful eyes, wide in wonder as they first saw him, as though he were a creature of dreams, not nightmares . . .

His hands came to his face, blotting out the light on the water. Each time he had found her, that innocent wonder had been in her eyes. Each time, she had died because of him.

And here he was, about to try fate again.

Chapter Five

The sun was rising. Tresand knew it, felt it in his blood, though not a ray of light could penetrate into the house. He'd had it built to his own design even before he first set foot on the island 40 years ago, overseeing all the details, such as installing shutters and blinds that only opened at specific angles. It was safe, even under the brilliant Maui sun. Yet his blood would ever be aware of that sun. Wary of it.

Ah, but he'd chosen this place, a small pleasure to help make an eternity alone bearable. After all, sun was sun, whether in Alaska or Hawaii. And here, the nights were always long, always warm. Perhaps he was getting old, but he'd grown tired of the harsh winters, the cold, driving rain.

Besides, living in such a prime vacation spot had other benefits—the endless stream of tourists passing through, for one. That escort ad had worked well, but he did not need it, not really. Blood was easy to come by in these fast-paced, enlightened times. All it usually took was one visit to a night club. His victims never remembered more than a dream, if even that. And his control had been commendable, too. He'd not killed, not for over a hundred years. . . .

Catherine.

His mouth tightening grimly, Tresand purged the image of a moonlit night on a distant mountain plateau from his mind, and stared into the mirror. His own eyes gazed back at him, looking so very human behind the modern miracles of colored contact lenses. Expelling a harsh breath, he turned away.

Without those contacts, she would not have smiled at him last night when he'd agreed to her proposal. She would have run from him, screaming, and it would have been safer for her by far.

Cursing, Tresand headed into the basement for tools and wood to patch the splintered railing before the rising sun could cast light onto the terrace. And after that, perhaps, he would use the self-control he'd had centuries to cultivate to sleep away the day. It was either that or pace a furrow into his living room floor.

He heard the crunch of gravel beneath tires long before the car came into view on the driveway. The white Geo rolled to a stop beside his battered 4Runner; a young Hawaiian got out, staring at the front-end damage to the truck. Tresand heard his low, appraising whistle before the youth came toward the house and disappeared from view on the patio stairs.

"Living dangerously, are you?" he cheerfully greeted Tresand a moment later, tilting his head to indicate the brightening sky. "Well, here you go, old chap. This'll have to do you for a couple of days, 'cause I'm not back on shift at the hospital till Thursday. What hit the truck?"

Tresand took the metal briefcase from Kimo's hand, set it down, and ignored the question. Last night had left him on edge and short of temper. He glanced at the truck.

"Keys are in it," Tresand said. "Take it down to the shop when you get the chance. It should make it that far."

"Fine!" Kimo threw his hands up in mock exasperation. "Don't tell me. But if some old lady's out to sue your butt for traffic violations, don't expect me to take the rap and go to court for you! Loyalty only goes so far, you know."

Tresand actually smiled at that. He leaned back against the patched railing, crossing his arms over his chest. "Telephone poles don't go around suing people. No little old lady is looking for me, I promise."

Kimo pursed his lips, a sly grin teasing at the corners of his mouth. "Yeah? What about a young, pretty one?"

Tresand's smile froze at the unexpected retort. Then he straightened, his frown slowly shifting from puzzlement to enlightened outrage.

"She was at the hotel yesterday, looking for an escort service," Kimo went on. "I slipped her your—"

"*You* gave her that paper?" His temper fraying, Tresand advanced on his confidant. "Bloody hell, I should tan your hide for that mindless trick! I couldn't figure out how she got hold of that ad. You know I haven't run the damned thing in two years! What the hell did you think you were doing—"

"Take it easy, Alec." Kimo grinned, backing off a step, his hands raised defensively. "I figured, if she was looking for some company, she'd be better off with you than with old *Bruce* from Starlight."

"Like hell."

Kimo ignored Tresand's glare, and looked up into the rising sun. "You've been spending too much time by yourself, *tutu kane*. It'll be good for you to get out among the living again. Besides," he added, casually backing toward the stairs, "you could have refused her."

Tresand scowled at him with narrowed eyes. "What makes you so sure I didn't?"

Kimo shrugged eloquently, his brows raised. "I saw her face when she came back last night. She didn't look like a rejected woman."

The young Hawaiian was off and running before the last word had left his mouth, chuckling all the way.

"I knew I shouldn't have deprived that poor

tiger shark of his midnight snack!"

Kimo laughed aloud at Tresand's growl, and waved once before jumping into the red 4 × 4 and coaxing it up the driveway.

Tresand stared after him, frowning severely, until a grin softened his harsh mien. He should be grateful to that old shark, really. Without it, he'd never have found the crazy kid who was to become that rarest of mortals—a loyal, trustworthy friend.

He picked up the briefcase, staring at it pensively. For almost a decade now, Kimo had been bringing him blood. It made life easy most of the time, especially after he had given up his escort service.

Sighing, Tresand let his gaze wander to the edge of light that had crept onto the far side of the terrace. Beyond, the first rays of the morning sun turned the rippled sea into a glittering field of light, reflecting the cloudless sky above. Like the color of her dress last night, pale blue silk . . .

Brusquely, Tresand turned his back on the beauty of the dawn and strode inside, closing the patio door against the rising sun. With a bit of luck, he'd find sleep for the next 12 hours. Even the cascade of memories that would doubtlessly claim him was preferable to waiting for the day to pass.

Cailie woke to pure, iridescent blue shining outside the open drapes that rippled in the sea breeze. She yawned, indulged in a luxurious stretch, then sat up abruptly, all remnants of sleep driven away.

She'd slept through the night. All the way through it. She hadn't jerked awake during one of her dreams, shaking with fear or crying with the heartache of loss. For the first time in over 13 years, her dreams had been ordinary, forgettable, the kind she'd had before the riding accident.

Stunned, Cailie closed her eyes, then opened them again. She stared out into the bright morning, her thoughts swirling madly in her head, unable to find a solution, an explanation for the absence of the dreams. They'd been a part of her life ever since she'd come out of a three-day coma, courtesy of one of that cranky old mare's stunts. Her father had sold the horse even before she, a heartbroken ten-year-old, had been released from the hospital. No amount of begging, pleading, and arguing had ever changed his mind to let her ride again.

Cailie turned from the rising memories of her long-lost, beloved mare to the matter of her inexplicably missing dreams.

True, there had been only the occasional night where she'd woken up in tears or horror, yet unable to remember why. But not after her family had been killed. No amount of anti-depressants, sleeping pills, useless hours spent at a shrink's office had been able to give her even one night's reprieve from her dreams in the last five years.

And now they were gone, or more correctly,

had been gone for one night. Perhaps, tonight, they would return. . . .

Cailie shook her head, forcing her thoughts in other directions: to the beauty of the blue sky outside, and to the delicious fragrance from the plumeria on the bedstand. Scrambling from beneath the covers, she rushed out onto the balcony in her gecko T-shirt.

The glazed tiles were cool beneath her bare feet, anchoring her in reality as the diamond glitterings of light reflecting from a rippled sapphire ocean greeted her. She sighed, willing her cares to leave her, imagining the breeze carrying them off into the sun.

Her second cloudless day in paradise.

And 12 left.

Shoving aside the tendrils of darkness reaching for her, Cailie painted a smile onto her lips and walked back inside to get ready for a day of sightseeing and beachcombing and napping in the sun.

The digital clock radio on the nightstand read 5:58 A.M. Cailie stared at it blankly for a moment, wondering if the power had gone out during the night. But no, the numbers weren't blinking.

Belatedly, her brain kicked into gear and supplied the missing piece of information: crossed time zones. She'd set her watch onboard the plane, of course, but after that . . .

She shrugged. It certainly explained nearly dozing off on her way back to the hotel last night, and falling asleep the instant her head had touched the pillows. Usually she was quite awake until ten at least—but then, nine o'clock Maui time was really midnight as far as her body was concerned.

Cailie glanced at the clock again and smiled brightly to herself. Being wide and happily awake at 5:59 A.M. was quite an accomplishment. Her smile drooped at her next thought. So would being bright-eyed and bushy-tailed and all fired up to enjoy herself tremendously from eight this evening until God-knew-when in the morning . . . Maui time.

Sunscreen or no sunscreen? Cailie made a face, and stuffed the bottle of lotion back into her beach bag. Then she pulled it out again. The bright noon sun was stinging every exposed inch of her body, despite the soft, constant breeze coming off the water.

Sighing, Cailie began spreading the milky fragrance on her skin. What was the use in even trying to break free of crippling overcaution and imprisoning habits when she couldn't even handle the threat of a sunburn?

Well, at least she wasn't doing this for fear of skin cancer. Despite the fake suntanning back home, she might still burn if she wasn't careful— and that would put a definite "ouch factor" into her perfect vacation.

Besides, she'd only bought SPF 6 and it really was a wonderful body lotion.

Content with that reasoning, Cailie spread

her big "Maui" towel at the Sheraton end of Kaanapali beach and plopped herself down on it, brushing invading tendrils of sand off the edges.

The bright stretch of beach in front of the hotels could have come directly out of a tropical vacation commercial. There were people cliff-diving from the towering black lava, scuba-diving and snorkeling and feeding schools of colorful fish, lounging on the lawns and creamy sand, sipping drinks out of coconuts or pineapples or fancy glasses decorated with fruit and neon-pink umbrellas.

Cailie stretched out with a contented smile and closed her eyes, soaking up the glorious radiance of the sun. Time for a nap, so she could be awake enough to enjoy herself tonight.

Besides, she'd accomplished quite enough for one day, prepaying her hotel room for 13 more nights and accumulating the basics of makeup, something she'd stopped bothering with after the accident. The day had flown by, between lunch at the Rusty Harpoon, across from which she'd spotted the baldheaded eagle sculpture, and her unhurried exploration of Kaanapali beach and the shops and galleries in Whalers Village.

Her thoughts of the overpriced but artsy open-air mall nestled between the towering beachfront hotels grew fuzzy and then trailed off. Gently, the rhythmic, surging rush of waves and the low mumble of voices lulled her into sleep.

Cailie awoke at just past three, and within seconds of sitting up realized several things. One, she hadn't dreamed of her phantom—again. Two, SPF 6 wasn't quite what she had thought it would be. And three, she should have woken up an hour ago and turned over. That way, at least she would have burned evenly.

With another philosophical shrug, Cailie slipped into her cover-up, packed her beach bag, and headed down the walkway to her hotel. Up in her room, she drew the heavy drapes across the open balcony door, slathered her skin with after-sun lotion, and continued her nap on the cool satin comforter.

She woke at four-thirty, ready to take on the world. The after-sun lotion had worked a certifiable miracle, or perhaps the hours spent in tanning beds had paid off after all. And it was astounding, what undisturbed sleep could do for a person.

Cailie's smile faded slightly. She was almost—almost starting to miss the dreams and the phantom who haunted them; they'd been a part of her for so long. But now, there was Alexander, and another dream—a waking dream—to be lived.

By six o'clock, Cailie had scoured the hotel shops for a uselessly tiny but stylish purse to go with her blue silk dress, and hadn't been able to resist a full-length, sea-foam-green, tie-dyed pareu complete with instruction booklet.

By seven-twenty, she had watched a spectacular sunset, had tried on the new makeup, changed her hairstyle three times, and was considering running down to see if the hotel shops were still open so she could buy another dress, because she couldn't for the life of her figure out how that beautiful sheet of luxurious silk could be turned into even one of the exotic pictures in the pareu manual.

By seven-thirty, she was wearing her blue silk dress again, and worrying. It was quite conceivable that Alexander Creighton had changed his mind, and would not show up tonight. Perhaps he'd only agreed to her proposition last night because he was too polite to reject her outright.

Cailie gave herself a severe, silent tongue-lashing to shut down her litany of doubts, snatched up her new purse, and strode out of her room without a single hesitant glance at the mirror on the door.

She forced herself to take her time along the walkway that was all but deserted at this hour of the night. Oriental statues of dragons and buddhas dotted the lawn along the beachfront, waiting silently in pools of shadows cast by hotel lights.

Behind the shielding wall of greenery, the outside dining rooms of the beachfront hotels were marked by soft music and light. More than once, Cailie caught sight of arched bridges crossing lit-up pools and fountains, of bubbling waterfalls and tropical gardens studded with lights. One of them in particular she admired wistfully, a huge open hall with white pillars, fronted by a semicircle of palms arranged in a lit pool, and a waterfall cascading down a rocky wall. It looked like a ballroom out of a fairy tale, bathed in soft white light. All it lacked was the prince and princess dancing in the center.

Perhaps Alexander would take her to this place, tonight. . . .

Cailie shook her head, turned her gaze away from the image, toward the water. Pale white ghosts of anchored boats bobbed in gentle swells in the darkness. Closer to shore, the water glowed turquoise from the illumination of the hotels.

Better not to set her hopes too high. She'd dated enough, after all, to know that no real man could ever equal the phantom of her dreams. There was no reason Alexander Creighton should be any different, except that she was *paying* him to at least try.

The torches in front of Leilani's and El Crab Catcher flickered in the warm night wind, filling the walkway with shifting patterns of light and dark, casting shadows of an earlier age.

Almost there . . . Cailie's stomach tightened in an uneasy mixture of anticipation and dread of what tonight would bring. She followed the walkway into Whalers Village, past Leilani's and the noisily fluttering flags bearing the Whalers Village emblem, to where the eagle sculpture rose, bathed in spotlights, from a pool of cobalt tiles.

Seven-forty, according to her watch. Cailie strolled past the silver-and-brown 15-foot metallic work of art, to the Dolphin Gallery and back again.

Alexander Creighton wasn't early.

She ambled across to the other Dolphin Gallery, where the focus was on jewelry instead of paintings. She gazed at the complex, intricately woven necklaces of gold and shimmering glass, the broaches and bracelets of mythical beasts, and the beaded earrings that seemed to glow from within. After three minutes of staring at a plain gold ring with a glittering, exotically cut green sapphire, she summoned the sales lady.

Seven-fifty-four. Cailie strode out of the gallery, glancing again and again at the elegant ring gracing her hand, and toying with the long, delicate gold earrings. Feeling unaccountably cheerful, she returned to the spotlit eagle.

Seven-fifty-eight.

Good God, couldn't the man be even a *little* early? She'd never understood how people could cut it that close, risk being late, when it was so easy to just leave five minutes early, and get there. . . .

Cailie stopped dead in her tracks, shook her head, frowning. Then she slipped off her watch and, with a wide smile, dropped it into the nearest garbage container.

That was when she saw him.

The man striding across the central square below was the kind whose looks and lithe, fluid movements drew speculative glances from women and envious ones from other men. It actually took Cailie a number of seconds to realize that this was her escort, that she wasn't caught in one of her haunting dreams.

Incredibly, she had forgotten just how much he looked like her phantom. Or, perhaps, he simply looked even more like that specter tonight, dressed in dark gray rather than white. Only the memory of his midnight eyes served to remind her that Alexander Creighton was real.

He reached the top of the stairs, and continued toward her. His casual suit didn't have a wrinkle. Cailie found herself wondering inanely whether he was very, very rich, or simply an accomplished "housewife." But whatever the case, at that moment she was extremely grateful for every dab of powder and touch of mascara that would bolster her self-confidence about her own appearance. Though she should have bought another dress . . .

Cailie's muddled thoughts stopped altogether when, with casual grace, Alexander kissed her hand, then tucked it into the crook of his arm. She could feel the hard muscle beneath her fingers, and remembered silk and last night at the Hard Rock Café.

"Good evening . . . Catherine?"

The name jolted her back into reality. Nobody who knew her at all called her that. But then, she was the one who had left her full name on his answering machine, though God only knew why, and of course he couldn't know that she didn't use that name. . . .

"Cailie," she corrected, pulling herself together, cutting off the constant jumble of thoughts that kept her mind from dwelling on what she was truly doing here. Thankfully, her voice held steady. "Short for—"

"Catherine Linette," he finished with a maddeningly masculine little smile, looking not at all embarrassed. "Pray forgive my mistake. And do call me Alexander, or Alec, as you wish."

"Alexander." Cailie managed a nervous smile as he led her back down into the square, past the lit-up tree, up to the whale's skeleton that was displayed at the road entrance to Whalers Village. It hadn't been his mistake, of course, but she decided then and there that she'd forgive him almost anything, so long as he kept talking in that rough velvet voice.

But God, she didn't know if she could go through with this. Perhaps she could still call the whole thing off. . . .

"Have you had dinner yet?" Alexander's words interrupted the coward's voice that had again begun to fill her mind. "There is an excellent, quiet little restaurant down by the water in Lahaina."

Cailie nodded, keeping her eyes down. "That sounds wonderful."

"Good." He was smiling. She could hear it in his voice. "I've already made a reservation."

Cailie said nothing, only bit her tongue, and kept on remembering that she was having the time of her life.

He led her to the open white Jeep parked— illegally, she was sure, because she'd never even *think* of parking there—alongside the brightly lit main entrance to Whalers Village. Alexander opened the passenger door for her, even shut it behind her, before sliding behind the wheel.

"Thank you." Cailie consciously kept her lips curved up into a smile, for fear she'd be caught staring open-mouthed. She felt as though, in the space of less than two minutes, she had been whirled into another time, into an age of chivalry and courtesy she'd thought long lost to the present.

She risked an overt glance at him as he started the engine, reminding herself again that she had never seen this man before last night, that only by some quirk of chance did Alexander Creighton look like her phantom.

Still, she felt . . . safe with him. Embarrassed, yes, and nervous, most certainly. But inexplicably, irrationally, she trusted him, believed, even, that he would do his best to fulfill the chore she had set him last night. Because now, there was no trace of the man she had parted with in Lahaina last night. No trace at all of the cool, distant . . . employee.

Cailie banished the thought, and forced the smile back onto her lips. This was the beginning of her time in paradise, and by God, she *was* going to enjoy it!

She looked different tonight. Tresand studied her as she studied the menu. He noted her painted lips, her meticulously curled hair, the touch of blush, of eye shadow and kohl and mascara, the faint trace of an elusive fragrance hovering about her. He cursed the long, gold filigree earrings that caught the light and drew his eyes again and again to the slender line of her throat, and the gold ring with its sparkling green gem that made him too aware of every graceful motion of her hands.

She was prettier tonight, no doubt about it. More attractive, in a classy, glamorous way. But it wasn't her. He was willing to bet she'd spent more time with a curling iron and cosmetics tonight than she had in the past five years.

Tresand lowered his gaze to the menu before she could look up, catch him watching her, and become nervous again.

God, but she was jittery. He'd never known her like this, so painfully shy and uncertain. If only he could tell her at least some fragments of the truth, to put her more at ease. But he couldn't, of course. One sip of that poison was as deadly as the whole bottle.

And one slip of the tongue could bring disaster for them both.

The night air rushing through the Jeep revived Cailie somewhat. Shivering, she stared out at the ocean on Alexander's side of the road, snatching the occasional glance at him because she couldn't stop looking at him.

It was probably only the age-old truth that opposites attract. Alexander was everything she wasn't: exotic, alluring, dark, mysterious, and instantly and innately in control of himself and his surroundings on a downright uncanny level. While her face was an open book, Alexander's was like a carefully crafted mask. Not cold, or impersonal, just . . . controlled. Always that control. It hid any flaws or weaknesses and left only impenetrable perfection. Enchanting charm, irresistible . . .

His words cut short her musings. "My jacket is in the back seat, if you are cold."

"That's all right." Cailie snapped her gaze forward, to watch the centerline markings on the road blur past. Moments later, she'd molded into the seat again, her eyelids drooping.

She jerked upright. "I'm sorry . . ."

"Don't be."

Alexander's gaze touched her briefly. It was warm, not scornful and ridiculing, and another shiver coursed over her. She shook her head to clear it of the cobwebs of sleep.

"Do you—um, know of any interesting things to do around here? In the daytime, I mean? Besides—besides suntanning and beachcombing?" She smiled at him, doing her best to look awake, to get him to talk more, in that velvety voice of his.

Alexander was nodding, his gaze still on the road. "The diving is excellent here."

Cailie made a face. "I'd love to, but I can't—go down very deep. My—" She shook her head, cut herself off. This wasn't the time to list her medical excuses. "I'm afraid diving is not an option."

"All right, then. Try snorkeling. You needn't go deep, and you'll see just as much. Although"—he met her slightly unfocused eyes for an instant—"you still mustn't go out alone."

"But—"

He shrugged off her protest. "That won't be difficult. It's a very popular sport, and most people won't mind if you join them."

Cailie snapped her mouth shut, and said nothing. She would never, ever simply swim up to somebody and blurt out, "Hi, can I snorkel with you?" Especially not with a mask on her face that made her look like the creature from the Black Lagoon.

But Alexander didn't know that and she wasn't about to argue. She was far too tired to argue. Inexorably, her eyes slipped closed.

" . . . Honolua, north of here. Visibility's often poor for the first few yards, but there's an abundance of sea life. If you're interested in that sort of thing."

Cailie looked up, realizing she'd nodded off again. The bright lights of the entrance to her hotel blurred as she stifled yet another yawn. Then she frowned.

"How did you know where—" she started, fuzzily, but Alexander was already getting out.

"We'd better get you to bed."

His arm came around her, easing her out of the Jeep, drawing her against him. He walked her into the lobby, past the rattan sofas in the orchid garden, between the pools whose fountains and

96

blue lights had long been shut down. She shelved her half-forgotten question and yawned again, too tired even to be embarrassed.

By the elevators, Cailie pulled away slightly. "I can take it from here."

Alexander's midnight gaze caught hers, intent with concern. "Are you sure? I can—"

"No. I'm fine." She shook her head, then nodded. A sweet, elusive scent drifted on the air, distracting her already wandering mind. "I mean, yes. I'll make it. Really. I'm just—tired."

Her head tilted sideways a bit as she looked up at him, blinking. He nodded once, an indulgent smile curving the corners of his mouth. Cailie bit her lower lip. God, he was too devilishly handsome when he smiled like that.

"I will see you tomorrow night, then. In the lobby, same time."

She beamed at him, glad she had enough presence of mind to keep her mouth shut over her wandering thoughts. "That'd be nice."

"One more thing."

Before she knew it, he brushed her cheek lightly with the backs of his fingers, a gentle, all-too-brief caress. Cailie caught herself just as she would have turned her face into his touch.

"Colors and paints are not for you, Cailie. Leave your skin naked to the starlight and your hair free in the night wind. There is more beauty in that by far."

Holding her gaze, he lightly kissed the back

97

of her hand, then turned and strode out of the lobby.

Cailie stared after him blankly, a vague frown creasing her brows as she tried to decide whether she should feel complimented or insulted. No. She was far too tired for either.

Leaning against the cool marble wall and yawning again, she waited for the elevator. It seemed like forever before it arrived and she was once again in the dark sanctuary of her room. She didn't turn on any lights, only hung the "Do Not Disturb" sign out and pulled the heavy balcony drapes shut. And before crawling into bed, she shoved the newly bought cosmetics and crazy-glue hair spray from the bathroom counter into the trash bin.

Alexander's last remark danced through her thoughts as she plummeted toward sleep, smiling. He must be a poet, this twin of the phantom from her dreams. Either that, or a used-car salesman.

Giggling, Cailie slipped into a dreamless sleep.

Tresand silently stepped through the open balcony door, and slipped between the heavy drapes into a room as black as night. With slow, hesitant steps, he crossed to the bed.

She lay on her side, her back to him, deeply asleep. Her nightshirt still lay folded on a discarded pillow. The covers had drifted down to her hips along her back, but she'd twined her hands in them, hugging the bunched-up sheets to her chest and resting her head on them.

A Deeper Hunger

The slow, steady beat of her heart filled his senses, a seductive, primal rhythm calling to him. He sank onto his heels beside the bed, his gaze intent on her small, heart-shaped face so peaceful in repose.

A thousand questions, a thousand pleas, old and new, clamored in his mind. He shut them all away. He had given voice to them before, and they had brought only anguish and death.

With a trembling hand, he reached out and traced a dark gold strand of her hair lying against the covers. She stirred in her sleep, then stilled. The faintest trace of a smile curved her lips, and he wondered what her dreams were. He imagined easing the covers away from her, gliding his hands over her skin, tasting its living heat and silken texture, and slipping into her dream. . . .

He snatched his hand back and cursed silently, his mouth tightening grimly as he stared down at her.

So trusting, so fragile, so . . . human. Mortal.

Tresand shut his eyes. He could feel the warmth radiating from her skin, the glow just short of a sunburn. Bitterness welled in him, a flood tide so deep he could drown in it.

A child of the sun, this one. As she always had been. So filled with light, with love, with fragile life . . .

He surged to his feet and paced silently toward the balcony door. From the threshold, he cast one last glance back at the peacefully sleeping woman.

"May God have mercy on us, *mo chridhe*."

Then he was a shadow in the night, slipping away before the sunrise.

Chapter Six

Cailie lay awake in the still-dark room, watching the digital numbers change on the clock radio as the minutes slid by. The balcony drapes banned the bright sunlight that would normally have woken her hours ago, allowing only a light sea breeze to carry the delicious scent of the plumeria blossoms through the room.

Her phantom had remained absent again last night. If she'd dreamed of anything, she couldn't recall it.

Her brows furrowed. It was . . . disturbing, this sudden loss of her haunting dreams. She should be overjoyed, she knew, to be rid of them finally, and yet . . .

She sighed impatiently. She had Alexander now, to take the place of her phantom. She no longer needed those dreams.

Cailie stretched, yawned, relegated the worrying about her dreams to some back corner of her mind, and thought instead of Alexander.

Last night's dinner had been awkward, the stroll down Front Street almost fun. As with so many things in her life, the evening had ended just as she was finally starting to really enjoy herself. Her blasted shyness had remained—until he'd taken her dancing.

Cailie sighed and turned onto her back to stare at the ceiling, her lips curving into a dreamy smile. It had been every bit as magical as her vision of a fairy-tale ballroom had been, and Alexander had played the perfect prince to her Cinderella.

He was a born dancer. It hadn't mattered that she'd never learned to dance that way, that she didn't know the steps and her balance wasn't the best. He'd swept her away into the flow of the music, had made her oblivious to everything except the lean strength of his body against hers, and the graceful magic of the dance.

And then, at about two o'clock, her get-up-and-go had packed up and left. Her body had wanted—no, *demanded*—its nine hours sleep.

Cailie's mouth turned down as she recalled her inane mumblings on the drive home. Alec had been wonderful about last night, hadn't even laughed at her, but the embarrassment of nearly nodding off on her feet was not something she cared to repeat.

It was too bad, really, that his time was so

limited. It would have been nice to have him show her around the island in the daytime too. But perhaps he had a full-time job during the day. Perhaps he was squiring around some other woman. . . .

Cailie cut off the thought and rolled out of bed, detouring to yank open the curtains before heading for the shower. There must be a hundred better things to do in paradise than harbor jealous notions about, of all people, a male escort.

Shopping sounded like an excellent way to start.

The sun was long past its zenith when Cailie cautiously parked her white Probe on the nearly nonexistent strip of shoulder lining the road a hundred feet above the azure waters of Honolua Bay. Her beach bag bulged with her purchases from the Cannery Mall: fins, mask and snorkel, a concise guide to all things living and dying in Hawaiian waters, and a small bottle of suntan lotion with SPF 15. The gorgeous white dress she had also bought hung in the closet in her hotel room.

Gingerly, she picked her way down the uneven, broad dirt trail leading to the bay. An abundance of gigantic, moss-and-vine-covered trees and shrubs wove into an airy green tunnel which ended rather abruptly at a dilapidated, half-sunken concrete boat ramp on a rocky beach.

Cailie slipped the thongs off her feet to test the

strangely murky-looking shore water, and leaped back three feet. This was Hawaii, for God's sake! The water was not supposed to be cold!

Dismayed, she took in the number of scattered red and white dots out in the bright blue bay marking snorkelers. They couldn't all be wearing wet suits! Besides, there were children playing in the water too, a little ways down the unremarkable shore, where a young couple was setting up a picnic.

Perhaps she was just spoiled by the warm water at Kaanapali. Frowning pensively, Cailie picked her way over the large rocks to a shady spot beneath some trees. Considering the lack of white sand, the chilly water, and the dearth of parking available on the hazardous road whose every second curve sported a "Blow Horn" sign, it was amazing that there should be anyone at all on this beach.

But both Alexander and the lady in the ABC store where she'd bought her gear had praised this marine park as a wonderful place to see fish. Perhaps that was what drew all these people.

Cailie shed her cover-up, determined to discover the attraction of this beach. Armed with her fish chart and mask, she reluctantly left her beach bag behind and waddled down to the waterline in her flippers.

The last time she'd tried this particular sport was ten or 12 years ago on a school field trip. She'd loved the freedom the snorkel gear gave her in the water, but the one thing most prominent in her memory was the red ring left by the face mask, and the laughter of those who hadn't gone into the water.

Gritting her teeth, Cailie waded thigh-deep into the bay, more than content to be on her own this time. After a long breath, she launched herself into the chilly waves and surged to her feet again instantly, spluttering from more than cold.

Poor visibility!

Muttering unintelligible imprecations through her teeth clenched around the mouthpiece of her snorkel, Callie mentally dunked Alexander. Curse that man for his euphemisms! He was probably hoping she'd drown in this mud so he wouldn't have to put up with her anymore! Poor visibility indeed.

Disgruntled, Cailie reluctantly lowered her face beneath the surface again. The murky, silt-laden cold fresh water mixing along the shore had all the clarity of a brick wall.

She straightened, stared out over the inviting, sky-reflecting surface of the bay. *That* water looked perfectly clear and the only way to get out there was to muddle through this mess. Of course, she could always turn back. . . .

With an expression of disgust, Cailie pushed off again, into the bay. Her arms and the laminated fish chart outstretched in front of her, she paddled for all she was worth. Her breath rasped eerily under water. She couldn't see her hands in front of her face, couldn't see the bottom that was less than three feet below her, couldn't see anything but brown mush.

Her heart was pounding triple time. She loved water, but this wasn't water. This was pea soup! Panic grew silently in the back of her mind, painting improbable but nonetheless utterly vivid graphic images of a huge, gaping, tooth-filled shark's jaw suddenly appearing in front of her face, or any imaginable and unimaginable deep-sea monster materializing out of the murky haze without so much as a second's warning.

Suddenly, she could see bottom, and boulders lining the sandy sea floor. Fish gracefully darted through the rapidly clearing water. Amazingly enough, she wasn't even cold anymore.

Cailie slowed her breathing, until her brain could reacquaint itself with the notion of having her face underwater and getting air at the same time. In a matter of moments, she was gliding through the water as though she'd never been on land.

Enchanted, she paddled along the side of the bay, over colorful reef formations and such a multitude of fishes, she gave up on trying to identify them and simply marveled at their existence. On the far side of the cove, the rusted skeleton of a car that had apparently not made the sharp turn north of the bay was buried among huge coral boulders, disintegrating and now part of the reef.

When Cailie finally got her head out of the water, shivering from head to toe, it was almost dusk.

A Deeper Hunger

Cailie turned back toward the shore, eyeing it with no misgivings. She could try her luck on the boulders rising into cliffs on the sides of the bay, or she could cross the mud belt again.

Forcing a grim smile around the snorkel, she started toward shore. The water grew opaque, then murky, and Cailie raised her head above the water, the fish chart held before her as a shield. Yet the specters of tooth-filled jaws still lingered in her mind, luring her face below the surface again. In the end, she nearly had a head-on collision with a large rock in just over two feet of water. But then, of course, she hadn't known she was that close to shore.

Her knees scraped, Cailie collected her shredded dignity, packed it up along with her gear, and headed back to the hotel.

Enough adventuring for one day.

She was early. Tresand knew, because it was three minutes to eight as he pulled up beneath the light-studded monkey-pod tree in front of the main entrance to her hotel. She was already waiting for him outside the lobby, looking like a vision in a sheer, shimmering gown of white.

He felt his chest grow tight. They'd painted angels like this, in the early days of Christianity.

She came toward him even as he shut off the Jeep and got out.

"Hi."

Tresand took in her shy, unpretentious smile, her softly falling dark gold hair, the fresh, radiant glow of her skin, and drew savage rein on himself. The hours of light had rarely seemed so endless, knowing she was so close, yet so utterly out of his reach.

"Cailie." The word was too gruff by far, his smile more than a little strained. "You are beautiful tonight."

She looked down, blushing in delightful counterpoint to the snowy dress, but he caught her chin and kissed her cheek, lightly, as an old maiden aunt might do. Then he ushered her into the Jeep, and pulled out onto Nohea Kai Drive.

Whalers Village was a ridiculously short distance away, yet driving was infinitely preferable to walking down the beach with Cailie. Tresand didn't trust himself that far, didn't trust himself to be alone with her, even in the darkness of a public beach.

Not yet, at least. Not while the wonder, the agony of finding her, was so new. Not while he could still see that lifeless body in his arms, up on the mountainside, see it so clearly as though it had been yesterday . . .

"Did you get out today?" His question was too abrupt after their moment of silence, but Tresand didn't care. It forced him out of his dark memories, into the present. His mouth tight, he turned off onto the main road.

Cailie was nodding when he glanced at her, catching her windblown hair in her hands.

"I went to Honolua, as you suggested. It was incredible! Well, once past the mud wall, that is." She shot him a sidelong look through her veil of hair, and hesitated as though expecting something.

Chagrin, presumably.

Tresand only nodded, biting back a smile. There must have been a heavy runoff from the cane fields again.

Cailie sent him another glance, then went on with undaunted enthusiasm, counting off her discoveries. "I saw moorish idols, angelfish, trumpetfish . . . and those big, silver ones, I forget what they're called . . . Oh, and that fish with the funny name, humumuku . . ." She shook her head, looked at him for help.

Tresand raised his brows, feigning ignorance. Her curiosity was disarming, but he wasn't about to start in on Hawaiian fish names. Although, if it came right down to it, that was probably one of the safer topics they could get into tonight.

Cailie shook her head again, a studious frown settling between her brows. "I'll have to look that one up again when I get back. But it's Hawaiian for a pig's face—or something like that. Oh, and there was this huge, neon-striped parrotfish, chomping away at the coral. Did you know—"

"Yes," Tresand interrupted brusquely, pulling off the Kaanapali Parkway and into the parking lot behind Whalers Village. "Fascinating creatures, parrotfish."

He found a parking spot in record time, and ushered Cailie out of the Jeep. He placed her hand on his arm and drew her into the shopping square, determined to forestall the inevitable conversation on the sex changes of fish. "How do you feel about Mexican for dinner? Chico's makes wonderful fresh fruit drinks."

Cailie stared at him for an instant, and then, to his amazement, erupted into laughter even as she quickened her step beside him.

After four days of living in paradise, Cailie had gone back to her true former self. Days of luscious meals with *haupia* for dessert, too many Lappert's ice cream cones and no hard workouts conspired against her, sneaking to put back some of her long-lost pounds. But the airy, loosely flowing lavender dress she'd bought this morning did a truly admirable job of hiding her indulgences.

She absently stirred the whipped cream into her mango smoothie, frowning at the calm, sparkling waters of Lahaina from her window spot on the second story of the Cheeseburger in Paradise. A multitude of boats anchored in the deeper turquoise water beyond the reef bobbed in the gentler swells, while surfers down by the *Carthaginian II* caught the breakers rising toward shore.

Sighing, Cailie tucked wayward strands of hair behind her ear, for the dozenth time. The stiff breeze that came off the water constantly tugged at her hair and dress, and blew off course the sparrows streaking through the busy restaurant.

If Alexander had noticed anything about her

extra pounds, he'd not said a word. Quite the contrary, actually. His every glance, every touch, told her without words that he found her beautiful.

Cailie's gaze followed the sign hanging over the table next to her out the window. "Lanai & Nautical Miles," it proclaimed. In the distance, against the hazy backdrop of the island, one of the huge white cruise ships was slowly passing by. Janey would be on a ship like that right now . . . Cailie mentally shook her head, snapping herself out of her incipient reminiscencing.

Alexander Creighton . . . She'd been thinking about him, about what an extraordinary man he was, and what heady magic he could weave, without the least effort. While she'd been mortified with embarrassment on their first evening, she had nevertheless eagerly awaited their second encounter. And today . . . today, she could hardly wait until evening came. She'd been sleeping in till ten, which was really no loss of a day, since most shops didn't open till 11, anyway. And she didn't need that many hours of sleep, not anymore, not since her dreams had disappeared.

Cailie shook her head, refusing to get on that train of thought. She smiled, recalling how well she'd made it through last night, with only a temporary low spot around two o'clock.

And the night had been marvelous. Alexander had been charming, funny, ridiculously gallant. He no longer seemed a stranger to her, but a long-time friend, companion.

It was an experience every woman should have

at least once in her life, Cailie mused wistfully, to be treated like someone precious, like a lady of days gone by. To have a man be the perfect gentleman, ever attentive and chivalrous, from opening the car door to kissing her hand when greeting her and bidding her good night.

And that was as far as Alexander had ever gone. He wasn't like some of the younger self-centered or arrogant man she'd met at dance clubs or bars, or like the lascivious older men who had, inexplicably, inevitably come on to her the few times Janey had talked her into going to a local night club with her, in the time between husband number one and husband number two.

Cailie shook her head. No, Alexander was nothing like those men. Not once, in all their hours together, had he suggested anything improper by word, deed, or glance. She felt safe with him, felt cherished and protected. She felt closer to him, after only these few shared evenings, than she ever had to another man—even to Kyle, whom she'd dated for over two years before the accident. With Alexander, she felt like a fairy-tale princess being courted by her knight in shining armor.

Yes, that was something no woman should be cheated of. And the bitter knowledge that everything was an illusion, bought and paid for, was kept securely shut out of her thoughts as she watched the waves break against the sunny Seawall and let the day's long hours heighten her anticipation of another night in paradise.

Chapter Seven

Cailie spent the remainder of the afternoon wandering through Lahaina—again. She toured most of the historical sites, and drifted through the art galleries, jewelry shops, and boutiques listlessly, feeling alone. Even the cheerful, lacy flower-print dress she'd picked up in one of the shops in the Wharf Center couldn't bolster her spirits.

As she passed the corner of the Pioneer Inn, where the parrots chatted noisily on their stands under a large umbrella, the man in the khaki tropics outfit turned toward her, smiling as he snatched up a rainbow-plumaged bird by its beak and transferred it to his shoulder.

"Held the birds yet, miss? Come hold the birds, and we'll get you some fantastic photo postcards you can send home to astound your family and friends!"

Cailie shook her head and waved him off, struggling to maintain her smile despite the bitterness brought forth by the man's harmless words. He couldn't know that none of her friends even knew she was here, couldn't know that there was no family left to whom she could send a card.

She released a slow, ragged breath and stared into the sky beyond the Seawall, ignoring the small plane towing a banner proclaiming "T-Shirt Factory 53% off Sale." She sought solace in the assurance that dusk was near, and that the loneliness of the day would soon be forgotten.

Less than four hours later, after an elegant dinner at the seaside hotel dining room she'd so admired two days ago, Cailie was once again ambling down Front Street, arm in arm with Alexander. The colorful awnings had disappeared from the shops since sunset, but downtown Lahaina was just as lively after dark as it was in the daytime, and somehow, even more tropical. But to Cailie, Lahaina wasn't even on the same planet now that Alec was with her.

Strains of live rock 'n' roll from the Cheeseburger in Paradise floated down from the corner building to accompany them as they strolled along the Seawall. A warm wind swirled the full skirt of her new lacy flower-print dress around her legs, and carried the delicious smells of a grill. Further down, the occasional large wave was dousing the sidewalk with spray.

"And that stand selling parrots—you know the

114

one, over there in the little market square?" Cailie gestured loosely across the street, to the shops already closed for the night, and went on without waiting for Alexander to reply. "Well, the salesman was trying to get this bright green bird to say 'aloha' to a bunch of tourists, and the parrot suddenly turned on him and squawked at full volume, 'I wanna be a lawyer!' You should have seen the—"

Cailie broke off as Alec abruptly stopped partway down the Seawall and turned to look out over the ocean, his expression distant.

She flushed and clamped her mouth shut. Good God, she'd been babbling again. Yet Alec said nothing, only drew her forward until she stood between him and the balustrade, then braced his hands against it on either side of her. Banishing her embarrassment, Cailie closed her eyes and leaned back slightly, into him, basking in the heady sensation of being surrounded by his presence.

"Look."

Guiltily, Cailie craned her neck and glanced up at Alec. He was staring out over the water. Her gaze followed his down toward Lahaina harbor, where the moon stood like a floodlight low in the sky, so bright it painted the boats at anchor offshore a ghostly white. Cailie inhaled softly as she found the replica brigantine moored in the harbor.

"That—oh, Alec, it's magical!" Its rigging illuminated, the *Carthaginian II* hovered on the black

115

water sparkling with reflections, a ship of lights, something ethereal out of a dream.

"It looks so ordinary in the daytime," Cailie marveled softly, staring still, as if mesmerized by the play of lights on the water and the moonlight glittering on the tiny ripples. "Not very pretty at all, just cold metal that's starting to rust. But now . . ." She sighed, smiling wistfully up at Alexander. "The night hides so many faults, doesn't it? It takes the ugliness into itself, and keeps it from being seen . . ."

The sudden tautening of Alexander's body made her keep the rest of her musings to herself. Yet he said nothing, only drew her along the Seawall, arm in arm, as before.

"How would you like more history tonight, Cailie?"

Because of his tension, she'd expected his voice to be gruff, even angry perhaps, but it was as warm and smooth as ever. Willingly losing herself in it, she met his eyes dreamily.

"I love history." And she loved his voice, his midnight eyes. Loved him . . .

Reality intruded with a cold blow, scourging the smile from her face. Good God, what ridiculous thoughts! Cailie felt heat rush into her face. What she loved was the character her wishes had created, the character that a man by the name of Alexander Creighton was playing so perfectly.

" . . . to La Perouse," Alexander was saying. "The moon is nearly full, and it will be high in the sky by the time we get there."

116

Cailie forced a smile. "Sure." Alec's arm tightened around her waist, and her smile turned bittersweet.

"Do you have a pair of running shoes back at the hotel?"

Cailie stiffened in silent mortification. Oh, God, here it came at last, the inevitable remark about her lack of exercise. She swallowed hard, kept her gaze on the sidewalk, and shook her head. "No."

Alexander shrugged, his step quickening. "Then we'd better find you something in town before the shops close."

He led her across the street toward the Wharf Center. Birds chattered noisily in the lit-up banyan tree, and occasional cockroaches skittered across the sidewalk, but Cailie hardly noticed. Her feet dragged with reluctance. Yet she did not break away from Alexander.

"You needn't worry about the dress—it'll be fine. But you'd break your ankles in those thongs on the lava fields."

Cailie ground to a stop, stared up at him. He was smiling, his midnight eyes glittering with a teasing light. Touching his lips to her brow in a brief, brotherly gesture, Alexander drew her forward again, and Cailie matched her stride to his, grinning like a fool.

What had sounded like a good idea on the lit streets of Lahaina was beginning to give Cailie second thoughts as the drive to La Perouse went on . . . and on.

Cailie knew the coast road from Lahaina, descending into the isthmus. But it was different again at night, for the ocean was hidden from view most of the way. They could have been driving through the middle of a red dirt-and-lava desert, for all she could see.

They crossed the cane- and pineapple-field filled isthmus, continued southward along the coast, through a moonlit plain. To their left, Haleakala came into view, ringed with silvery clouds that cast ghostly shadows in the bright moonlight. Only the occasional position lights of an arriving airplane and the steady path of a satellite mingled among the stars. Closer to the ground, road-marking cats' eyes, headlights, and distant city lights disrupted the night.

About half an hour after leaving Lahaina, a sign proclaimed, "Wailea Makena End of Highway 1 Mile." The road streaked through a forest of light from fancy hotels fronted by blooming hedges and ground-lit walkways, light-studded trees, and golf courses with sprinkler systems. One of the hotels, a huge, pseudo-moorish structure in white, looked like a fairy-tale palace out of 1001 Arabian Nights, with spires and domes, all lit up. Ahead, in the distance, towering clouds rose above the treetops.

Cailie sat silently beside Alexander, fidgeting with the ring she could wear only in the cool of night, when her fingers returned to normal size. The fragments of their conversation had trailed off as her attention had become more

118

and more absorbed by the landscape. Now the darkness of the night grew complete, no longer broken by the hotels' lights. Yellow signs warned of "No Outlet" and "No Sight Distance," even as the two-lane road curved, rose, and fell like a writhing snake.

Then came the ominous sign, "Narrow Road." The centerline vanished, and with it the cats' eyes and shoulder reflectors. Black walls overgrown with oleander sprang up on the right, alternating with houses and black lava bays as the road twisted onward. The beams of the headlights revealed a surface that consisted more of patched potholes than actual pavement. Out over the water, the intermittent flash of a lighthouse marked an island in the black ocean of night.

Cailie tensed even as Alexander slowed the Jeep. Trees, wall fragments, houses, and breaker-washed, rocky coves came at her out of the darkness of each curve, without warning.

Then suddenly, they were out in the open, and everything was flat. Black fields stretched on either side of the road, up the slopes of Haleakala and down to the sea. Insects whirred through the beams of the headlights, shadows shifted eerily among the yellow, dry grass and the boulders of lava on the roadsides. The only remainders of civilization were the telephone poles lining the road and the dot or two of light low on the slopes of the extinct volcano.

Suddenly the bumpy remains of pavement were gone, and the Jeep crept along a path of crushed lava. The road was so poor, it didn't dawn on Cailie that they'd turned off onto a parking area until Alexander shut off the Jeep.

If Makena had marked the end of the highway, they had just reached the end of the world.

Cailie shivered. Certainly, the moon was full. It even shone brightly enough for her to see the cloud bank on the horizon, to see the harsh, rugged black lava fields that stretched back from the ocean into the hills.

It was not a particularly inviting landscape, especially at night. There wasn't a single light here, not a single sign of human habitation since they'd passed those last houses miles ago. Without the illumination of the headlights, even the poles and cables were invisible. The only sound Cailie could hear was the roar of breakers exploding against an invisible shore not far away, and the incessant whine of cicadas.

She took a deep breath. "Alec? Are you sure this is such a good idea?"

"You won't forget this place," he reassured her in a low voice, finding and squeezing her hand for a moment. "Come."

Cailie bit her lip, then watched him get out, inordinately glad to hear his voice again. Theirs had been a companionable silence, true, but it had been silence all the same. At least, though, the eerie landscape had prevented her from dwelling on other thoughts.

Reluctantly, Cailie left the security of the Jeep, and instantly understood Alec's insistence on solid footwear. Though light as pottery shards, the rough, cutting lava would have been a nightmare in thongs. Even so, the land looked like something out of a horror movie—a travesty of freshly tilled soil, frozen into sharp, jagged rock.

"This is one of the latest flows from Haleakala," Alec noted conversationally, taking her hand and starting down some invisible path amidst the harsh surface. "The lava is only two hundred years old, give or take a decade. Up there, somewhere"—he pointed toward the rising hills—"are burial caves, and a place where human footprints are said to mark the lava flow."

He paused, then chuckled. "A friend of mine was up there one time, climbing through the lava tubes. He didn't realize what he'd found until he came across the first row of skulls. He made it back to the car in record time that day. But then, he never was one for history."

Cailie didn't comment, only held on to his hand with grim determination and followed in his steps. She could see next to nothing, didn't know what her next step was going to bring, and thinking about skulls and boiling rock made her skin crawl.

"You sure you know where you're going? We could have brought a flashlight . . ."

Alec's quiet chuckle shut her up. God, what a coward he must think her!

"Don't worry so much, Cailie. I have excellent night vision. I won't let you fall."

Cailie bit her lip and frowned. The rushing of

waves was just off to their right now, loud and irregular. She could see the white shimmer of breakers not 30 feet away, and further out, the river of moonlight reflecting off a rippled sea.

Suddenly the ground beside her exploded into a roaring tower of white water. With a screech, Cailie jumped, right into Alec. He should have been bowled over by her momentum, face-first into the sharp lava, but he caught her against him and steadied her.

The thunder and geyser subsided simultaneously. Within seconds, the night had grown quiet again.

"Alec!" Cailie exhaled sharply. "Alec, what the— what was that?" Trying to quiet her pounding heart, she clutched Alexander's arm. Her legs felt unsteady, watery.

"That, my dear, was a fairly large wave in one of the blow holes. There are lava tubes—"

"Don't you 'my dear' me!" The smile in Alec's voice made Cailie stiffen and pull away from him. Embarrassed, she stumbled past him, but he caught her arm before she'd taken more than two steps along the narrow path.

"Hold, Cailie. Unless you care to chance riding the air on one of those waves, of course."

The humor had left his voice. She fixed him with a mutinous stare, but nevertheless let him resume the lead. "I don't think I'd call this place romantic."

"Oh, it can be, I assure you," Alexander countered, smiling again. She could hear it in his voice, and squashed a rising tendril of jealousy even as he grew serious once more. "But foremost, it is a place of history."

Cailie scowled into the night. Just ahead, the path widened abruptly, into the moon-pale sand of a small lava cove. Past that, it seemed to disappear into a thicket of trees. She walked closer to Alec, uneasily eyeing the overgrown area.

"And it is a place of darkness," Alec continued, his voice more resonant now, deeper. His arm around her waist tightened, fitting her against his side more closely as they followed the uneven, rocky path into the trees. A canopy of intertwined branches reached like bony, grasping fingers against the starry, moonlit sky, weaving shadows on the path. The wind rushed through the trees, filling the air with ghostly creaks and groans that blended with the surge of waves into an eerie concert.

Cailie shivered, but said nothing. She was trying very hard to stifle her rising fear, an unnamed fear, born of darkness and shadows and of walking along an uneven path in the middle of nowhere. There was a presence in this place, an ominous sensation. She struggled to ignore it by concentrating solely on the sensuous closeness of Alec's body, which was also all that was keeping her from falling flat on her face on the winding, treacherously rock-studded sandy path. Every now and then, something plopped down on the ground from the trees above, pods of seed presumably, but it only added to her skittishness. She wished they were back out on the lava plain, where at least the light of the moon could touch them.

"See the ruins?" Alexander nodded into moon-shadowed hollows beneath the branches. "*Kiawe* grow from them now, with their roots climbing the tumbled rocks."

Cailie, despite her fascination with history, had no wish to see the remnants of those black lava rock walls. She did not look too deeply into the darkness beyond the path. This place was too oppressive, too dark.

After an endless walk, which could have been no more than 20 minutes, a sharp right curve led out of the trees and onto the sandy beach of a lava bay.

Cailie felt as though a black shroud had been lifted from her soul. The night wind fingered softly through her unbound hair, carrying the sound of breakers and the sweet scent of some night-blooming tree or flower. Ahead, the sea shimmered like quicksilver beneath the full moon.

She summoned a vague smile, resisting the urge to stop and shake the sand and rocks out of her new running shoes. This, now, could be romantic—even if there was the occasional, faint odor of some dead fish washed up on shore, when the wind shifted.

Alexander released her abruptly and halted a half step ahead of her.

"This bay . . ." He tilted his head, as his voice

trailed off. Cailie frowned at the cold set of his features, silvered like those of a statue by the bright moonlight.

"Over two hundred years ago, this shore was blasted with grapeshot at the command of an American merchant's captain. Here, and at Olowalu, natives were massacred in revenge for a stolen cutter and a dead ship's guard. But this place . . . harbors more memories."

Never taking his gaze off the ocean, Alec gestured landward, into the grove from which they had just emerged. "The natives sought refuge from the British here, in later years. The population is estimated around ten thousand during some periods. And again, there are ruins, crumbled walls . . ."

Cailie glanced around, alarm blossoming silently in her soul. All thoughts of how beautifully Alec's voice intertwined with the sound of the waves were gone from her mind. Gooseflesh was rising on her arms, icy shivers coursing down her spine. She shifted uneasily, warily, feeling no desire to know more of this place's history. Not here, not when it was so close, so overpowering.

"I think I've had enough of history for tonight," she muttered faintly, rubbing her arms for warmth, though the tropical night was not cold.

Alexander turned from the water and looked at her with the oddest expression, as though he had momentarily forgotten she was there, as though he had been miles and years away, in his mind.

The mask fell again, instantly.

"Of course." Nodding, Alec drew her close once more and started back down the path in silence.

Cailie did not prod him for conversation. Just before the trees gave way to open sky again, they passed a cove littered with what looked like bleached skulls in the moonlight. Coral rubble most likely, Cailie told herself. But she couldn't help the shiver that ran over her again at the thought of skulls and burial caves. Alexander must have felt her shudder, for his arm tightened around her.

"I am sorry, Cailie." He sighed, his voice quiet, soft. "I should not have brought you here."

She studied his face for a moment, finding it inscrutable. Frowning, she gazed out over the moon-bright water visible beyond the lava shore now that they were clear of the trees. "Why did you?"

Alexander sighed again, and ran a hand through his hair. "It is not . . . easy to explain," he offered haltingly. "Perhaps it would not even make sense to you."

Cailie tilted her head at him. "Try."

They'd reached the narrow trail again, and Alec kept his silence until they reached the Jeep, until they had bumped along for some miles on the patchwork road.

"Have you ever been in a castle, Cailie? An ancient cathedral?"

Taken aback by the question, she shook her head as he glanced at her. That response seemed

126

to sit ill with him, for his hands clenched the steering wheel.

"I've seen them in movies, though, and in history texts," Cailie was quick to add, seeing his knuckles grow white by the dashboard illumination. "Both castles and churches. I've always wanted to go to Europe and see real ones."

A short laugh broke from Alec's lips, the sound cold and harsh. Cailie stiffened in her seat. "What?"

Alexander shook his head, relaxing his hands on the wheel again. "I am afraid we would have no common frame of reference to make sense of any explanation I might offer," he informed her with an almost mocking smile.

Cailie shut her mouth before she could make some inane retort she'd most likely regret later. Then she frowned at him. "Try harder. I really would like to know."

Alec glanced at her before turning his attention to the road again. His features were unreadable. "Did you hate it so much?"

"I . . ." Cailie shook her head, startled by his suddenly too-soft voice. "I didn't say I hated it. It just wasn't what I'd expected." She shrugged, stared ahead into the darkness now pierced by the occasional house lights. The wind ruffled her hair over her eyes; annoyed, she caught the strands in one hand.

"How about a graveyard? A cemetery? Ever been in one of those?"

Cailie drew a tight breath, and swallowed hard

as a knot formed in her throat. "Yes."

Her voice must have carried more than she'd wanted it to. Without even looking at her, Alexander stopped the Jeep, and shut off the engine. Then he turned to face her.

"How did it make you feel?"

Cailie studied the flowers on her dress, avoiding his penetrating gaze. The cicadas were growing too loud, unnerving her. "I don't think I want to discuss this."

Alec caught her hands, lightly, his warm strength enfolding them. Reluctantly, she turned toward him and looked up. His face was sculpted from hard planes and shadows, looking almost inhuman in the darkness.

"I am not talking about mourning the dead, Cailie. Few have buried as many friends as I have, and I do not like to dwell on it any more than you do."

He released her hands, and brushed a strand of hair back from her face. She nearly flinched. The intensity of his voice, his gaze, should have been frightening.

"I am talking about what remains after a hundred, a thousand years. That which endures through time. The stone, grave marker, or tower wall. The metal, be it grapeshot or bronze torc."

Cailie stared at him dazedly, uncomprehending, yet mesmerized by his voice, by the light in his near-black eyes.

"You felt it tonight. I know you did, Cailie. It's why you wanted to leave."

"I don't like places of the dead," she retorted faintly, barely suppressing a shudder. In her mind's eye hung the image of an old cemetery full of graves, some decrepit and overgrown, others carefully tended, and three new plots, overflowing with flowers, as though death could be disguised into something beautiful.

"Few people do, Cailie," Alexander replied gently. "It reminds them too much of their own mortality."

Cailie shut her eyes. She would never be buried in the cold ground, as Mom and Dad and Beth had been, left to rot. . . .

"Cailie, don't."

His words were soft, urgent, pulling her out of the horror of her memories. She snapped her eyes open, blinked away the rising tears, and met Alec's compassionate gaze with a mutinous one. She had not come here to be reminded of the past.

But Alexander was relentless now.

"Look deeper than the fear, Cailie. Think not of a tomb, but of a castle. Or a church, or a tower keep, built a thousand years ago, and still standing." He leaned back, watching her, his eyes intent, his voice rich with emotion.

"Think of walking through the tall oaken gate, along twenty feet of solid stone wall. Ancient stone, worked by men long forgotten. Yet the castle still stands. That"—he gently caught up her hands again—"is what I wanted to show you tonight. The power of the past, for it will ever haunt the present. And the power of the present, for it will one day be the past. It will endure."

He inclined his head slightly. "To stand amidst such with understanding is unsettling, to say the least. It is to know humility and sublime glory in the same instant."

His gaze somber, Alexander brought her hands to his lips. Cailie felt tears burn again behind her eyes at his words, at the enigmatic truths behind them. God, it was almost as though he *knew* why she'd come to paradise. But, of course, he didn't . . . couldn't.

She nodded faintly, without meeting his eyes. "I think perhaps I understand."

Alec smiled, a barely perceptible curving of his lips as he released her hands and started the Jeep again. "Then I am glad I brought you here."

Chapter Eight

Tresand knew that she wasn't, however. Or at least, not entirely glad that he'd brought her. Or perhaps she just wasn't sure yet if she was or not. But she did not have the understanding with which he'd hoped to gift her with tonight. Tresand knew it as surely as he could feel her heartbeat, faster than usual with agitation. But he didn't know what to do about it.

The drive out from La Perouse was too long. Though she kept her silence for a good half hour, past the "Caution—Simulated Moon Surface" sign and the hotels, and the lights of Wailea and Kihei, she was still uptight. Part of it, perhaps, were memories his words had raised. Part of it, most surely, was the atmosphere of the deserted lava fields, for much of the tension had left her once they'd reached the Piilani highway again.

But some of it had remained.

By the time they turned off toward Lahaina, Tresand could no longer stand her agitation.

"You're still troubled," he ventured gently, watching her out of the corner of his eye.

At first he thought she hadn't heard him, for she did not acknowledge his words. Then, abruptly, she turned to look at him, her eyes carefully guarded.

"What can I do, Cailie?" he prompted when she still kept her silence.

She sighed and sat back to stare out at the road again. "Tell me what happened there. At La Perouse."

His gaze snapped to her in surprise. She met it with a level one of her own, though her smile was less than steady. "You know the history of the place, don't you?"

Tresand shrugged. "I do. But—"

"Then tell me. Please. It was only *there* that I didn't want to know what happened. And you have a voice made for storytelling, Alec. I'll listen anytime you have one to tell."

He glanced at her again, the bitter taste of regret suddenly in his throat. God, if only she knew the tales he could tell . . . He pushed the thought aside. "You're sure?"

"Yes." She was still smiling at him, that uncertain, bashful smile. Yet there was a kind of relief in her features now. Relief to be distracted from her own thoughts? Tresand cursed silently. What was the nameless demon that haunted her?

But he would not ask—not now, not ever, if he had any sense left in him. He could not get too close to her, or he'd never let her go. And history would repeat itself, as it always had. Nay, he'd not risk her life again.

He stole a deep breath and fixed his gaze on the road. "Very well, you shall have the story. Though there's not that much more to tell, in truth. Back in January of 1790, a Captain Simon Metcalfe arrived to barter with the natives. The news spread, and a chief from Olowalu showed up with some men in a canoe after dark. They stole one of the ship's cutters and killed its guard, then burned the crewman and dismantled the skiff for its iron before returning home.

"The next morning, Metcalfe found his man and skiff missing. Cook had been killed only eleven years earlier, under similar circumstances beginning with the disappearance of a cutter, and Metcalfe more than likely recalled that incident. In any case, he tossed the local ladies off his ship, fired at the village, and sent his men to burn what remained. After he found out about the canoe from Olowalu, he sailed there to meet with three of the chiefs. The reward he offered for the return of his man was a musket and eight cartridges, a bar of iron, and a piece of Bengal cloth. The same reward stood for the return of his cutter."

"Must have been a charming fellow to work for," Cailie muttered dryly.

Tresand, seeing her frown, nodded. "Doubtlessly. Later on, one of the chiefs came aboard to give Metcalfe a piece of broken keel and two charred thighbones. The Hawaiians, you see, believe that the essence, the soul of something, is contained in its bones, and as far as the chief was concerned, he'd fulfilled his side of the bargain. Metcalfe kept his rage bottled up. He invited all the villagers to come out to trade, and when hundreds of them were in the water between the ship and the shore, he let loose with every gun and cannon onboard."

Tresand watched her as he spoke the last words, but she accepted the story with the poise of one used to the harshness of true tales. The shadows he'd sensed in her earlier had receded far beneath the surface again.

"There have been much worse massacres in the course of history," Cailie commented finally, as though realizing he was waiting for her to say something.

Tresand's whole body stiffened slowly, inexorably, until he thought he would shatter under the onslaught of the past. "There have."

The words were harsh, dry, all he could wring from his throat tightened beyond pain. He focused on the road, while her innocent words released a torrent of images in his mind, images from a time no more remote than the Olowalu massacre, but half a world away. Images of a nation of people rising up in hysterical blood-thirst, guillotining thousands . . .

He clenched his jaw, struggling futilely to keep

the memories from welling, but it was a battle lost before it ever began.

As though it had been only yesterday, he saw the gendarme's lascivious grin as Tresand had handed him the pouch of coins, the leering chuckle, the quip that *mademoiselle* was seeing so many admirers tonight, he was tempted to visit her himself. Tresand relived the shock and horror and agony of cradling her ravaged, violated body gently in his arms, muttering soothing nonsense and oaths under his breath, swearing he'd find and kill every one of the revolutionaries who'd touched her, while she sobbed quietly, incessantly in his embrace. Like a lash, the memory of his own voice drove through him, a shaking voice, promising her everything would be all right, promising her that his blood could save her life. Though the guillotine would end the existence of one of the Blood as surely as it would do a mortal, he swore that he would tear down the Conciergerie with his own hands before he would let them hurt her again. Empty, helpless words all, cut off by her raspy voice, hoarse from screaming, begging him to let her die, in the name of the love they'd shared, to *please, God, just let me die.* . . .

It had been his fault, again. Had he refused to stay in Paris, even after he'd found her, had he been strong enough to walk away from her, they'd never have become lovers. Then the Tribunal could never have accused her of impurity in body or thought, or of disobedience to her father, who had been executed three days earlier for having been overheard to reminisce fondly about the times under Louis XVI.

Tresand forcibly relaxed his hands around the steering wheel, to keep himself from crushing it. All he'd been able to do, in the end, was hold her. Shelter her from the biting cold of winter housed in the stone floor of the cell, touch her gently, soothingly, and tasting his own tears, fulfill her pleas.

" . . . bastard."

He flinched at the coldly spoken word; his head snapped around to focus on the woman beside him. "What did you say?"

She gave him an odd look, then stared ahead into the night again. "I said, I hope somebody did him in. Metcalfe."

Tresand nearly choked on the bitter taste of relief and regret welling inside him. He'd thought she had, somehow, remembered, but of course, she couldn't. Not unless he loosed those memories her immortal soul held hidden . . . Unthinkable. He snapped himself out of it, seeking distraction in the safe, impersonal historical tale himself.

"Eventually," he replied to her last remark, forcing his voice to remain even. "But there is an epilogue to this incident too. On an earlier visit, Metcalfe had alienated a Hawaiian chief, who swore to avenge himself on the first white men he'd encounter. While Metcalfe was slaughtering natives at Olowalu, this chief was doing away with the crew of the *Fair American* . . . whose captain was none other than Metcalfe's son."

Cailie scowled at this information. "It wasn't his fault his father was such a . . . horse's behind."

One side of Tresand's mouth quirked up. "No."

"But then, life's seldom fair, isn't it?" she replied softly after a moment, meeting his gaze when he looked at her.

Tresand's jaw clenched at her words. Shadows lingered in her eyes again, shadows she was battling valiantly to keep at bay.

He cursed silently. They were almost at her hotel, and he did not want to leave her like this. Did not want to reaffirm the truth of her words, to her and himself, by leaving her. Yet she was infinitely safer alone with those shadows than alone with him.

So he only took her hand, solemnly bringing it to his lips. "No," he agreed just as softly. "It seldom is."

Chapter Nine

The sun sparkled brilliantly on the turquoise water as Cailie strolled along Black Rock beach, dangling her thongs by two fingers, walking where the flooding of waves cooled the bright, hot sand. Tourists old and young played in the mellow surf, couples strolled through wave-washed sand, hand in hand, oblivious to the crowds along the shore.

Cailie looked away from two lovebirds embracing in chest-deep water, and watched instead the catamaran further down the beach, maneuvering cautiously in the swells to keep from being run aground. Passengers in flower-print polyester shirts and bikinis skimpier than the one she wore were wading waist-deep into the water to board.

She wanted more. It felt like stepping off the

towering, rugged black lava cliff at the north end of the beach even to admit that much to herself. But it was the truth. Her former contentment with Alexander's unfailing courtesy and respect, with feeling protected and cherished, waned with each solitary moment she spent wandering down this beautiful shore. The sultry breeze was like a lover's caress, whispering secrets against her skin, taunting her with what lay just beyond her reach.

Yes, she wanted more, wanted what those lovers all along the shore had. She wanted a touch born of hunger, of passion, instead of courtesy and propriety.

And it was all Alec's fault, in a way. She had never wanted from any man the things she wanted from him, had never felt close enough to a man to want them. But then, no other man had looked like her phantom. No other man had melted away her shyness and innate distancing with his . . . his most convincing mimicry of love.

Cailie frowned severely, erasing those caustic words from her mind. This was her doing, her plan. She was only mocking her own choices.

With a sigh, she turned her steps toward the water, until she was strolling knee-deep in the waves. An elderly couple, dressed from head to toe against the sun, passed her; two young boys, chocolate brown, stormed into the water ahead.

Today was the beginning of her last week. Her last week!

The past two nights with Alec had been as fascinating as her previous ones, and had never again been as strange and unsettling as that excursion to La Perouse. But the days . . . the days grew more empty and dull with each sunrise.

Why couldn't he offer, just once, to spend more time with her? Couldn't he see how much she thrived on his company, how much she looked forward to it each day?

The ugly demon of jealousy that had reared its head while she'd had lunch at Chico's came to life again, goading her emotions into undesirable directions. She had no right to be angry with him, had no right to envy other women he might have taken there.

She sighed, pushing away her rising anger. Alexander was what he was; she had accepted that the day she'd hired him. And he wasn't guilty of anything other than extreme propriety.

She'd survive the four endless, lonely hours ahead, just as she'd survived them yesterday and the day before. And she should be doing more than passing time! She should be living life to the fullest in these days.

Quickening her step, Cailie pulled the white cover-up out of her beach bag and shrugged into it, leaving her thongs off until she reached the scorchingly hot cement walkway leading back to Whalers Village, past scores of sunbathers dozing on beach towels and the nylon decks of beached Hobie Cats. Though she well knew the shops and galleries by now, she made herself roam the open mall twice, ambling through the whaling museum and admiring the sensuous, frankly provocative acrylic sculpture turning slowly on its pedestal in one of the galleries' display windows. Despite outrageous prices, she bought a violet-aquamarine silk scarf and matching barrette, and spent half an hour braiding her hair and pinning it up.

The sun was setting in the haze obscuring the horizon as she made her way back toward the hotel. Anticipation and a shadow of inbred dismay at her plans for tonight quickened her stride across the still-warm sand.

Tonight, she would ask Alexander to change their arrangement—change it to what her original plan had called for, what she'd been too cowardly to propose then.

Let him think her greedy, or worse. He did not know that this was her last week. And she wanted more, wanted it all. She wanted to drown in his illusion of love, and forget that she was living a lie of her own making.

Dinner was a casual affair at the beachside lounge of one of the best sunset-viewing spots in Kaanapali. Cailie thought it a rather ironic choice, especially since the sun had set over an hour before they'd arrived at the restaurant. The meal had been wonderful, as usual, but the new pumps she'd bought yesterday to match her new rose silk dress hurt her feet, and the uneasiness rising with each thought of her intentions made her fidget with her ring and hair and nearly pull apart her braid.

She looked up from studying the wood grain on the table, met Alexander's warm gaze, and blushed. It was so easy to forget those mesmerizing eyes, that cool masculine beauty which so often made her think of "Beauty and the Beast," with the roles reversed. During the day, when she was alone, she could plan. But now, face to face with him, her heart beating rapidly and her cheeks flushing at the mere thought of what she wanted to say, no words would come.

"Have you made it out to Hana yet?"

Cailie shook her head and summoned a flustered smile. "I just stayed around Kaanapali today, actually. You know . . ." She stole a deep, fortifying breath. She had to start somewhere, and this was as good a topic as any. "I've heard so much talk about the gorgeous sunsets up on Haleakala. I—I don't know where you work, but couldn't you—I mean, maybe—just take one afternoon off, and . . ."

The suddenly measuring look out of his cool, midnight eyes choked off her voice and made her cheeks flame brighter. Good God, she was sounding like a shrewish wife. And he really had made his hours perfectly clear the first night they'd met. This was definitely not the way to lead into what she wanted to discuss.

Cailie surged to her feet, too quickly, jolting the small table.

"Oh, blast!" The floating candle sizzled and drowned as her hands flew to steady their teetering, empty glasses. "I—I'm sorry. I had absolutely no right to say what I did, and it's certainly none of my business how you spend your days. I really don't know what got into me!"

"Breathe, Cailie."

Alexander's hands closed over her fluttering ones even as he spoke, his warm, long-fingered hands that were so very gentle in their strength. He rose in a smooth motion that made her own seem all the more clumsy.

Cailie sucked breath into her empty lungs. Her gaze flew from their entwined hands up to his face. The torchlight painted enticing shadows onto his features, but could not mask the crinkling of his eyes.

"You're laughing at me!"

He lifted her hands in his, then touched his lips to the vein-traced back of her stiff hand, just above where the green sapphire gleamed in the dancing light.

"Yes. You are a delight, Cailie."

Embarrassed, she tugged on her hands, looking anywhere but at him. The surf, she noted, was particularly loud this evening. She squinted into the darkness beyond the flickering torches, beyond the white masts of beached Hobie Cats, stared at the boats anchored out on the black water beneath the starry sky.

"As for your previous questions, I am on a

deadline and really cannot take any time off."

Reluctantly, Cailie tore her gaze from the horizon. "Oh."

Alec was smiling, that teasing, masculine little smile. He gently nudged her back down into her seat, keeping hold of her hands as he sank into his own chair again.

"I write, Cailie," he offered before she had to ask. "Texts on history. The invasions of early Britain, at the present."

History! That perked her up. "The Romans? Like Hadrian's Wall, and such?"

"A bit later than that. The Norsemen."

"Vikings?"

Alexander nodded. "They are called that, yes."

Cailie latched on to the subject of history as though her life depended on it. Since they weren't visiting any more battle sites, it would be a safe enough topic, one on which she could at least converse—she hoped—without making a fool of herself.

"I've always been fascinated by history, Alec. Well, pre-twentieth-century history, anyway. But then, you probably gathered that from the other night, though I guess I didn't do too well at La Perouse. But I'd love to see some of your work, especially the—"

The minute change in his expression sent Cailie backtracking again, and her gaze down to the table top. "I'm sorry, I—I didn't mean that the way—"

"Cailie."

144

She looked up at him only when he raised her chin with gentle fingers.

"Why don't we go for a walk and talk about history."

"Yes!" Cailie was on her feet before the word had left her lips. It sounded like an excellent idea to get away from even the soft illumination of the restaurant, into the darkness which would hide the embarrassment still to come—if she could ever summon the courage to bring up her intended topic. Her last attempt at leading up to it had certainly been disastrous.

Alexander took care of the bill, then led her across the walkway onto the soft, satiny sand. In the distance, the intermittent dots of torches traced the outline of the black lava cliff from the Sheraton down to the waterline.

They left their shoes beside one of the beached Hobie Cats, and, arm in arm, like the couples Cailie had so often seen on the beach in the lonely hours of the day, they strolled along the shore. Tropical fragrances and the occasional aroma of roasting meat wafted on the warm wind, mixing with Hawaiian music and sporadic laughter from beachside luaus.

Alexander angled them away from the walkway and the well-lit hotels, until they were ambling through cool, wave-washed sand, walking somewhat lopsided on the steep berm.

Somewhere between Whalers Village and Black Rock, Cailie managed to regroup her scattered wits. Still, they hadn't spoken a single word on history, hadn't spoken a single word, period.

"Um . . . Alec?"

"Hmm."

"I—really, I didn't mean to intrude into your privacy—"

Alexander stopped, then turned her to face him. The dim light from beyond the walkway gave his features a cold, dangerous edge. "Stop apologizing for everything you do and say, Cailie."

He tucked an escaped, windblown strand of her hair behind her ear, let his fingers trail down her cheek, taking the sting from his words. "I don't know what you're used to, but I for one will not jump down your throat at the merest provocation, imagined or otherwise. I am not waiting for your first faux pas to cry off this engagement, Cailie. Not," he added, moving along the sand again, "that you've committed any."

She cringed inwardly at his words, yet matched his stride. His arm came around her waist again, quite naturally, drawing her more closely against his side.

So he was going to see their arrangement through, was he? Well, he might change his mind, if she could only get the blasted words out.

"Alec?"

"Yes?"

"I . . ." Cailie bit her lip, stared into the silent night sky. One of the bright stars was flickering distinctly, changing from blue to orange to yellow. She wasn't going to ask him why he'd kept such a scrupulous distance. She wasn't going to ask if she wasn't attractive enough for him, even if it killed her.

This was her time in paradise. Her dream to live, a final dream of life, of love. And she wanted more.

She slowed her step.

They were closer to the cliff now, closer to darkness, to solitude. The bay was painted with golden streams of light from the clifftop torches; the waves were longer, gentler, as they glided onto the more shallowly sloping sand.

Cailie stopped, disengaging herself from Alexander's light hold. He watched her, with an impassive yet attentive gaze.

"You've been the perfect gentleman since the first night we met," Cailie began, feeling her short nails burn into the palms of her clenched fists. "The storybook knight in shining armor, noble and gentle and chivalrous."

She looked down, tracing patterns into the wet sand with her toes, not wanting to see his expression at her words. A large wave surged onto the shore, coming within inches of her feet. She watched the last trace of foam seep into the sand, then shrugged.

"I really wish your armor weren't quite so . . ." She looked up, blushing. "Spotless."

Alexander's unexpected laughter brought another rush of heat to her face, but she didn't lower her gaze.

"Ah, Cailie, I have kno—found many a knight

whose armor was, in that respect, very badly tarnished indeed."

Cailie bit her lip, unable to escape his laughter-bright eyes, wondering if he was making sport of her. Another wave rushed onto the sand, swirling water around her ankles. She stared along the beach, back toward Whalers Village, where the wet sand gleamed in the shore lights' colors.

"No, Cailie," he replied softly, as though having read her mind. "I am not laughing at you." But then, perhaps the darkness did not hide as much of her flaming face as she had hoped.

Alec drew her to his side once more, and resumed walking. "But by God, you amaze me sometimes."

His voice was rich with laughter still. Yet he held tight when she would have pulled away in embarrassment.

"Alec—"

"No, don't blush again. Not that I don't enjoy seeing that innocence in you," he added, dropping a kiss on her hair. "But for one so very shy, you do come up with some incredible feats of courage."

Cailie clenched her hands into burning fists, and looked up at him defiantly. "And what about you? How much courage would it take for you to—to—"

Before she could force the words out, the world suddenly spun around her. She was pulled up against the solid expanse of Alexander's chest, captured by an arm around her back. His free hand slid through her hair, cupping her head, holding her steady as his mouth devoured hers with the ferocity of a dying man seeking salvation.

Cailie knew the beach was by no means deserted, knew they were not the only ones in the warm embrace of darkness. But her proper, shy, timid self suddenly didn't give a tinker's damn about who might see them, whose brows might furrow at their behavior. It wasn't as though she'd never been kissed. Alec had kissed her before too, on her cheek, her brow. But this . . .

Her world narrowed to the hot, hard wall of his chest pressing against her, to his shockingly intimate possession of her mouth. A soft sound of pleasure and surprise rose from her throat as he slowed the kiss, deepened it, stealing the very breath from her.

Abruptly, he pulled his head away, his arms tightening around her shoulders and low back as though he meant to meld their bodies into one. Cailie's face heated at the sudden, new awareness of his body, taut and aroused, fitting so perfectly against her, at her own body's instant, unexpected response. She could hear his heartbeat, hard and quick, and felt the pounding of her own match its beat.

"Not nearly so much as you seem to think, Cailie."

She'd never heard his voice like this before— so husky, breathless, when he was always so very much in control. It didn't matter that it took her almost a full minute to remember her own words, and realize that he had replied to her question. It didn't matter that her braid had come loose and her hair was tickling her face in the night wind, and that the scarf once intertwined in the braid would probably be floating out on the next wave. Her fingers had better things to do, curling against Alexander's back like the kneading paws of a kitten being stroked. She felt a slow shudder go through him, and his arms tightened around her.

Nothing mattered, save this first taste of fire, this shattering of ancient boundaries and inhibitions. This was passion, hunger, desire, so bright and vivid it could compare only to her dreams.

Yes, this was what she'd wanted, what she wanted more of.

"God, Cailie, you don't know what you're asking."

His voice was thick, gruff, almost angry, but she didn't care. She only wanted to stay in that close embrace for the rest of the night, never to be cast back into the world of cruel reality. The phantom in her dreams was gone, and all she had left was this illusion of love.

Yet Alexander gently put her at arm's length. Gathering her composure, she straightened and looked up at him somberly.

"Oh, but I do know, Alec. And I only have a week left. Friday is our last night."

Chapter Ten

Tresand stared down at her for long, tormented seconds, watching the fragile light in her eyes slowly dim.

One week left. Only one week, and he would lose her again. Seven nights—seven nights to glory in a love that was meant to outlast time itself. Seven nights to endure the agony of holding inside the truth. Seven short nights, and another eternity alone.

"Cailie—" His voice broke. He squeezed his eyes shut, enfolded her silently into a gentler embrace. She moved against him with a soft sound, clinging tightly as though afraid he would push her away again.

That should have been the least of her fears.

Tresand drew an unsteady breath. The heat of her body burned him through the silk of her dress, wreaked havoc with his breathing. He looked down at her, nestled so perfectly against him, flushed with the first taste of the fire that ran so quickly, so easily between them, and bit back a groan. "God help us both, Cailie."

"Then . . ." She tilted her head up at him shyly, her lips bruised, her eyes huge, full of starlight. "Then you'll . . ."

Tresand met her hopeful gaze steadily, thought of all the centuries he'd had to learn to master himself, his body and mind, and meticulously gathered every shred of self-control he could grasp.

"Yes."

Her smile would have put the sun to shame. Feeling as though he'd been stabbed in the gut, Tresand forced himself to release her slowly, gently, reluctantly. He snatched up the scarf slipping out of her loosening hair, and tucked the piece of silk into his shirt pocket. Then, keeping her curved possessively against his side, he started back toward Whalers Village.

"Alec?"

He tightened his arm around her waist. "It's still early, Cailie. And this beach is becoming too crowded for my tastes."

She choked back laughter at his words. A tight smile tugged at Tresand's lips in reply, yet by the time they'd retrieved their shoes and were heading into the parking lot, he hardly felt like smiling. Three minutes later, southbound on the coast highway, his carefully made plans of remaining in public places with her lay shattered all around him.

"Are you mad at me?"

"Mad at you?" Taken aback by her quiet question, Tresand glanced at her. She'd been sitting so silently beside him, leaving him to his self-reproach, that he'd not sensed the tension, the uncertainty rising once again within her.

"Of course not." The twist of his lips fell short of the reassuring smile he'd intended.

"But you're upset about something."

Tresand shot her as long a look as he dared without going off the road. She continued staring straight ahead, avoiding his gaze. Her hands were torturing the silk scarf he'd returned to her some minutes ago.

"I have a lot on my mind right now," he finally confessed, managing a crooked grin in an attempt to lighten her troubled gaze.

Her brows knitted in a faint frown. Still, she did not look at him. "I'm not sick, you know. In any way."

The first curse escaped before he could catch himself. His knuckles white around the steering wheel, Tresand bit his tongue, forced himself into silence. Almost there. Almost . . .

Dust billowed as he turned off onto the dirt road skirting a cane field on the ocean side of the highway. The trade winds had risen since sunset; they ruffled the cane and the trees, filled the night with shifting sound. After a few hundred yards, he cut the Jeep's headlights, shut off the engine, and

153

turned to face his still and silent passenger.

"Cailie . . ."

"It's okay, really," she countered, suddenly occupied with stuffing the silk scarf into her purse. "If you've changed your mind—"

"Bloody hell." He couldn't take this anymore. Biting back another curse, Tresand leaned over and shut her up with a kiss and pulled away, much too soon for both of them. Not nearly soon enough.

"Now bloody well stop belittling yourself," he ground out, gathering his mantle of control more tightly around him. One of them had to keep a level head, and it certainly wasn't going to be in her power to stop him if he lost his.

"There is an old sugar mill pier further down the road," Tresand commented tightly as he got out and came around to the passenger side, resorting to neutral conversation to keep his mind off the raw carnal hunger fanned to life by that simple kiss. "But it's hell getting through the tangled shrubs and *kiawe*. This path is bad enough."

"It's very windy here. Not at all like Kaanapali or Lahaina." Cailie was standing beside the Jeep, staring around wide-eyed, trying to look past the night-black, ten-foot wall of cane growing directly beside the dirt road. "And I can't see anything."

A sharp rustling in the cane field sent her scrambling halfway back into the Jeep before Tresand could utter a word. Smiling, he caught her hand in his, and drew her down the road with him. "Relax. It's probably only a mongoose."

154

"What—what's a mongoose? And how big is it?"

"They eat the cane rats." Tresand bit back a grin at her sudden start. "Look it up in an encyclopedia, Cailie. That can be your day trip tomorrow—researching dangerous wildlife of Maui in the library."

She made a face. "I thought the only dangerous things in Hawaii were sharks and scorpions."

Tresand pressed his lips together and said nothing. That kind of irony was enough to put his hunger on ice and make him silently list dozens of reasons why he should be dragging her straight back to the Jeep, driving her back to her hotel, and telling her in no uncertain terms to find some other "escort."

Yet he did nothing of the kind. He released her hand, and strode ahead into the black, tangled mass of trees and shrubs on the seaward side of the road. The tree crickets fell silent around them.

Cailie followed wordlessly for all of two minutes. Then she made up for it.

"Where in the world are you taking us?"

"You'll see." Tresand continued through the thicket, along the invisible path. Behind them, the crickets resumed their song.

"No, I can't. That's half the problem. I'm not a cat, Alec. I can't see—ouch, dammit! And you said this trail wasn't tangled?"

Tresand turned back to her, helped her disentangle the silk dress and her skin from a *kiawe* branch, while waiting for her to comment on blow holes and thorny trees, or on the ruination of her dress. She didn't.

"It's only a little farther."

She mumbled something under her breath, but gamely pulled away from him and stumbled on ahead in her pumps, through the tall, dry grass and intertwined trees and bushes. Tresand watched her with a slow smile.

"For someone who can't see in the dark, you're doing a remarkable job avoiding the tree trunks."

"Wait till I find something the right size to hit you with."

He should not have heard that low mutter, would not have, were he human. As it was, Tresand bit his tongue and swallowed his laughter. Then he caught up to her.

Waves silvered by the moon rushed gently onto a sand and rock beach that appeared from one instant to the next out of the tangled growth.

"Thank God! There's an end to this after all."

"Almost." Tresand pointed along the shore. "Turn left."

Cailie sent him a martyred look, but did as she was told. Twisting and contorting, he followed her along the overgrown waterline. A black-crowned night heron perched on a *kiawe* branch watched their passage motionlessly.

The wind was gentler here, its force broken by the line of trees and scrub. It underscored the pulsing whisper of waves, the chirping of night insects and whistling of geckos. Here and there the faint scent of unseen spider lilies drifted by, an elusive perfume on the warm wind.

"Hold, this is it." Tresand caught Cailie's arm before she could round another overhanging tree, and led her to an old log beached on a sandy piece of shore. Tangled greenery and the occasional palm surrounded the tiny spot, framing the sky in shifting silhouettes. The moon, bright as a distant searchlight in the sky, lit up cloud fragments and cast the shadows of branches onto the sand.

Tresand sank down on the driftwood and leaned back against a vertical branch stump, guiding Cailie down in front of him. She sat stiffly at first, then acquiesced to the light pressure of his hands and curved her back gently against his chest.

Tresand sighed and closed his eyes, reveling in the fragile peace of the moment. It felt far too right, holding her here, in the night that was his world, in the sanctuary of shadows.

He stiffened slightly, staring into the darkness with cold, bleak eyes. No. It was wrong, all wrong, for she was a child of sunlight, a creature of dreams and not nightmares, a woman who deserved a man who could give her a good life, be a father to her children, grow old with her.

"What!" Cailie suddenly jerked back with a cry, snapping Tresand out of his thoughts and clipping him in the jaw with her head. The scurrying shadow on the ground vanished into an invisible hole in the sand.

"What in the . . . Oh, are you all right? I'm so sorry . . ."

"I'm fine." Smiling, Tresand tightened his arms around her to keep her from fidgeting. How utterly boring his life had been all those decades! How lonely, all those centuries that he'd searched for her but had not found her.

He tore himself away from the past. "And that poor creature you nearly scared to death was a ghost crab. But don't worry, they won't hurt you. They're more skittish than you are."

Cailie grumbled something to herself, but slowly relaxed against him. The tension suffusing her body had little to do with nocturnal crustaceans, Tresand knew. She was waiting for him to make a move, impatient and afraid all at the same time.

He inhaled deeply and closed his eyes again. Her heartbeat, the silent rush of blood through her body, was a seductive siren song weakening his control. Yet this last week was for her, only for her. He had waited a century to find her again. He could wait now, would wait for the pounding of her heart to slow, for her to find peace with herself. Then he would feel the throb of her pulse catch the beat of his own heart, heavier, faster. . . .

"The stars look different here."

Tresand's eyes snapped open. A crooked grin tugged at his lips, mocking only himself. Ah, but she couldn't see his face.

"You're not used to this latitude." It was

an innocent guess, yet Tresand caught himself before he could unconsciously probe for more information about her home. "We're just far enough south to see the Southern Cross. Over there, above Kahoolawe."

Cailie nodded, staring at the horizon. "I've never seen it before."

Tresand cursed silently. He felt her stiffen against him, as if from an unpleasant memory, but could not fathom her thoughts. He could only tighten his arms about her minutely, comfortingly.

"Relax, Cailie."

She nodded again.

Tresand didn't push her. He simply sat with her, watching the stars glitter behind the black silhouettes of swaying leaves and palm fronds. He could make a fair guess at the battle she was waging with her timid self, but it was not one in which he could interfere. So he only held her, gently, patiently, as her nervous tension slowly drained away in tiny increments.

Finally she sighed deeply, turned her cheek against his shoulder, and stared up into the twined branches above them. Tresand smiled faintly, admiring her courage and spirit. Such a hard step to take for one so bashful.

"It's so beautiful here," Cailie whispered dreamily. "Such a beautiful place to spend eternity . . ."

Tresand stiffened as though struck. Ice formed in his soul, spreading through his body, claiming him. His breath caught in his throat and stole his

159

voice, so that he could not even defend himself.

God. What had he said to give himself away? How could she have found out?

"It somehow feels right, you know, to think that all life came from the sea," Cailie continued in the same soft, dreamy tone. "That returning to it would complete some endless, timeless cycle."

Tresand frowned harshly. She was patently oblivious to his alarm. Puzzlement took the place of dismay as he stared down at the top of her head. "What in the world are you talking about?"

As though rising from a trance, Cailie shook her head, and glanced at him over her shoulder. Her lips were curved into a wistful smile, more bitter than sweet.

"Nothing. I'm just thinking out loud. Babbling. It's nothing, really." She pointed across the bay. "Look. What are those lights?"

Frowning still, Tresand glanced up at the intermittent white points that snaked along the far shore. He sighed, reluctantly following her change of topic. "Headlights. It's the coast highway."

"Oh." She nestled closer against him again. "And that out there? A cruise ship?"

"Mmm-hmm."

She pushed no further. The distant ship moved slowly along the black boulder on the horizon that was Kahoolawe, while silence of words again settled between them. Tresand listened to the chorus of tree crickets rise, and suddenly fall quiet.

"Alec?"

He smiled. "Cailie."

She shifted, turning her head so she could see him. A tiny frown hovered between her brows, and she pursed her lips. The line of her throat, slender and pale in the moonlight, doubled Tresand's heart rate. She wore no earrings tonight, but it made no difference. Tresand gritted his teeth until his jaw ached.

"When are—I mean, um . . ."

He met her hesitant gaze, watched her catch her bottom lip between her teeth and look away, out to sea again.

She wasn't going to say it, Tresand would swear to that. Not that she needed to. She had conquered her demons. Now it was up to him to retain control over his own.

Tresand drew an unsteady breath, let his hands, which had been holding hers, slowly drift up her rib cage. He heard the tiny catch of her breath as his fingers brushed the undersides of her breasts, but shifted his hands to her arms, her shoulders, massaging lightly.

"I will not rush you, Cailie." His hands rose higher, tracing the fragile column of her throat, slipping through the cool silk of her hair. "But neither will I deny you. Whatever you wish—anything, everything . . . If it is in my power to give it, you shall have your heart's desire."

She turned even as he pulled her around to face him, her fingertips tracing his features hesitantly, like butterfly wings beating against his skin, her

161

blue eyes huge, questioning.

"I don't know, Alec," she finally whispered, her eyes closing as she burrowed against his chest. "I don't know what I want anymore."

Tresand enfolded her in his arms, felt her arch closer at the touch of his hands along her back. There was something in her words that didn't ring true, something more than was obvious to him, yet he wouldn't question her. Not now—not ever, if he had any sense left.

He kissed the crown of her head, savoring the faint fragrance of roses in her hair, the sheer touch of it against his lips. She looked up uncertainly, and he brushed his mouth against hers lightly, again, then again. He knew now what he'd guessed before. She was an innocent, yet searching so desperately for love that she would buy what she thought was an illusion. Yet he could not allow himself to linger on that, or to think of the loneliness that must be in her life to have driven her to this. Because his flawed logic would seduce him into thinking that he could keep her from the loneliness and the heartache, that he could give her love, forgetting that he had ever brought her death.

Drawing harsh rein on himself, Tresand captured and banished his turmoil, kept even the hunger of his desire shut securely inside, and let her explore at will with bashful curiosity the shivers of sensation his mouth and hands could awaken in her. He'd not lose control again, as he had at Black Rock beach. This was not the night for passion. It was the prelude to ecstasy.

So he touched her softly, gently, showering her with lingering, slow kisses, creating embers never quite allowed to flame but hot enough to melt away the darkness from her eyes. They had forever, here in the soft shadows of interwoven branches, beside a sea darkening as the moon set.

Desire rose higher, burned more brightly in his flesh, clamoring for more than these sweet, undemanding kisses, for more than light and gentle touches. Yet he backed off even more, lightened each caress, until he could sense the change in her, the serenity that had stolen her wariness, her doubt, until she lay soft and pliant in his arms, peaceful now, no longer afraid.

He held her quietly, for time out of time, in their sanctuary of shadows and whispering waves. She slipped into sleep eventually, curled trustingly against him, and still he held her.

Such a brief moment of eternity they'd been given together. Yet the certainty that at least they would have that much put a bittersweet smile on Tresand's lips. There was hunger, and passion, and desire, yes. But those were fickle, temporary. They were prey to pain, to deception, to death. The achingly pure emotion that wrenched at him now, again, after centuries, was something as eternal as the power of his blood.

But dawn was less than three hours away and he had long since learned the folly of racing the sunrise.

Tresand rose with Cailie still in his arms, and carried her the short trek back to the Jeep. She woke when he deposited her gently into the passenger's seat, clung to his arms, unwilling to be put down.

"I don' wanna go back. I wanna stay here. Sleep here. With you."

"I know." Tresand only smiled at her drowsy protests. He knew she meant it, knew how sterile and silent the confines of a room could be after the sultry night wind and the whisper of waves. He thought about taking her home, thought about holding her against him, skin to skin, in the large hammock on the shore, watching over her while she slept, and shoved the thought away as though it had burned him.

The sun would rise too soon. He'd take her back to her hotel, see her settled into bed, and get the hell out before he did something stupid.

She was dreaming of her phantom again. But this time it was different. This time, he had midnight eyes, like Alec. This time, heaven above, his touch was so sweet. Never before had her dreams been like this. His hands on her bare skin were like silk brushes, his mouth like the bright fire of the sun. She couldn't remember where she was, didn't want to remember, because conscious thought might chase away this dream.

The heat of his body, smooth skin and leashed power, was all around her. He was raining soft kisses over her face, her eyes, down the column of her throat and the valley between her breasts. Tremors started somewhere deep in the pit of her stomach, spreading outward until her breathing grew ragged and she trembled at his touch. She felt the thick strands of his hair slipping through her fingers as she pulled his head closer, and heard the sound of her own husky moan echo shockingly through her dream as the heat of his mouth shamelessly bathed her in fire.

Yet this was a dream. There was no need for shame. She twisted wantonly beneath him, craving more of his touch, more of the fire. His mouth was on her shoulder again, then her neck, titillating nerves she had never known existed. Burning ice shimmered down her throat, along every nerve in her body. She turned her head, laying bare her throat to that addictive touch.

Sharp teeth nipped her again, creating almost pain for an instant, then flooding her with wracking shivers of ecstasy. She was weightless, floating, spiraling into a burning kaleidoscope of color and light, soaring higher with each heartbeat, until her whole being shattered into bright, splintering sensations.

Then a deeper darkness came, taking all awareness.

Tresand paced the shoreline in front of his home as he watched the stars fade in the pre-dawn light. Soon, the sun would soar into that sky, heralding another day in paradise.

Six nights left.

Cursing, he whirled and stalked back the other way, kicking at a piece of coral washed up on the beach.

There was no excuse for what he had done. He should have tucked her into bed and left. Just like that, as he'd told himself he'd do.

But he hadn't. He'd undressed her as he would a child, had slipped her into the T-shirt folded atop her pillow, placed her beneath the covers, and scattered the handful of plumeria blossoms from the bedside table over her. Even then, he should have gone.

But even in sleep, she had clung to him. And though he'd pulled away, he had stayed, and watched her curl up on her side and sink deeper into sleep.

At first, she'd looked like a child—vulnerable, guileless, without cares or fears. Yet as he watched, his perception changed. He saw a woman curled into herself, with the covers drawn tightly around her to shut out the world and all its cruelty.

Aye, she had known that, must have tasted of it all too deeply, to be so innately defensive, so painfully self-conscious. To come to this place, searching for what she could not find in her own world.

How much courage would it take . . . ?

Memory of her words had been his undoing. A crimson fog of rage had flooded his mind. He'd wanted to hunt down and kill every person who had ever hurt her, who had ever laughed at her or made her cry.

166

He had wanted to envelop her in such caring and love and pleasure that she would forget the pain which held her even in sleep. He had wanted to bring back the fragile trust and gentle smile that had so transformed her on the beach.

And, God help him, he'd done just that. He had loved her, not fully, or in any way she would find a trace of in the morning. The small puncture on her throat would be healed even before full light.

Six nights.

Tresand stopped pacing and stared out over the gray ocean, and cursed again.

He would come to her in her dreams every night, were it his choice. Love her and leave her, and send the memory of their time together into some distant corner of her mind. Because he could not trust his control around her when she was awake. He could not trust himself to pull away again and again, to deny the silent longing in her eyes, when he wanted nothing more than to fulfill that longing and lose himself in the love that had not died, though her body had been consecrated to the earth time and again, in the cycle of life and death. She was a fire burning all too brightly in him, a hunger deeper than that of the Blood—one that must never be quenched while she was yet human, yet alive. Too often in the centuries gone by had he given in to the longing, had he shared her life, foolishly hoping again and again that mortal and monster could defy a cruel God, that, this time, they could have

167

at least the span of a short, mortal life together.

Now he knew better. And he would walk into the sun before he'd repeat the mistakes of his past. Aye, she'd talked of the ugliness which the night hid, but she'd never had an inkling of the scope of her words.

The brightening of the eastern sky intruded into his thoughts, awakening an awareness deep in his blood. Slowly, Tresand returned to the house. All too soon, the first fingers of light would touch the beach, confining him to the shadows once more.

The shifting wind carried the faint perfume of plumeria blossoms to him, and he cursed silently. Never again, even should he live to see another thousand years, would he be able to breathe in that scent and not think of her.

He ran a hand through his hair, his breath catching raggedly as he remembered the hours past. Remembered the innocent honesty of her touch, her response.

She'd nearly woken, at first, had smiled and stared up into his eyes as though welcoming him into her dreams, as though he belonged there. But he'd not dared let her realize the truth, had guided her back into that semiconscious world where sensation was pure and untainted by logical thought, where memory intermingled with the images of dreams and fantasies.

God. He'd not tasted blood in this way for centuries. In slow, shared love, shared ecstasy. Not since the times he'd secretly visited her in her family's castle in the Cotswolds, bringing forbidden pleasure in dreams fading by morning light.

Tresand slammed the patio door shut behind him. He had over twelve hours to gather the strands of his fraying control, over twelve hours to come up with some sort of plan that would keep his sanity intact for the next six nights.

After that . . .

After that, what would it matter?

Chapter Eleven

Cailie blinked at the LCD of the clock-radio on the nightstand.

12:28. And the little red light was on the P.M. spot.

She stretched luxuriously, then snuggled under the covers again, reveling in the sweet scent of the blossoms scattered on top of the bed. It really was time to get up, if she wanted to do any sightseeing today. But she was still so tired.

Cailie frowned. She had dreamed of her phantom again last night. No. She had dreamed of Alexander last night. Alexander . . .

She shook her head, flushing crimson as hazy memories of the dream surfaced in her consciousness. Dream . . . Of course it had been a dream. Alec had done no more than take her home and sprinkle blossoms over her bed after a few shared kisses on the beach.

Another wave of heat suffused her face as she remembered that, remembered, and wished he were here right now, so he could start this day as he'd ended the last.

Cailie couldn't decide whether she was embarrassed, horrified, or shamelessly wanton. In the end, she closed her eyes, pulled the covers over her head, and opted for another hour of sleep.

Dinner was going to be impossible.

Cailie sat silently across from Alexander, toying with her empty wine glass, studying its smooth surface.

She was nervous. Again. She knew she shouldn't be. It was silly and naive and immature, but she couldn't help herself. Each time she looked up at Alec, to find him watching her attentively, she remembered last night—and remembered that dream.

And each time she remembered it, she blushed to the roots of her hair, got all flustered, and quickly studied her wine glass again.

This evening was going to be a disaster. Good God, even meeting his eyes was going to be impossible!

"Here you are. And have you decided on dinner yet?"

Cailie shot the waiter a panicked look, but fortunately he was busy placing two half-full, round-bellied glasses on the table.

She frowned at the snifters, mesmerized by the deep red glow of the liquor in the soft lighting, wondering when Alec had ordered the drinks. She'd never touched alcohol in his presence; surely he would have figured out by now that she didn't drink.

"Another few minutes, I think."

"Very good, sir."

Cailie glanced from Alexander to the disappearing waiter and back again. When Alec offered the first glass to her, she stiffened reflexively.

"I—I'd rather not, thank you."

"I know you don't drink." His lips curved into a faint, teasing little smile. "But I know of only one other way to relax you, and that would be somewhat inappropriate in the present surroundings."

Flushing with memory, Cailie shook her head, though her gaze remained on the dark red liquid shimmering in the glass he still held out to her. "No."

Alexander set the snifter down in the middle of the table. He did not prod her for reasons, did not again invite her to drink. After a moment, her shoulders slumped slightly and her mouth softened.

"My . . . parents and sister were . . . killed by a drunk driver."

Still he said nothing. Cailie did not look up at him, only caught her lower lip between her teeth, worrying at it while her fingers compulsively stroked the smooth surface of the empty wine glass.

"It happened just over five years ago. We were on our way to her wedding . . ."

Alec's hands caught hers around the slender stem of her glass, held them until she met his gaze.

"It was only a suggestion, Cailie. If it disturbs you, think no more of it." Releasing her hands, Alec rose in a smooth motion and scooped up the glasses, setting them down on an adjacent, empty table.

Bitter laughter crowded at the back of Cailie's mind, but she only nodded soberly. Of all the rules and habits she'd left behind when coming here, this one was not open to compromise.

Alexander reclaimed his seat and her hands. "Now, do you think we might have a nice, romantic dinner, and afterwards go for a stroll on the beach?"

Cailie nodded, her brows furrowing lightly in puzzlement. That was precisely what they'd been doing for most nights, so why would he ask such a silly . . . A smile dawned slowly and banished her frown.

What an incredible man, this Alexander. He'd made her forget to be nervous.

"Enough of a walk yet?"

Watching the waves sink into the sand at her feet, Cailie nodded. They'd waded up and down half of Kaanapali beach by now, arm in arm. And she felt like the lovers she'd seen in the sunshine now. Well, almost like them.

She looked up at Alec. His face was shadow and moonlight, planes and angles, framed by strands of ebony hair shifting in the wind. She remembered last night, on that secluded shore, and drew a quick breath. "Where are we going tonight?"

"Your choice, Cailie." He glanced down at her, his generous mouth tilted into a crooked smile. Turning toward the walkway where they'd left their shoes, he added, "You probably know this island as well as I do by now. Where would you like to go?"

Whatever you wish—anything, everything . . . If it is in my power to give it, you shall have your heart's desire. Such heady words, to replay over and over in her mind. Too heady. Too dangerous, too shameless by far for her to even consider taking him up on that promise . . . But she had only six nights left.

She slowed, then stopped. Alexander released her arm, turning toward her, his gaze intent.

"Your choice," he repeated quietly, then lightly brushed a fingertip across her bottom lip.

Cailie drew in a soft breath and captured his hand before he could take it back. His eyes were midnight fire, burning down into hers. She remembered the kiss he'd given her last night on this beach. Swallowing hard, she dropped his hand and looked away over the endless waves rushing to shore. The wind was soft against her face, feathering her hair. She could almost make herself believe that she was alone, that not a soul would hear the words she was about to speak.

"I . . . would like to . . . stay home tonight."

The touch of his hands cupping her face, raising it so she would meet his gaze, was nearly as hesitant as her voice had been.

He brushed her mouth with his, briefly, fleetingly, the touch of a smile playing about the corners of his lips. "Yes. I would like that." Then he straightened and tucked her hand into the crook of his arm.

Floating in suspended reality, Cailie held on to him, her eyes softly blurred as they walked along the shore. Yet under the bright lights of the hotel lobby, the fragile magic of the starlit beach splintered into a thousand painful, mocking shards.

Cailie kept her gaze fixed ahead of them as they made their way up to her room. She pressed her lips tightly together, because her anxiety inevitably manifested itself in verbal nonsense. She never bit her nails or chewed on pencils—just talked. Incessantly. And usually inanely. And this, all things considered, was *the* most nervous she should ever get without becoming downright hysterical.

Cailie congratulated herself on arriving at her room without saying a single word. Her hands fumbled with the key card a bit, but finally the lock opened. She rushed into the room, flicking on the lights, and went to shut the balcony door so insects drawn by the light couldn't get in.

"Don't. Leave the door open."

Even as he spoke, Alexander turned down the

175

light, until the room was barely brighter than the night. Cailie smiled vaguely, didn't touch the glass door, and instead opened the heavy drapes. A soft sea breeze wafted through the drawn sheer curtains, raising gooseflesh on her arms.

She inhaled deeply, trying very hard to tell herself that she shouldn't be nervous, shouldn't be embarrassed, shouldn't be shocked by what she was doing.

She didn't believe herself for one second.

Alexander was still standing in the middle of the room, watching her with shadowed eyes, waiting for her to make the first move.

She stared back at him, motionless, wide-eyed. They both knew why they were here. Why couldn't he be a little less the gentleman and just sweep her up in his arms and be done with it?

"Maybe . . ." Her voice disappeared into a squeak. She cleared her throat, then gestured vaguely. "Could you . . . maybe . . . just . . . hold me? For a while?"

Alexander nodded thoughtfully, then nonchalantly shrugged out of his shirt, kicked off his shoes, and made himself comfortable on the bed, resting his shoulders against the headboard. With casual grace he snatched up one of the plumeria blossoms from the bowl on the nightstand, slowly twirled it between his lean, strong fingers, while watching her with faintly raised brows.

Cailie flushed a deep rose, and glanced at everything in the shadowed room but the half-naked man on her bed.

He was stunning. Beautiful. Like the phantom of her dreams. Yet Alexander was real, as real as his midnight eyes. Made of flesh and blood, not twilight memories.

God. She couldn't possibly be doing this!

"Cailie."

"Alec, I think—"

"Don't think." He smiled disarmingly, invitingly, motioning her closer. "Come here, Cailie."

She looked at him, thinking how unfair it was that a man could go out for dinner every night and still have a body like that. Then, before rational thought could intrude, she rushed into his arms.

"Much better." Alec settled her against him, tucked the blossom behind her ear, and touched his lips to her forehead. "Now try to relax."

She nodded, but relaxing was quite out of the question. For one thing, because his back still rested against the headboard, her head lay against his shoulder at an uncomfortable angle. For another, it was still rather shocking to be held this close, to see her hand settled with such familiarity against his chest. Perhaps it was because she could so clearly feel the taut strength of muscle beneath her fingertips, or because his flesh was so smooth, so warm . . . so pale.

A thin frown appeared between her brows. Even in the darkness of the room, her own new tan stood out against his lighter skin tone.

Then she smiled at herself, at her naive assumption that everyone in Hawaii would be permanently tanned. Of course, if Alec worked such long hours indoors each day, researching and writing, it was no wonder he had even less of a tan than she did. Perhaps only the tourists and surfers and the independently wealthy were permanently tanned. Or maybe Alexander was simply one of those smart, foresightful people who didn't intend to die of malignant carcinoma before their time.

"Alec?" She tilted her head up at him. He met her gaze, his brows raised.

"I'm getting a crick in my neck."

He chuckled. His gaze followed the somewhat strained line of her throat, and something dark momentarily flashed across his features before his smile returned. Then he shifted down on the bed and cradled her against him again.

"Better?"

"Much." Cailie smiled as she nestled closer, deciding that this was definitely an underrated activity. It was heaven, being enfolded in his arms. She'd never felt like this with Kyle—had never felt so right, as though they truly *belonged* together. In Alec's arms, she felt safe, sheltered from the knowledge of how this week would end.

"Alec?"

"Mmm."

She had to get away from her thoughts. "May I ask you something?"

178

His chest rose on a deep breath. "Go ahead."

"Where are you from?"

"England, originally."

"I thought so. But you don't have much of an accent."

He shrugged. "I've been away for many years."

Cailie sighed, wishing he'd keep on talking in his warm velvet voice, instead of making her prod for each word. "What's it like?"

"Green."

Propping herself up on her elbow, she frowned down at him. "Maui is green too, and I'm sure the two islands are not at all alike."

He pulled her back down, one hand skimming along her shoulders, down her back. She shivered with the sensation.

"You should go there someday. See it for yourself."

That shut her up. For about five seconds. But his soothing touch helped her forget the harsh reality that his last words had brought crashing down on her again.

"Why did you move here?"

"I like the warm nights." The smile was evident in his words—mirth, and something else. . . .

Cailie nodded thoughtfully as she watched the curtains dance in the breeze, gossamer webs glowing a ghostly white in the moonlight.

"I guess you are a night owl at that. Must be nice, having your own schedule. But you don't get out in the sun enough, you know. You're—"

"I think you've had your twenty questions, Cailie."

The sudden chill in his tone startled her. "I—of course. I'm sorry, I didn't mean to pry—that is, I—"

"Relax, Cailie. You talk too much when you're uptight."

The words were in his usual rich, smooth voice, all harshness gone from it, as though she'd only imagined it the instant before.

"But I'm not—"

The touch of his lips silenced her. It was the kind of kiss she remembered from late last night, undemanding, slow, gentle. This was what she'd wanted. This was better even than hearing his voice. Besides, she wasn't paying him to talk. The thought made her jerk away from him. It made her feel soiled, cheap, contemptible.

"No, Cailie. Never that."

Alexander leaned over her, held her though she ducked her head and tried to shift away. Yet his embrace did not allow for embarrassment or shame, and his touch thoroughly dispelled all rational thought.

If he had been undemanding before, he was fierce now. His kisses were no longer slow and languid, his hands no longer gentling, calming. Cailie's eyes closed as she moved helplessly against him, surrendering to the hunger he roused in her. A low sound of pleasure caught deep in her throat.

Yet his touch suddenly disappeared, and his

weight shifted away, off the mattress. Cailie looked up, dazed, bereft, trembling.

He stood in the shadows beside the bed. Stripping.

Her eyes grew huge. Then she dropped her gaze to the floor, acutely aware that she'd been staring. Her hands clenched the covers.

"Do not look away, Cailie. Not unless you cannot stand the sight of me."

The husky timbre of his voice sent a shiver over her skin. She shook her head wildly. "I—no, it's not that at all!" Her eyes wide in dismay, she carefully met his gaze. "It's just—"

"Hush." He reached his hand out to her. "Stand up. And don't look so frightened. I won't bite."

The words sounded ironic, not flippant. Cailie summoned a tremulous smile, placed her hand in his, and let him pull her to her feet. Pull her against him, burning her with the heat of his body, through the lace of her flower-print dress.

"Alec . . ." Her eyes closed, her breath breaking.

"Beautiful." He spoke the word into her hair, then whispered in a lilting language she did not know as he smoothed his hands down her back, arching her close. Cailie felt the slight tug as the zipper of her dress gave, felt the lace slide down her arms, felt his hands on the ties of her bikini.

Galvanized into motion, she tightly wrapped her arms around Alexander's neck, panicking.

He touched his lips to her hair. "Don't hide from me, Cailie."

181

She could hear the smile in his voice, knew she was being silly, but she didn't budge. She'd never gone this far with Kyle, or any of the men she'd dated. For one thing, she'd wanted a lasting love and couldn't imagine any man wanting to be awakened every night by the screams or sobbing of his wife when she came out of her nightmares. But more than that, being with any of those others had never *felt* right. And the irony of this, of feeling as though she belonged with this stranger she had hired, was too much to bear. She simply couldn't make herself step back and face this moment she'd brought about, face *him*, as a lover might. . . .

Before she could trace that mortifying thought to its conclusion, Alexander scooped her up into his arms.

"Alec, no" Appalled, Cailie struggled to get down, suddenly mindless of her state of undress. She was no piece of fluff, especially after all those fancy dinners. "Alec, put me down before you hurt your back!"

He froze in mid-stride. Cailie caught her breath, hearing her own words from a different perspective, suddenly afraid she'd mortally wounded his pride.

She could feel him begin to shake an instant before his laughter burst forth.

"I—"

"Good God, Cailie, you say the damnedest things," Alexander choked out, landing on the covers with her in a tangle of limbs and dress.

182

"You must be nervous again. But we'll work on that, never fear."

Before she had a chance to get her bearings, he'd done away with the last of her clothing, and covered her body with his own, with nothing between them but building heat. Cailie's breath was ragged at the purely sensual shock of it, then unraveled softly as wonder bore her higher. There was nothing but his touch, and the bright flame of desire rising sharply to eclipse all else.

She bit her lip and met his gaze, her voice unsteady. "I think I know now how little Red Riding Hood felt when the wolf stood over her."

Smiling, Alexander touched his lips to her abused ones, soothed them with the tip of his tongue. "The wolf never got this far."

Cailie closed her eyes and arched into his touch as he wrapped his arms around her, molding her body against his. It was like her dream, the touch of fire, stroking along her skin, waking a flame that shivered along every nerve in her body.

She blinked her eyes open, met the almost frightening hunger in his gaze, and smiled. "Pity little Red."

Chapter Twelve

From the shadows of his living room, Tresand stared at the sun, high in a cloudless sky, and pondered the criminal idiocy of his actions. He'd lied to her, had taken her blood—again.

A slow shiver coursed over him even now with the memory of it. Too addictive, the taste of her love, the vibrant fire of it in her blood. He was playing with his own damnation, with her safety, testing the limits of his control again and again.

And Cailie . . . He shook his head, incredulous still. Even while struggling with her own shyness, she had worried about his back.

Aye, the love was there. The love she'd always given him, the love that had never died. But then, he'd already known that, had tasted it all too clearly last night, and the night before, and in nights uncounted in the centuries past.

Tresand shut his eyes and turned away from the bright azure sky spanning the white-capped ocean.

He had no right to place her life in danger, to tempt history to repeat itself. History. Ah, curse history.

The images welled in his mind, unstoppable, as they always were. The memory was crystal clear, tangible in its vividness, of his bursting into that night-dark chamber, hauling out of bed and slamming against the wall the writhing shape of the glass-blower Antonio, nearly breaking his fragile, human neck with the violence exploding within him.

The maniacal laughter had washed against him like acid. He'd cut it off with a tightening of his hand, as he had watched the eyes of the scrawny old man grow huge, glazed with his insane jealousy.

She's gone, Nicolò, gone into the Bocca di Leone. *You knew she was mine. Mine, by right and custom! But you stole her from me. I warned her, time and again, of the danger in associating with you, damned Genoese spy! But she wouldn't listen. Left me no choice. The Black Councillors took her this morning.*

More choking laughter. *Ah, they're so quick, efficient. They do not waste time on a public trial, or on bringing forth the offender to hear her sentence, for there can be no appeal. You'll never even find her body, Nicolò. They don't mark the graves of traitors!*

Tresand unclenched his hands, which had

curled into fists, and breathed deeply. Lying, scheming old bastard. It had been one of the only times he'd killed a man slowly, deliberately, feeding on pure terror that carried over into madness before death stole his revenge.

But it hadn't brought her back. Nothing ever had, in all those times.

Aye, he should know better. He'd learned that bitter lesson all too often. Yet like before, so again now, he could not deny them the few moments they might have together. He could no more walk away from her than he could stop the sun from crossing the sky.

Like day and night, they were. Able to touch, so briefly, but never allowed to exist together by the whim of a cruel fate.

With heavy steps, Tresand retreated into his bedroom, turned down the blinds until all light was shut out. In darkness, he awaited the coming of another night.

Only five remained.

"Alec!"

With a slow smile, Tresand turned his back to the black, torch-lit wall of lava rock at the north side of Kaanapali beach. Cailie was waving at him, coming toward him on the soft sand with a bouncy stride. For a heartbreaking instant, it was like a mirror of a scene from a millennium ago: the fluttering lavender of her dress, her hair loose about her, though she should have been crossing not a beach but a summery field on a hillside miles from a doomed Norse city. . . .

"Hi." She stopped a half step before him. The white pumps in her hand silently landed in the sand.

Tresand snapped himself out of memories and into the present. "Good evening, Cailie."

She looked up at him with an odd flicker of emotion, then smiled shakily and raised hesitant hands to his shoulders.

With a gruff sound, he wrapped his arms around her and brought his lips down to taste her innocent hunger, craving the addictive rush of passion.

Again, there was a wistfulness beneath her smile, that deep, hidden sadness he could not fathom. Perhaps it had been there all along, perhaps it was only that he'd not felt it before, had not been able to, before tasting so deeply of her blood. He would not be able to sense it clearly, unless . . .

His breath caught at the instant, graphic image that sprang into his mind, so vivid he could almost feel the touch of her mouth against his throat, the drawing of ecstasy—communion, completion . . . damnation.

He tore himself away from the scene, mentally flaying himself for even daring to conceive it. It took far too much control to still the slight tremor of his body, to keep leashed the hunger and desire, to take no more than a simple kiss from her here.

Oh, it was too sweet, this life with her. Too

right, too easy to forget what the truth was. And too easy to forget that she must never know that truth. That she must leave . . . would leave. Soon.

Tresand reluctantly lifted his head, surrendering the heat of her mouth, the softness of her body against his. He needed distance, needed to reestablish the control that became so frayed near her. He picked up her shoes, slid an arm about her waist, and started toward the path leading up and across the lava cliff. "Did you have a good day?"

She smoothly curved her body into his side and beamed up at him proudly. "I drove the road to Hana today."

"And made it back in one piece. Congratulations," he teased, his heart wrenching at the transformation last night had wrought in her. No longer the bashful, timid creature, afraid to live . . . He pushed the thought from him. Five nights, and she would be gone.

"Don't be silly. It's a perfectly good road." She shrugged. "Well, most of it, anyway. And it's no worse than that stretch to La Perouse." She glanced at him mutinously, before her smile broke through again. "But that—the jungle there is incredible! It rained most of the day, and all those waterfalls—"

"And potholes, and washouts," he said, keeping a straight face, stopping to slide the pumps onto her feet before they ascended the sharp lava path. "Yes, I know. Did you get the T-shirt with the number of bridges and curves?"

Cailie shook her head. "No."

"What, your suitcase isn't big enough to hold any souvenirs?"

She stiffened abruptly. Tresand felt her sudden anguish only too clearly, and still, he could not fathom its origin. Disturbed, he ushered her along before him, up the rough, torch-lit steps.

"Don't you like Hana, Alec?"

Already, she had relaxed again. He forced away his frown of concern, lest she look back and see it. "Did I say that?"

Cailie tilted her head and glanced at him, her lips pursed. "Well . . ."

Chuckling, Tresand gently pushed her forward again. "It's a long road to nowhere, Cailie. Did you even find Hana?"

She nodded, but he could hear the sheepish smile in her voice. "Well, actually I almost missed it. It's not exactly a big city."

"Few people I know would call it a city." The path had widened, enough to allow him to walk next to her, draw her body close to his.

"But it's very pretty. And I loved the Seven Sacred Pools. The coast is so wild there, and the grass so springy to walk on, and the waves so huge . . ."

Tresand stole a glance at her. She was so vibrant and alive. He thought of the coastline she described and remembered that shore in Ireland, high on the cliffs, where death had found her yet again.

" . . . and anyway, did you know there's no such

thing as the Seven Sacred Pools, that somebody made the whole thing up to attract tourists?"

Snapping himself out of the past always so near, Tresand forced a smile. "It worked, didn't it?"

Cailie frowned at him, nodded with a disgruntled sound, and abruptly changed the topic. "What's for dinner?"

Tresand couldn't help himself. He grinned down at her, curving her against his side selfishly. Already they were close to the parking lot where he'd left the Jeep. "What would you like?"

"How about pizza?"

"Pizza!" Tresand missed a step, stared down at her, appalled. The light of the hotel complex topping the cliff cast her face in shadows. She shrugged defensively, backtracking.

"Well, or something else a bit more casual. To make me more appreciative of these fancy dinners again. Not that I don't enjoy them . . ."

"It's all right," Tresand assured her, shaking his head in exaggerated exasperation. "Though I should like to bypass pizza, I'm sure we can find something a bit more . . . casual in town."

Four hours later, after dinner at the Cheeseburger in Paradise, Cailie still felt her lips curve into a smile when she thought of Alec's reaction to her suggestion of pizza. Strangely enough, she'd never thought he would have likes and dislikes, as everyone else did. He'd seemed too perfect to have any of the normal quirks and failings of ordinary people.

"We'll be there in a few minutes."

Cailie nodded as she watched the mountains of lights that were hotels pass by behind groomed golf courses, and gradually give way to trees and shrubs and darkness. Alexander turned off at a shopping center, and followed a narrow, winding road through a residential area, before more hotels appeared on the horizon again.

Strange, that there should be such a comfortable, easy silence between them. It had been like this from the first, as long as she wasn't nervous and blabbering. Quiet, companionable minutes, sometimes hours, when not a word was needed. And it was deeper now, since—since last night. It was as though she had known Alec all her life, as though he were the missing part of herself, and the more she let herself be at ease, the more complete this extraordinary communion grew.

It was amazing, what money could buy.

Cailie hated herself for the thought the instant it escaped into her mind. In one heartbeat, she'd managed to turn to ashes all the fragile joy and wonder in her soul.

Alexander pulled off into a dead-end road and parked the Jeep. Woodenly, Cailie got out, mindless of the gentle, warm wind and the soft, fragrant night air. How easy it had become to take paradise for granted.

"Smile, Cailie."

Alec's voice was like warm honey, so compassionate and caring, as though he could sense the darkness that had claimed her yet again. It made her feel like crying, like throwing herself into his arms and begging him to say that this role he played was real. That the end wasn't only a few days away.

"Come." He caressed her cheek lightly, tucked her hand into the crook of his arm, and started down a cement walkway flanked by hedges and palm trees.

The rhythmic pounding of waves filled the night. They rounded a corner, and the beauty before them took Cailie's breath away.

At first, all she saw were lights—an ocean of lights, white and green, orange and red and amber. They were painted onto the gently rippled water in the crescent bay, multi-colored paths of light reflected from the shore. Waves broke into moon-bright foam on the harsh black rock flanking the points, rolled as smooth breakers onto the golden sand fronting the inevitable luxury accommodations.

Breaking her gaze away from the bay, Cailie noticed Alexander standing beside her, his shoes in hand. She followed suit, then let him lead her down the steps and bare, smooth rock onto the sand. It was cool, dry, and softer than satin.

Keeping her close to his side with an arm around her waist, Alec drew her slowly down to the waterline and strolled with her through the wet, clinging sand.

The beach was deserted, but Cailie didn't mind. All the better to have all this to themselves, to be alone in the moon-bright tropical night, on this magical, light-washed shore. Alone with Alexander.

He suddenly stopped, turning his back to the soft beach lights. Cailie glanced at him, found him smiling enigmatically.

"Look down."

She did, and with a sound of wonder dropped to her knees in the wet sand shadowed by Alec's body.

"I have seen breakers aglow with this living light, Cailie . . . or the sea in the wake of a ship, when the night is dark enough."

"It's—like a fallen star!" She glanced up at the diamond-studded sky, bright with the moon and silhouetted cloud fragments, then back down into the night-dark sand which harbored a single grain of brilliant blue.

"A star, yes," Alexander echoed softly, crouching down beside her, his words all but lost in the drumming of the surf. "A star the color of your eyes."

Cailie met his gaze, and caught her breath. He'd looked at her like that last night, with those bottomless midnight eyes, looked at her as though she were the most desirable and precious thing he'd ever found.

Cailie dropped her gaze to the dot of blue fire in the sand, her eyes filling with bitter tears. Yes, it was amazing what money could buy.

"Here."

Alec picked the bioluminescence out of the grains of sand, brushed it off on the back of her hand, and rose, drawing her to her feet. She kept her head down, blinking away tears, brushing with one hand at the sand on the edge of her dress.

"It is a tiny animal, washed ashore."

Struggling to banish reality, Cailie stared at the fragile light on her hand, then whispered, "Is it dead?"

Alexander shrugged and started down the beach again, his pace slow, his arm around her possessively. "Hard to tell at that size. Just because it's glowing doesn't mean it is still alive."

"But it will die out here, won't it?" She looked up at him, already knowing the answer.

"Perhaps. Perhaps it will survive until the tide creeps up again, or a large wave washes it back into the ocean."

"We should put it back." She gazed down at the tiny star on her skin. It was magical, a mote of fairy dust. But it was a living thing.

Resolutely, she met Alec's gaze, feeling her sadness shadow her smile. "I—it's so beautiful. But I don't want it to die because of that."

Even as she spoke, Alec stopped and stooped to retrieve another creature of light. He dropped it onto her hand, beside the other glowing dot of blue.

"There are probably hundreds of them along

the beaches, Cailie. You cannot return them all to the sea."

Cailie dropped her gaze. Return to the sea. Yes, that would come soon enough. But not yet. Not yet . . .

She straightened and met Alec's eyes intently. "We can try."

He held her gaze a moment longer, his expression unreadable; then he nodded wordlessly.

They combed the shore twice, collecting grains of blue fire. Cailie couldn't get over Alexander's extraordinary eyesight, for while she had to be right on top of the bioluminescence to see it, Alec could spot one five yards away.

All the stars, however, went into Cailie's keeping, and by the time Alec guided her up to the dry stretch of sand on the far side of the beach, her cupped hand was full of wet grains of sand and light.

"Now what?"

"Now we take them back into the sea."

Raising her brows, Cailie watched as Alexander started to strip. She didn't realize she'd been watching with bated breath, mesmerized, until Alec straightened and faced her, still in his briefs.

Color rose in her face. She whirled away, not wanting to face his amusement. Green and amber lights from a hotel on the point filled the glittering water, and the moon, low behind her, cast ghostly shadows of palm trees onto the sand.

Alec came up behind her and ran his hands

along her spine in a light caress before slipping open the buttons of her dress. Cailie jumped, almost spilling her precious burden. "What—"

"Come now, Miss Good Samaritan. Surely you realized that you'll have to get wet to return your little charges. If you just toss them in, they'll be washed up again by the next wave."

Cailie snapped her mouth shut, then let him slip the dress down her body shivering from the night wind, from the trailing touch of his hands. Nervously, she toyed with the string ties of the bikini that had become her standard underwear.

"But isn't—isn't it dangerous to go swimming at night? What about sharks? They feed at night, don't they?"

"I usually swim at night, and I haven't had any trouble yet."

He urged her closer, and she could see the flash of his teeth in the moonlight as he drew her toward the water, his smile somewhat strained. "Don't worry, I'll protect you."

"Alec, there's nobody else in the water. I don't think—" Then she cut herself off harshly. She was doing it again, letting caution dominate her. Well, no more!

Without another word, she waded into the low surf ahead of Alec, her hands high and cupped together around her blue stars. After a few steps, the sandy ground dropped off abruptly, and Cailie suddenly found herself in four feet of water.

She gasped as she splashed forward two steps

to regain her balance. The water wasn't as cold as Honolua, true, but the hour was late and there was no trace of that bright Hawaiian sun to warm her skin. She shivered convulsively and rose on her tiptoes to escape each surging wave.

"Is this far enough yet?"

Alexander stopped, his eyes dancing with laughter. "Cold?"

She clenched her jaw to keep her teeth from chattering. "N—not at all."

In reply, he enfolded her in his arms. The heat of his body was like that of the sun, soaking into her skin. Cailie blushed despite the cold. She must be terribly wanton, to so delight in his touch, in the feel of his hard, lean body against her own.

"Better?"

"Just tell me I can dump these guys now."

"No."

Cailie stared at him, frowning. Alec released her to the cool water, then took the grains of light out of her hands.

"But—"

"Hush. Be still."

She obeyed for two whole seconds, until something brushed against her calf and twined around her ankle. Her resultant leap almost landed her on Alec's shoulders.

"There's something in the water! It—on my leg—"

Chuckling, Alexander set her down again, reluctantly, it seemed, but in no way alarmed. "Relax, Cailie. It was only seaweed."

Her heart was beating almost too loud for her to hear him. "How can you be so sure? You—"

"Cailie." He fished around beneath the surface with one hand, then straightened, holding out a brown, dripping mass to her, mirth alive in his eyes. "This is what attacked you. There are whole mats of it in this bay."

Cailie poked at the fibrous lump with one finger, then glared at Alexander. "You don't believe in warning people, do you?" she muttered grumpily, caught between embarrassment and ire.

His face was utterly sober when she looked up at him. No trace of laughter remained. "It's something I should learn to do, isn't it?"

"Yes." Cailie nodded vigorously, though she had the feeling his question somehow hadn't been directed at her. She cast a meaningful glance at the bioluminescence still in Alec's hand.

"Are we going to let the little ones go before they shrivel up and die?"

"Yes." Watching her intently, Alexander placed a drop of blue fire on her cheek, another on her forehead. Cailie stood shivering in the chest-high waves as he scattered grains of light over her skin, arms, chest, and face, leaving fire of more than one kind in the wake of his touch.

For a moment, he simply stood and looked at her, transfixing her with a smoldering gaze. His features were harsh, set, sculpted from obsidian as he closed the scarce distance between them.

"Now," he whispered, his lips almost touching

hers. "Close your eyes and take a deep breath."

Cailie stared at him dazedly, hardly able to breathe at all between the cold water and the heat of his body so close to hers. Forgotten was her ire and fear, burned to ashes in a reawakening fire. His hands rose to her face, his fingertips sliding into her hair, and her lips parted as his mouth came to hers, hot and achingly sweet, doubling her heartbeat. Her eyes closed of their own accord, her awareness focusing inward, on the flood of sensations, the rhythm of touch and taste. She moved her hands up his chest, and twined them around his neck.

The water was rising higher around her, and amid the heady rush of passion, Cailie suddenly understood. She felt Alec's hands glide down her back, felt him gather her close to him, and held on tightly.

As one, they sank beneath the waves.

Chapter Thirteen

Cailie broke the surface gasping for air, swiping water from her eyes. Beside her, Alexander rose from the sea like Triton in the flesh, his hair and skin wet and gleaming in moonlight.

Breathless, her eyes wide with excitement, she smiled at him. "Are they all gone?"

He nodded somberly. "And you? Are you still cold?"

His hand rose and traced her cheek lightly. Despite her shivering, Cailie shook her head. "I'm getting used to it."

"Good."

Alec moved against her again, rained butterfly kisses on her face and throat and shoulders, his hands warming her skin wherever they touched. She clung to him, reveling in the heat and strength of his body, all too aware that the trembling inside her had little to do with the chill of the water.

When Alexander caught her up in his arms, she held tightly to him. He carried her out onto dry sand, and let her slide slowly down his body and to the ground. Cailie's knees were already less than steady, but he did not let her go, only continued his sensual assault. His hands wove a heady magic across her skin, and his kisses stole her breath away.

"Alec, this is a public beach . . ."

Her gasped, half-hearted protest had no effect. The hot touch of his mouth moved down her throat, slowly, sending tendrils of fire shivering through her body, until she clung to him for fear of falling. His lips traced lower, still, across her collar bone, and lower. . . .

"Alec!" Cailie pushed against him, with enough conviction that he straightened. "There's someone on the beach!"

"Easy," Alexander hushed her, never even following her horrified gaze down the shore, to where a solitary couple strolled along the waterline. He fitted her against his side and calmly headed for one of the beach showers, gathering up their clothing on the way.

The spray felt like slivers of ice. Cailie rinsed off with record speed, but before she could step, dripping, into the lavender dress, Alexander caught her arm.

"Wait."

Crumpling up his shirt, he used it to dry the

beading drops of water from her body. Cailie stood still, shivering, letting him do as he would, watching with mesmerized intent the ripple of muscle beneath his wet skin glistening in the moonlight. Though his hand never touched her skin, her breathing grew more unsteady with each gentle swipe of that soft cloth, her heartbeat heavier, faster.

As though sensing the leap in her pulse, Alec met her eyes with an unreadable glance. Then he stepped back.

"Now, put on the dress, if you must."

She stared at him, her eyes wide, dazed. "What? Oh. Right."

Feeling heat rush into her face, Cailie fumbled into the loose cotton while Alec rinsed off. She was still struggling with the buttons down her back, her fingers uncommonly clumsy, when Alec stepped into his slacks and slung the damp shirt over his shoulder.

"Here." Alexander turned her away from him, brushed her hands aside, and did up the buttons. His hands lingered warmly on her shoulders even after he was finished; Cailie felt his mouth on her nape and shivered.

"You would prefer the privacy of your room?"

Cailie froze as the meaning of his words sank in, blushed furiously, then nodded. She was beginning to understand, though, why Janey had wanted to come back to the islands for her second honeymoon.

Alec drew her against him and started down

the shore, passing where they'd left their shoes on the way to the parked Jeep.

"Your choice, Cailie. But tomorrow, if you wish, I shall show you a different beach. It is not as groomed as this one, I'll admit. It has pebbles and *kiawe* thorns as well as sand. But it is not a public beach. And nobody will disturb us there."

His control was slipping, had been, ever since that night ten days ago when she'd walked back into his existence. And the proof of that lack of control was right here, right now, tonight. Yesterday, he'd made a promise to her—and now he was fulfilling it.

Tresand shifted down into third gear as he turned off the highway onto his street.

"Almost there." He glanced at Cailie, then back at the road. Catching her hand in his, he reassuringly touched it to his lips.

Her wavery smile brightened fractionally.

Tresand smiled back, never once showing a trace of the battle still raging in him.

Oh, he'd cursed himself a dozen times since last night, for not keeping his mouth shut and for letting hunger and passion conquer his common sense. God, but he'd thought he would know better.

He'd been wrong.

The thought of bringing Cailie to his sanctuary, of spending the night making love to her in the privacy of his beach, of seeing her naked in the moonlight, her skin glistening with crystal drops of water, should not have affected his reasoning.

Ah, but it had.

So he was taking her home, and would fill that place of safety with memories to haunt him each time he looked out over the moonlit ocean, each time he walked along the sand, each time he felt the breeze on his skin.

Nay, he should never have spoken those words. But it was far too late for should-have-beens. Too late for a great many things.

All that remained was creating memories so glorious and pure they would be enough to carry him through the rest of eternity.

Chapter Fourteen

Cailie was half a step behind Alexander as he rounded the corner of the house in the uncertain light of an outside lantern and started up the steps to the back door.

A flash of metal in the darkness beneath the terrace caught her eye, a flash that turned into a deadly blur of motion.

"Alec!"

He didn't reply—couldn't. There was a sickening thud, then the sound of a body falling heavily.

A scream lodged in Cailie's throat, choking her. She wanted to flee, but her feet carried her instead to Alec's crumpled body. A thin trickle of blood, black in the shadows, marred his forehead and stained the cement walkway.

"Oh, dear."

Cailie shrank back at the gruff voice so close. The sight of a short, archaic creature standing not three feet away tore a cry of shock from her. Nothing this old should still be living, never mind swinging a sword with such agility and power.

A sword. God help her.

"Alec!" Her hands were on his shirt, frantically shaking him, though her widened stare never left his grandfatherly assailant. "Oh, God, Alexander, wake up!"

Alec didn't stir, but the wizened old man cleared his throat, shifting to lean his elbow on the hilt of the sword that was nearly as tall as he.

"'E'll be all right, lass. Just a knock on the 'ead. 'T willna kill 'im."

Outrage roared white-hot through Cailie. She surged to her feet in a rush of mindless fury, topping the stranger in black by half a head.

"You! You would have—would have—*murdered* him!"

The wiry little man straightened huffily. "Well, 'tis dreadfully sorry I—"

"Sorry!" Cailie blazed, glaring at him incredulously. "Sorry! What—who the hell do you think you are? You almost killed him, and you've got the gall to just stand there and say you're *sorry?*"

He shrugged sheepishly. "'E did ask me to do it, ye know. I didna realize 'e'd changed 'is mind again, but I canna say I'm sad to 'ear it."

Cailie halted in mid-attack. Utter stillness descended on her. "What do you mean, he asked you?"

A Deeper Hunger

Looking decidedly uncomfortable, the would-be assassin shuffled back a few steps to examine the closed hibiscus blossoms framing the stair banister.

"'Twas some time ago," he hedged.

"Keep talking."

He hesitated, then shook his head, gesturing to Alexander. "'E's coming round. Best step back."

Cailie shot him a scathing look and defiantly dropped to her knees beside Alec again, her hands gentle on his shoulders. "Alec? Can you hear me?"

"Come on, Alec, wake up."

The voice was close to him. Disorientation vanished, memory struck home with crystal clarity. Tresand was on his feet, launching himself at the bearer of the ancient samurai sword with the inhuman speed of his kind.

"Easy, lad!"

The little man gave up the weapon without resistance. Tresand checked the automatic reflex of his blood, controlling the urge to kill.

This was no enemy. The old man had given it his best shot, and if not for Cailie's cry, he would have succeeded.

Tresand smiled wanly. So here was another source for the restlessness, the undeciphered tension that had been with him for the past day. There was more cause for it than just his decision to bring Cailie to his sanctuary. . . .

He sighed. "Aramond."

The ancient man clasped Tresand's out-stretched arm tightly. Tresand met his dark green eyes—colored contacts, as his own—and noted the passage of millennia carved into the somber, weathered face. Yet none of the fierce spirit had faded from the sharp eyes behind their disguise, from the classical features that had ever caught the ladies' eyes. Ah, but Daria had always been possessive of her mate, even when they were half a world apart. Tresand smiled.

"'Tis sorry I am, my friend. To be so late. To fail ye . . ."

With a sound too close to laughter, Tresand pulled Aramond into a bear hug. Then he noticed Cailie, standing with her back pressed against the house wall, her eyes huge. Holding her gaze, he clapped Aramond on the shoulder and stepped past him, to gather Cailie into his arms just as something like a sob broke from her.

"Oh, God, Alec, I thought he'd—"

"Hush. Everything is all right." He tucked her head against his chest and touched his lips to her hair, absorbing her trembling. In his embrace, she steadied quickly.

"Alec? Who—who is that—man?" She shook her head, as though hearing her own question for the first time. "I know, it's none of my business. But shouldn't we call the police—or something?"

Smiling, Tresand gently set her at arm's length, and shook his head. "He's an old friend, Cailie. And no, there's no need to call the police or the nearest mental institution. This . . . It was only a . . . practical joke, of sorts."

At her scowl, he drew her away from the house, past Aramond, at whom Cailie shot a distrustful look. Holding her close to his side, Tresand walked with her onto the lawn.

"We test each other sometimes. It is an old game, Cailie."

"But you're hurt. And he would have—"

"No, he wouldn't." He touched the drying blood at his temple, the skull fracture already healing.

"This is only a scratch. Besides, if he'd wanted to kill me, he could have done so while I was unconscious. And he didn't, did he?" Tresand glanced back toward Aramond, a frown high between his brows, then met Cailie's gaze again.

Reluctantly, she shook her head. Scowling into the darkness by the house, she offered, "I suppose you'd like some time alone with your . . . friend."

Tresand stole a deep breath, then nodded. This was not at all how he'd expected the evening to pass. Ruefully, he turned her face toward him with a light touch on her cheek.

"Only if you do not mind. It has been . . . a long time since we saw each other. But he can come back another time."

Cailie shrugged. "Go ahead."

"Thank you." He touched his lips to her brow, then caught her shoulders and pointed her toward a cluster of coconut palms at the border of lawn and sand.

"See those? Between two of them is a large,

comfortable hammock with a perfect view of the ocean. I won't be long, I promise."

"All right."

Tresand released her after a brief kiss, and watched her walk away without a backward glance at him. Reluctantly, he turned and strode back to the house.

Aramond was sitting on the bottom step of the terrace stairs, his arms folded across his chest, his head hanging.

"Lord above, Tresand, I'd no idea she was with ye. I couldna just destroy ye before 'er very eyes!" He looked up, his time-lined features grim, the hint of a grin playing about his mouth. "Besides, I thought ye might 'ave changed yer mind, what with 'er 'ere."

Tresand met the vivid green gaze for a long moment. Then he sank to the ground by the stairs, his back against the house wall, expelling his breath in a long rush before he wearily closed his eyes.

Aramond. God, what a luxury to speak without words again, to touch so easily, so clearly, another's mind. It had been over two centuries since he'd had that pleasure, over two centuries since he'd been with another of the Blood. Longer than that, since he'd heard from Aramond.

How very good it is to see you again. Tresand smiled vaguely. *And you've been traveling again. That accent is horrid.*

Oh, is it now? came the perfect Oxford English reply. *I'm afraid my Norse is a bit rusty, but I can certainly regale you with Gaelic, French, Italian, Arabic. . . .*

Tresand cut him off with silent laughter. *Another day, my friend.* He hesitated. *How is Daria?*

Aramond grunted. *Not to worry, lad, she's well as ever. Doesn't look a year older than she did when I met her, I swear.* He chuckled at Tresand's wordless laugh. *She nearly had my head for tracking you down, you know. Said if I killed you, I shouldn't bother to show my face again.*

She's still bossing you around, is she?

Aye, when I let her. Aramond sighed, straightening where he sat. *But I must apologize for being so late in responding to your call. I was . . . indisposed, one might say.*

Two hundred and twenty-six years is a long time to be indisposed, Tresand teased with a grin, his eyes still closed, understanding perfectly. *But you concealed yourself well. I did not know you lay in wait.*

There was a distinct *harrumph* from the wizened creature on the stairs. *As if ye would, if I didna want ye to!* The accent was back in full force. *I may 'ave been a century late, but ye'll not be teaching me new tricks, lad! Don't ye be forgetting who ye're talking to!*

Aye. An antediluvian fossil of a—

"Ye'll take that back!"

Tresand snapped to attention too late. Before he could so much as spring to his feet, the sword previously lying on the ground ten feet away was in Aramond's hands, unsheathed, the point lightly resting against Tresand's chest.

"Not a very effective threat," he commented drily, "but passable speed."

With another "harrumph," Aramond straightened and sheathed the blade again, grumbling. *Look who's slowing down with old age.*

Tresand chuckled. Aramond frowned at him.

"How's the head?"

"Were I mortal, you'd have been successful in your task," Tresand replied without rancor.

Aramond grunted in agreement. *Aye, I'd thought as much. 'Tis not often I've seen one o' the Blood drop like a stone.* He leaned against the wall, looked at Tresand somberly. "Ye've changed yer mind, then? 'Tis 'er, no?"

Tresand shut his eyes and sighed. *Aye.* Meeting Aramond's gaze, he nodded, repeated his thoughts aloud. "Aye, I've changed my mind. For now, old friend."

His gaze traveled to the woman in the hammock, and softened. "And aye, 'tis her. Again."

Aramond chuckled, and Tresand could sense the relief in his old mentor, the approval that he had chosen to go on yet.

"Quite the spitfire, she is. But then, she always was, eh? Ye should 'ave seen 'er, after I missed me aim—thanks to 'er, no less. She didna even try to run. Came after *me*, she did. Reminds me of Daria. More fire than sense sometimes."

Aramond shook his head, smiling still, but said no more about Cailie. Tresand, inordinately thankful for small mercies, made no attempt to hear his friend's thoughts on the matter. There was turmoil enough inside him already when it came to Cailie.

Thinking of her, Tresand rose. The night was passing all too quickly, and there were too few hours left to let them slip away.

Will you stay for a while?

Aramond shrugged. *Perhaps. 'Tis a nice place, this. And warm. Daria would like it.*

Smiling, Tresand clasped Aramond's proffered hand.

"Aye, I too like my comforts in my old age." With a nod at the house, he offered, "My home is yours, if you wish. It is private enough here, and safe, at all hours of the day."

"Ah, nay, I couldna do that!" Shaking his head, Aramond started up the driveway, raising his hand in farewell. *Especially not when ye've yer lady with ye!*

Aramond!

There was only faint, silent laughter in reply, and a certainty that he would not be gone so long. Tresand stared after him for a moment, then turned on his heels and strode across the lawn to the shore.

"I heard you fought like a lioness over my fallen body."

Cailie jerked upright in the hammock, startled by the sound of his voice. Smiling, Tresand caught her up in his arms before she could get herself tangled in the large, loose webbing, and gently set her down in front of him.

She pulled away immediately. "That's not funny!"

Tresand summoned a straight face, glad to have distracted her from worry. "Aramond thought it exceptionally so."

"You're laughing at me." She scowled fiercely.

"He also thought it exceptionally courageous. And more than a little foolish, considering who it was you might have been risking your life for."

Cailie stared at him silently for an instant, frozen. "Oh, Alec—" Choking on some emotion he couldn't fathom, she flowed back into his arms. Then she stiffened.

"That cut . . . It should be disinfected, and you ought to see a doc—"

"It's nothing." Tresand intercepted her hand, brought it to his lips, grateful that, in the concealing darkness, she had never clearly seen the extent of his injury. "It has already stopped bleeding, Cailie. You won't even notice it tomorrow. Trust me."

"But—"

"Don't worry about me. I'm a fast healer."

She wasn't content with that, but let it go. Tresand heaved a silent sigh, hoping she'd not bring up the injury again tomorrow, when not a trace of it would remain. He did not want to take her memory of this. Bad enough that she'd witnessed Aramond's attack—but so long as she accepted the explanations he offered, and didn't think too much about what had occurred here tonight, he'd not tamper with her memories.

"Um, well, you can take me home if you want, you know. I could even call a cab . . ."

Tresand shook his head, then kissed her crown.

"No. There's no reason for you to go, unless you wish to do so. I'll certainly understand if you would rather not spend any more time here." His brows raised, he met her gaze. "Your choice, Cailie."

She remembered the words, he could see it. He could sense the catch in her breath, the leap of her pulse, at even the memory, still, of that night, and the ones since.

Ah, but he too could not claim indifference. He wanted her, needed her, more with each night. And there were five hours yet until the threat of dawn would force him to return Cailie to her hotel room, to the world of sunlight.

"You said nobody would disturb us here."

A bitter laugh broke from Tresand's lips. He shook his head, then rested his forehead against hers for a moment. "It seems I lied. Would it help if I told you this was the first time this has ever happened?"

She moved softly against him, closer, a tiny smile evident in her voice. "I might forgive you. But only because he didn't interrupt anything."

Tresand chuckled, even as she turned her head into his shoulder, hiding. Before she could blush over her own bold words, he scooped her up into his arms and strode down onto the sand.

"And not a word about my back," he growled

softly against her ear, then bit it lightly. She squeaked, squirmed in his hold, but didn't struggle.

A few feet from the waterline, Tresand stopped and slowly let her slide down to her feet. Her eyes were wide, locked to his, as he slipped the gauzy sun dress over her head.

"Alec . . ."

He brushed her lips with his, once, then again.

"This isn't a public beach, Cailie," he reminded her huskily.

She swallowed, nodded, and blushed, but did not avert her gaze as he shed his own clothing. Tresand smiled. She'd come a long way in the last few nights.

He raised his brows. "You?"

Her eyes grew bigger yet, and the blush staining her cheeks, visible even in the moonlight, darkened several shades.

Tresand's smile widened. Well, perhaps not so very far after all.

He moved closer, tugged on the tie of her bikini top, toying with the string. She stiffened, but made no move to stop him.

Tresand let the string drop, then moved around behind her, letting her see the rippled sea, glowing silver and black in the pale light of the moon, and the distant, dark shore of the bay.

"Show me that you want this, Cailie. That you want to feel the starlight and the night wind on your bare skin. That you want to go into the sea as though you had been born to it. You won't be cold, I promise you."

He placed his hands just over her shoulders, feeling the warmth of her skin, a hair's breadth from touching.

"Show me that you trust me. That you are not afraid of my touch, of the fire that burns so very brightly just beneath the skin . . ."

He saw the tremor of her hands as they undid first the knotted bow between her shoulder blades, then behind her neck, and more hesitantly still, the ones on her hips. Each time she brushed against him, it was a sliver of lightning passing between them, heightening awareness, feeding a hunger deeper than that of his blood.

Finally she stood, trembling, waiting, staring out to the sea. His gaze caught on the faint tan lines along her back and buttocks, harsh reminders of the unbreachable abyss between them. Of what he was. What she was . . .

He shut his eyes and leashed the anguish, the hunger. He let his hands come down on her shoulders and draw her back against him, absorbing the tremor of desire that coursed over her, trembling in turn as his body tautened in response. He touched his mouth to her nape, tasting the faint salt of her skin, too aware already of the quickening beat of her heart, the breaking of her breath, the throbbing artery in her throat.

Tresand released her and threw his head back, his eyes squeezed shut, breaking the contact between their bodies, struggling for breath. It was too closely linked, the hunger of passion and of blood. With her, it was almost inseparable. Dangerous . . .

"Alec?"

He snapped his eyes open just in time to find Cailie turning toward him, her hands clenched in front of her chest.

Uncertain again.

Tresand cursed himself in as many languages as he could recall on the spur of the moment. He caught her hands in his, brought them to his lips, and kissed the pulse points of her wrists.

"Do not doubt, Cailie," he whispered into her palms, then drew her closer, closer still, until not even the night wind could pass between them. He found her lips, and released her hands. They clasped behind his neck, then roamed restlessly, urgently down his back.

"Hold on to me." Lifting her against him, Tresand strode into the water.

He knew the shore, knew where the coral rubble and the rocks and the sand were. He walked down a wide sand channel until the water reached his chest, and slowly let Cailie down.

She shivered, clung to him, hands and lips, skin to skin, her eyes dark pools of desire and of shadows he could still not define. He stroked her skin, pearly smooth in the moonlight, with relentless tenderness, denying his own hunger, summoning iron control.

He could banish the darkness behind her

trusting blue eyes, could make her forget her cares and fears, here in the velvety embrace of night.

He was the bringer of dreams, if only till the morning light.

Chapter Fifteen

Two hours till sunset.

Tresand roamed the shadowed garden on the east side of the house, pacing amidst the skillfully cultured foliage and tropical blossoms. He caught the scent of plumeria, and let his eyes close as he drew the fragrance deeply into his lungs.

The night rose in his memory like a blazing phoenix from the ashes. Tresand clenched his fists as he stared hard into the surrounding foliage with unseeing eyes.

God, he should never have brought her here. It would tear him apart to let her go. He could feel the pain already, the grief, rising in him as a tidal wave rises from out of the ocean.

But he had no choice.

He turned on his heels, and with quick strides

headed for the garden door. In the living room, he began to pace again.

Almost seven. Damn, but what was keeping Kimo? He should have been here half an hour ago.

Tresand paused in mid-step, growing still as a statue for a span of seconds. He searched for the first tendrils of hunger, and found them vague and restless in his blood. Not anywhere near strong enough to fray his control, and yet . . .

Oaths tumbled through his mind. He'd promised Cailie they'd stay in tonight. Order room service for dinner, and watch the stars from the balcony of her corner room, and listen to the steady rumbling of the surf.

The silent oaths took on sound. Tresand stared out into the darkening sky over the mountains, his hands clenched into fists. There would be more than the hunger for blood to test his control tonight.

And there would be hell to pay if Kimo didn't show up soon.

Callie woke alone, again, as she had the past eleven days. Yawning, she squinted into the bright daylight that streamed in through the sheer balcony curtains and flooded the room. The drapes were still open; they'd never bothered drawing them last night.

She blinked at the clock. 2:42 P.M.

Good God! She hadn't slept in this late yet! But she was so tired.

She yawned again and stretched. A smile curved her lips at the realization that beneath her was not the hotel's linen sheet but heavy, luxurious silk.

The pareu.

Cailie sighed, and let her eyes drift closed again. Dreamily, she rubbed her cheek against the heavenly fabric. Alec had showed her how to transform the length of silk into all the exotic dresses listed in the pareu manual—and then some. If she'd known he was an expert in the matter, she would have made that quip about being ignorant of how to wear a sheet much sooner.

But they'd used it as that too, in the end.

Flushing, she recalled last night, in her room and out on the balcony, recalled the endless hours of silent touches, of kisses that turned her blood to wine, and such drunken passion that she had no memory even of Alexander leaving before the morning light.

And there were only two nights left with him.

And only three days in paradise. Shoving away the rising panic that welled in her, Cailie tossed off the light blanket and surged out of bed. Even before the few plumeria blossoms remaining on the covers had scattered onto the carpet, she plopped down on the mattress again.

The dizziness faded almost instantly. Cailie rose again, more slowly this time, and the lightheadedness did not recur. Frowning, she made her way out onto the balcony.

God, that was all she needed—some tropical bug to make her last days in paradise miserable. It would be the ultimate of fate's tricks . . . but with her luck, more than likely.

She shook her head irritably as her gaze wandered over the azure ocean, down to where the massive waves pounded against the golden sand. Along the walkway, the red flags were up and fluttering in the wind, warning unwary tourists of the heavy surf. Of course that didn't stop the die-hard water babies from body-surfing, or the inexperienced tourists from getting washed up on the beach, in all sorts of painful-looking positions, by a towering wave.

Cailie smiled crookedly as a stocky lady in a hot pink bathing suit picked herself up off the sand.

Yes, she knew just what that felt like. There was nothing quite like the adrenaline rush that one got standing in three feet of water, unable to move due to the undertow of a rushing, oncoming seven-foot wall of water. More than once, Cailie had thought she'd see her end in that unstoppable force of nature. But six turbulent seconds later, her skin sand-burned from being propelled up onto the beach by the wave, and sand in her bathing suit and absolutely everywhere else, she'd shoved her hair out of her face and rushed back into the water.

So much for crippling overcaution.

Cailie's proud smile was interrupted by a most unamused rumbling from her stomach, reminding her in no uncertain terms that she'd missed not only most of dinner, but also all of breakfast and lunch.

Forty-five minutes later, she was in her favorite window spot at the Cheeseburger in Paradise, nibbling on cheese fries and sipping her mango smoothie. She was just about ready to leave when the waitress showed a young couple to the table across from her.

It was the woman sitting facing her who caught Cailie's attention. She was very, very beautiful, with short, bouncy black hair, porcelain skin, huge, dark eyes, and a radiant smile lighting up her features. She was also very, very pregnant.

Cailie froze in the motion of getting up from her seat. Something like a keening wail was growing in volume inside her head, making it pound painfully. She snapped her gaze away from the young couple, but not before the dark-haired man had sat down beside the woman and, smiling fondly, placed his hand against her distended stomach. He said something, too softly for Cailie to hear, and both dissolved into laughter.

Cailie didn't feel like laughing. She felt like she had that time she'd sailed off her horse and landed face-down on the hard ground, stunned, unable to get air into her lungs.

Rising abruptly, she fumbled a number of bills out of her purse, left them on the table, and escaped into the thankfully empty ladies' room. The colorful walls and dim lighting made her feel as though she'd just trapped herself inside her own mind.

A Deeper Hunger

Pregnant. The thought reverberated through her like thunder. Bracing her hands on the sink, she stared at herself in the mirror in utter shock. It was impossible. Wasn't it?

Her legs felt weak, even as her mind produced the perfectly logical answer to that question. She held her hands under the lukewarm water that passed as cold on the island, and splashed some drops onto her face. It didn't make the tremors inside her go away.

God. Back home, she'd never spent much thought on a family of her own, because she had never been in love, had never met a man with whom she wanted to share her life. Had never seen herself as a wife, as a mother.

Of course, in the past nights, those things simply hadn't mattered. This wasn't love—it was a fling. But biologically speaking, whatever she chose to call it would make preciously little difference.

She bit her lip, watching the blue eyes in the mirror grow huge as the thought reached its logical conclusion.

Could she go through with the last part of her plan if there was a new life inside her? But how alive could it be, after only a few days?

Cailie buried her face in her hands, her breath rasping in her throat. Then she dropped her hands and straightened. This was just life's irony again. And she was overreacting, as usual, making a mountain out of a molehill . . . or a baby out of a wish.

A wish?

Three minutes later, Cailie was stalking along Front Street, oblivious to the shops and tourists. By the time she'd reached her car, she'd twisted herself into such a knot, she couldn't even think straight.

She drove back to Kaanapali on autopilot. There she paced the beach, up and down the stretch to Black Rock, burning nervous energy in the deep, soft sand. The flower-print dress was much too hot, and she finally returned to her room to have a shower and change into the aquamarine sun dress. Then she went down to the beach again and paced some more.

The sun seemed to hang in the bright blue sky forever, nearing the horizon at a snail's pace. Finally, it sank into the haze over the ocean.

Cailie stalked along the shore in front of her hotel, getting cool sand in her thongs, her turmoil twisting ever tighter. Perhaps she should see a doctor, and find out. . . .

"Good evening, Cailie."

She whirled around at the sound of his voice so close, her heart in her throat.

"Alec!" A shaky laugh tumbled from her lips. "You surprised me. Can't you walk like normal people? You know, with the sound of footsteps and all?"

He didn't point out the fact that they were standing in soft sand, but only smiled and drew her close for a quick kiss. "Don't tell me you're nervous again."

Cailie pushed away uneasily, unable to relax into his embrace.

"Alec, I—I have to ask you something. Something—uh—" She broke off, struggling to find the words.

Alexander brought her hands to his lips, and touched his mouth to the pulse points. "Then ask me, Cailie. Don't be afraid."

"But I am!" She looked away, into the night, then blurted out, "All these nights—we didn't—I mean, you didn't—and I'm not on—anything—"

He was frowning severely when she risked a glance at him. Cailie cringed inside. In his line of work, he probably took it for granted that the woman knew what she was doing and took care of matters—or not, however she was inclined. But still, with the kinds of diseases out there these days, he should be more careful—though she'd told him she wasn't sick . . . Her convoluted thoughts trailed off as she realized that Alexander was still watching her, waiting.

God, she couldn't look at him and say this. But she had to. She had to meet his midnight gaze as she whispered, "We could—I mean, I could—could be—pregnant. Couldn't I?" The words were not a question.

A multitude of sudden, unexpected emotions flitted over Alec's face, then vanished again before she could even be sure of what she had seen.

"No."

There was no doubt in that single word, not the slightest hesitation. Cailie stared down into the sand and drew a deep, slow breath, blinking to ease the sudden sting of tears behind her eyes.

So. There would be no last-minute escape. No reason for her to go on . . .

Alec's hands came to her shoulders, drawing her gently against him. "I am sorry, Cailie. I should have told you in the beginning that there is . . . no possibility of a child."

His voice was harsh, but not with anger. Cailie nodded, still not meeting his gaze. She shrugged helplessly. "It just—I realized that—we—I—hadn't been very responsible in the matter," she explained haltingly. Then, before he could reply in any way, she forced a cheerful smile onto her face, looked up at him, and blurted out, "Have you seen your friend again? And how's your head today?"

Her desperate attempt to change the subject wrought a sudden, cold distancing in Alexander. Cailie frowned in consternation, then sighed defeatedly. Trust her to make an awkward situation worse.

"Did I say something wrong? I didn't mean to pry, really."

But Alec shook his head at her apologies, his features already smoothing into something resembling a smile again. The mask of control never slipped for long.

"You didn't. No, he's not been by again, though I'm sure it won't be long before he will be. And the head's just fine, thank you." He held out his arm to her. "Now, shall we go?"

Nodding, she twined her arm with his, and let him lead her back up to the walkway, consciously forsaking reality to live in her dream of love.

"Hey, Alec!"

Tresand broke his stride, then glanced back across the deserted hotel lobby. Kimo was coming out from behind the registration counter, heading toward him.

"Man, you keep worse hours than I do!" The young Hawaiian grinned tiredly as he ran a hand through his short black hair. "Sorry I haven't been by, old chap, but I've been stuck on shift here. I won't be at the hospital till Saturday. But I'll come by after that, all right?"

Tresand grunted a reply, silencing the sharp retort that came to his tongue. Had Kimo shown up the other night, he'd never have taken so much blood from her—not enough to do her harm, but still, more than he'd intended.

The insistent ring of a telephone sent his confidant shuffling back toward the counter. Kimo raised his hand in salute without turning back. "See you then, Alec."

"Saturday." Tresand nodded, then continued out into the parking lot. Once in the Jeep, he slumped into the seat and buried his face in his hands.

A child. God above. He'd never even thought about the matter of a child.

Had she known? Could she have guessed, in that moment, that he'd have moved heaven and earth to make her concern a reality? To be mortal, and convince her to stay, whatever her future plans might be, to remain in the embrace of his love, raise a human babe with human eyes, and live out the rest of a puny life span by her side?

Nay, she'd not known. There had been too much anguish in her own eyes when he'd told her the truth.

And it had been his fault again, that pain. He should have been prepared for that question. Never mind that one tended to forget about the matter of a child, after a thousand years of living in the power of the Blood. He should have taken on the role of a mortal man more completely. A mortal man in his position would have said something at least, on their first night—or taken care of the matter so that she wouldn't need to question it.

Tresand choked on a deep breath as he forced himself to start the Jeep and head home. The sunrise would not wait for him.

Chapter Sixteen

Chapter Sixteen

Cailie stared out over the luminous ocean from the aerie of her balcony, watching a flaming sun sink into the low cloud bank on the horizon. Ragged tufts of white hung higher in the sky, closer, burning brilliant orange even after the sun had disappeared into the haze. The sky above was changing from blue to violet, slowly darkening to reveal flickering stars.

She watched the ships at anchor just off the beach, the sailboats with their masts bare, rolling in the low swells, and felt tears well in her eyes.

Such peace, such beautiful tranquility . . . Oh, yes, she loved this place, this shore, loved it more with each minute she spent by it.

She blinked away the tears, remembering her afternoon trip to the half-collapsed Mala wharf. Despite the threat of structural failure and local rumors of garbage dumping and sharks, and the "Warning" and "Restricted Area" signs, she had gone snorkeling there. She was getting amazingly good at it, conquering her innate caution with her will. And despite the shopping carts and old tires littering the sea floor, she had found magic.

Wending around the encrusted wharf pylons, in and out of the shafts of sunlight filtering through the hazy blue water to bright sand below, floating over fragments of cement blocks and pillars tumbled this way and that . . . It was like glimpsing the columns and walkways and tumbled walls of long-lost Atlantis.

It had fit perfectly with her melancholy mood, that comparison to a world in a watery grave.

Tonight was her last night with Alexander.

Cailie sighed. She'd cashed all her remaining travelers checks just before the banks closed, and most of the money was now in her purse, in an envelope with his name on it. She was quite certain that the sum was more than adequate, whatever the going rates for escort services were.

Still, if she'd had twice that amount left, she would have given it to him. Gone was the resentment that had risen again and again at the thought of having to pay to live this fairy tale. It was only money, after all—and she had no other way of repaying him, of thanking him, for bringing her dream to life so beautifully.

Tears blurred her vision again. She watched the stars brighten slowly through her brimming eyes, then finally went back inside. Leaving the balcony door open wide, she stretched out on the bed and stared up at the ceiling, comfortable with the darkness and the silence.

Alec had taught her that. That, and so much more.

Cailie shied away from the wistful thought, the fantasy that this could all be real, that Alec could really love her the way he did, that she could stay here and live in paradise forever. . . .

A sob choked her. Despair was rising like a tidal wave in her, escaping as solitary tears to slip from the corners of her eyes and trickle into the hair at her temples. This was the end of her fairy tale, the end of her dream. Tomorrow, there would be nothing left. . . .

Cailie sat up abruptly. She had to stop giving in to self-pity, for she had brought this about herself. Impatiently rubbing at her eyes, she pushed off the bed, strode into the bathroom, and brought a cold, wet washcloth back with her.

She lay with it over her eyes, concentrating on the fragrance of the plumeria blossoms filling the room, trying to let go of the anguish tearing her up inside. Alec would be here in less than half an hour, and if she kept this up, he'd take one look at her face and run.

God, but how had she ever thought to pull this off? She should have known she wouldn't be strong enough. She should have called him up and canceled tonight, should have done any number of things other than lie here and wallow in self-pity. Perhaps she could still reach him at home. . . .

The unexpected knock on the door snapped her straight up and off the bed. She shot a frantic glance at the radio clock. 7:38 P.M.

"Cailie?"

Oh, God.

"Just a moment!" She scrambled for the bathroom, then cursed with feeling the red eyes staring back at her from the mirror. But at least the rest of her looked passable.

Nothing left but to open the door.

"Hi, Alec . . ." Flustered, she stepped back to let him into the room. He was dressed sharply, as always. "You're—you're early."

He smiled as he met her hesitant gaze searchingly. "I did not want to waste a moment of our time tonight."

"Oh." She looked away, smoothing a nonexistent wrinkle out of the skirt of the sheer white dress.

"Any preferences for dinner?"

Dinner. Cailie kicked her mind into gear, shook her head, and snatched up her purse. Yes, they'd be going out to dinner.

Alec caught her before she could rush to the door, and turned her to face him. "Cailie . . ."

She met his gaze for an instant, and immediately wished she hadn't.

Such concern, compassion, warmth. Nobody should be able to act with such consummate skill. Nobody should have such a rough velvet voice, like sunlight reaching all the way into her soul. Nobody should be able to give so selflessly, love with such devastating tenderness, and yet have such control.

He even knew better than to ask her what was wrong.

Cailie suddenly pulled away from him. She couldn't go through with this last night. The bitterness, the despair that had become more difficult to hold at bay each day, each night, had finally won. And tonight . . .

"No." She couldn't do it. Fumbling through her purse, she fished out his pay.

"We can order room service if you prefer."

She shook her head. "No. This . . . here." She thrust the envelope at him, then quickly turned away, her hands clenched on her purse until she tossed it onto the bed. "Your . . . employment is over. I believe that should cover your—your fee, and any expenses—"

"Cailie—"

"No." She avoided his reaching hand, then squeezed her eyes shut, shaking her head. "I— I'm sorry . . ."

Her hands were shaking too, and she balled them into fists. Pain like she'd never known was burning in her throat, behind her eyes, tears that wouldn't come, so much sorrow and despair.

"Be still, Cailie."

Alexander's arms came around her gently, drawing her into the harbor of his embrace, surrounding her with invincible strength, with peace. She held still for endless, raw heartbeats, gathering strength from him, then pushed away, staring at the floor.

"No. I—I can't . . . You have to . . ." She sucked in a ragged breath, and steeled herself to meet his gaze. "Please, go. Now."

She should have known better than to look at him. Wordlessly, he caught up her hands, kissed them, and gently drew her against him again.

Her breath rushed out. "Alec, I—"

"Hush."

He brushed his lips across hers, again, then again, until she couldn't stop herself from seeking more than that fleeting touch. He met her hunger with intoxicating skill, drawing her into a gossamer web of sensations. His warm, knowing hands stroked along her arms, her back, lightly massaging her knotted muscles as she arched against him.

"Don't talk, Cailie," he whispered against her mouth. "Not of time, or of parting."

His black eyes half-lidded, he kissed her cheek, her forehead and eyes, traced the line of her throat with liquid fire. "This night is for you. It is forever. There will be no tomorrow."

His husky words struck her to the core, beating with cruel irony at the little of her strength that remained. She clung to him, because alone she would have fallen.

"Let it go. Just let it go, Callie. God, don't push me away—" His voice broke, husky, ragged, as fraught with emotion as her own had been—

as though all this had really meant something to him, as though he could no more stand to let her go than she could bear to end the fantasy. Ah, yes, he was good. She had bought the best.

But even that fact no longer mattered. Not tonight.

Cailie bit her lip, because she couldn't let the foolish, childish words of love be heard. Tears brimmed in her eyes, and she laid her head against his chest, surrendering control.

With a low sound, Alec swept her up into his arms and carried her out onto the balcony, into the warm night wind and soft moonlight.

"Just . . . promise me one thing." She kept her eyes closed, struggling to surrender herself to the sensations he painted so masterfully across her skin, her heart, her soul.

"Anything." He spoke the word without breaking his kiss, letting her feel the sound, taste the promise behind it. She drew an unsteady breath and did not open her eyes.

"Don't—don't say good-bye. When the time comes . . . just leave. Like all the other nights . . ."

With a sound that could have been a prayer or a curse, Alexander crushed her against him. He was trembling too, she realized, and wept openly, silently, at the beauty of this, of what she would never know again.

And he was right. The night was forever, and there was no tomorrow.

* * *

Cailie was far away, in a world of light and dreams, when Tresand rose without disturbing her and quietly dressed. Then he crouched beside the bed, gazing at her with glittering, luminous eyes, his hands knotted into trembling fists in an effort not to touch her one last time. If he did, he'd never be able to walk away.

"Beannachd leat, mo chridhe."

The choked whisper lingered in the room, in the shadows, long after the door had silently closed behind him.

Part 2
THE COMING
- OF NIGHT -

Chapter Seventeen

Cailie watched the sun set from the balcony of her hotel room. So quickly, the last light faded. So ruthlessly, so relentlessly, day turned into night.

She whirled around, strode inside, and pulled closed the curtains. The room grew thick with stifling shadows. In their embrace she undressed slowly, then stretched out on the soft king-size bed. And inhaling deeply of the sweet fragrance of the plumeria, she remembered last night, the nights before, the illusion of love. To think that, perhaps, some people really lived like that, loving and being loved.

Alec had never spoken of love to her, and for that she was grateful. His words had been of beauty, of elegance and fire, and all the things a woman yearned to hear, spoken softly, during

nights of stolen passion. Yet he had never pro-
faned the name of love, had never insulted her
with that lie.

Cailie rose from the bed hesitantly, to pack all
her belongings except for the green pareu into
the brightly colored beach bag and her carry-on
bag. Her gaze caught on the spiny white murex
doubling as a paperweight. Under it was an
envelope that held a brief note and an indecent
amount of money for the unfortunate soul who
came to make up the room tomorrow morning.

True, shells much like this were cheap to buy in
the local tourist shops. But this one was special.
It was hers. She'd risked life and limb today by
climbing down a hundred-and-fifty foot drop
to rummage through loose rocks, digging up
a multitude of beautiful shells. And then, with
tears in her eyes, she'd scattered them all back
onto the beach. All but one.

She picked it up, lightly stroking the fragile
spines. It was as large as her clenched fist, and
as dry now as her eyes. The lustrous glimmer
of the aperture had faded without the sheen of
seawater.

Cailie closed her eyes, and put the shell back
on the bedside table. It had looked so perfect as
a dashboard ornament in her car. . . .

Tears stung her eyes. It never had been hers, of
course, but she'd loved that car. It was gone now
too. The smiling man from the rental agency had
picked it up two hours ago, as arranged.

Heedless of the tears slipping down her cheeks,

she pressed her lips tightly together, wrapped the pareu around her shoulders, and with slow steps went to draw water for a bath. The final part of her plan would be done tonight.

In utter stillness, she sat on the rim of the tub, watching the steam rise from the stream cascading out of the faucet. Her tears ceased flowing. She thought of ghostly white breakers in the moonlight and of rivers of light painted on a night-black ocean, of gleaming silvered skin and the drunkenness that came from passion.

Doubts cut through her mind again, for the hundredth time, as she tried to rationalize them away with painful clarity. The dreams were gone now. She could go back, perhaps even live a normal life. No. She'd be forever dissatisfied, comparing the imperfect life and love that existed in the real world to that which Alexander had brought to life during the brief time they had spent together.

And it had been like a fairy tale. A fantasy, a lie, all of this, no more real than a mirage. She had come here with a purpose, and that had been met—more beautifully than she could ever have dreamed.

She'd had her time in paradise, and she would be true to herself now. Better that than go home to no home, and return to a life that wasn't worth living. A life inhumanly lonely, and darker than death for lack of the light which she had but glimpsed now, and that only through illusion.

Dreamlike, Cailie rose to wander through her

room once more. The warm wind rippled the drawn curtains and through the open balcony door. She smiled wistfully.

Alec had taught her something of her own beauty, her pride and dignity, that alone she would never have seen. Yet he was wrong about her strength, for she could not find enough of it now. Deep down, she had always been a coward, and facing the empty life she'd left behind two weeks ago, devoid now of even the love of her phantom, was more than she could bear.

Her hands were shaking, her eyes filling with tears she would not shed again as she shut the bathroom door behind her.

Tomorrow, her flight would leave without her.

Tresand had nearly paced a furrow into his living room floor by the time the last sunlight was fading into dusk.

He'd denied himself the taste of her blood last night, fearing that if he didn't, he would never be able to let her go.

Ah, but he'd been a fool. Nothing could make this parting easier.

On the glass table lay a pristine white envelope, his name scribbled on it in that childishly tiny script of hers. He had left it there, untouched, since he'd returned early this morning. He had no stomach to open it.

Tomorrow, she would leave for home. He did not know where that was, or to what life she was returning. He knew only that he would have no place in it.

His desire battled his conscience, and found it lacking. He wanted to go to her, wanted to tell her the truth yet again, and to pray to a God that had long since forsaken him that, this time, there might be a future for them. That, this time, she might understand the impossible, and . . .

A harsh sound escaped his throat. And what? Agree to live out her numbered days by his side, growing old and frail and finding only death, while time left him unmarked? Agree to become like him, a creature shunned and feared, ruled by an unholy hunger, forever hiding in the shadows?

Nay, he'd not condemn her to the latter or condemn himself to the former, not again. He'd thought he could do it once—that time in the mountains near Milano. She'd been in her late forties, an old woman in her time, twice widowed yet still countess of her own castle. She'd never cared about the gossiping that came from associating with a man looking less than half her age, a man who never stepped outside in the daytime. They'd had 15 years together, 15 peaceful, quiet years, while farmers planted and harvested crops, tended hillside vineyards, and faithfully followed the toll of the church bells to mass. Aramond had stayed too, for a while, before his wanderlust hit again. All that time, she'd understood about the Blood, had accepted the existence of it in an offhand, pragmatic manner that had shocked Tresand to the core.

Aye, 15 years of an ordinary, joyful, happy existence. Yet while time had stood still for him, she had remained inextricably caught up in its flow. Once, Tresand had begun to offer to her the unspeakable, only to have her stop him with quiet certainty. She had died in her sleep at the age of 62, and he'd still looked no older than 18.

Tresand released a deep breath as he shook his head. Nay, he'd never again condemn them to that parody of life.

And he should be grateful for the time they'd been given here now, for the chance to love, however briefly. He should be grateful that it would end so simply, without bloodshed this time.

He had to let her go—let her live, just as she had given up those tiny, brilliantly glowing creatures into the sea again rather than keep them and risk their dying. He had to let her live her own life, without his interference. There was no other choice.

Tresand stopped by the window, and stared down at the Jeep waiting in the driveway, waiting to take him. . . .

With a sharp expulsion of breath, he reached out and closed the blinds, cursing, even as the sound of another vehicle in the driveway reached his awareness. Moments later, Kimo was jogging up the back stairs, coming in through the kitchen.

"Hey, old chap! Not out working tonight? You

probably should consider it, you know. I got nothing for you from the hospital—" His brows rose. "Ah, it's payday, I see."

"Shut your mouth, Kimo." Tresand's already dark mood turned foul, ugly. He did not even look to see the cheerful Hawaiian amble across the living room and help himself to the white envelope.

If only he could go to her, just one more time . . .

"Holy shit! What was this broad, a millionaire?"

Tresand moved with blurring speed. He whirled, caught the front of Kimo's neon T-shirt, and felt the fabric rip as he slammed the young man up against the paneled wall before the last word had even left his mouth.

With considerable self-control, Tresand released him, then stepped back. "I think you'd better go."

"I think you'd better count this cash, *tutu kane.*"

Kimo retrieved the fallen envelope, but Tresand turned away.

"I don't want her money."

"Looks like she doesn't either."

"Get out, Kimo. I'm not fit company tonight." The emptiness inside him was growing with every beat of his heart, threatening to swallow his soul. How could he let her go?

How could he not?

"Dammit, Alec, get a grip! Look at this, for God's sake."

He stared blindly at the money Kimo thrust into his face. It was a lot of money, much more than he would have charged her, to make the charade seem real.

His hand took the bills from Kimo before his mind had formulated the thought. He would return the money to her. A perfect excuse to see her again . . . No. He'd have Kimo return the money to her. What good would it do, to torture himself like this? Yet still, his hand holding the bills did not move. His harsh look scoured a remarkably calm-faced Kimo, who, after a moment, turned away with a shrug.

"I'm off to the Big Island tonight," Kimo commented, pausing outside the kitchen. "I won't be back with rations till late tomorrow or early Monday. You gonna be okay for that long?"

Tresand's gut clenched at the thought of blood. Two days since he'd tasted the fire of Cailie's blood; one day since he'd loved her . . . left her. And though the hunger of his blood was appeased, there was yet another, a deeper hunger, one that would not release him—would never release him, not while he was left to face this existence without her.

Struggling with his composure, he nodded curtly in reply to his friend's question. Kimo shrugged again, and left the way he'd come.

Tresand's eyes squeezed shut. His head fell back. Control was slipping from his hold, one fine strand at a time, each fiber pulling a dozen more with it. Not long, now, and it would tear him apart.

Wise, prudent Kimo. He'd always known when to leave the beast alone.

A silent, mournful cry surfaced among his anguished thoughts, a soundless whisper so low he hardly was aware of it.

His head snapped up. It wasn't a cry. It was a good-bye, drenched in soul-crushing sadness.

At first, he thought it was his own soul, mourning her loss. Then, bit by bit, he realized that it wasn't.

"Cailie." He spoke her name aloud, followed the trace of her presence . . . and felt nothing but the faint pulse of her life ebbing away.

Such a beautiful place to spend eternity . . .

"Dear God, no!"

The words were no more than a whisper left in an empty room. Tresand was out the door with inhuman speed. He understood, suddenly, what Cailie had meant with that enigmatic statement. Understood the shadows and wistful sadness he'd sensed in her all along, understood why she'd never spoken of her past or her future.

Racing against time, Tresand prayed that the choice had not been taken from him yet again.

Chapter Eighteen

Not a soul saw him scale the outside of the hotel, he made sure of that. The balcony door to Cailie's room was ajar, the drawn curtains rippling in the night breeze. Tresand all but tore the door from its hinges in his rush to get inside.

It was like stepping into a tomb—a tomb of the newly dead.

A shudder gripped him, his fear grown tangible. The metallic odor of blood, undetectable to any mortal, intertwined with the sweet scent of the plumeria blossoms, hit him with an intensity that sent his senses reeling.

"Cailie!"

There was no one in the room. Tresand slammed open the bathroom door, plunged into the softly lit, steaming interior, and for one endless, nightmarish instant, stood frozen in time.

He had lived with blood for too many centuries to be sickened by the sight of it. He had even seen her take her life this way before, to keep him safe, in that cursed cell in Castile, five hundred years ago. . . .

"God, Cailie, no . . ." His paralysis shattered. Tresand scooped her from the tepid bath, the crimson-green silk pareau slipping off her like a shroud to disappear in the water. Shaking, he sank to the tiled floor, and cradled her against his chest.

Her heartbeat was nearly gone, a mere shadow of life echoing through a body as pale as a corpse. Tresand snatched up the discarded razor blade on the edge of the tub, opened the artery in his wrist, and pressed it against her slightly parted, bloodless lips.

"God forgive me, *mo chridhe,* but I can't let you go. Not again. God, not again, not again . . ."

Feverishly, he stroked her throat, waiting, hoping, praying that he was not too late.

She swallowed weakly, reflexively. Tresand's breath rushed from his lungs in relief. She would live. If her body did not reject the power of the Blood, she would live.

Oh, how very different he had thought it would be, her first taste of immortal blood. He shuddered, suddenly sickened by the memory of that other image, that dream of sharing blood with her in love.

His features hardened, he watched every moment of her throat, watched each swallow.

Bright red ran in tiny rivulets from the corners of her mouth, and spilled down her throat, between her breasts. He had to reopen his quickly closing artery twice, before he was certain she had taken enough. Enough of his cursed blood to be pulled back from the precipice. Enough to save her life, not to condemn her to endless night.

Already, the cuts on her wrists had stopped their sluggish bleeding. Soon, they would be closed. By tomorrow, not even the scars would remain.

Tresand swore, long and violently.

Tightening every muscle in his body until it screamed in protest, forcing the return of control, Tresand gently lowered Cailie to the floor. He tossed the pareu into the sink, drained the bath water, and rinsed the stains of blood away. Then he placed her back into the tub, and with painstaking care bathed her, then wrapped her in one of the thick towels and carried her to the bed. For an instant, he stood staring down at her, so pale and still amidst the white terry cloth.

Then he whirled away. His conscience would flay him alive soon enough for what he had done.

His thoughts kept carefully blank, he removed all traces of blood from the hotel room, rinsed out the pareu, and before packing it into Cailie's carry-on bag, removed the aqua sun dress. He frowned at the weighed-down envelope on the bedside table, then dropped it and the shell into the bag as well.

"Come on, love. You're leaving here."

His voice sounded alien to his own ears. He slipped the sun dress over her, then shouldered her carry-on and beach bag and scooped her up in his arms.

The corridor was deserted. Tresand carried her quickly to the nearest elevator, and once inside punched the button for the lobby. Before the doors reopened, he feathered Cailie's damp hair over her face, settled her head against the crook of his neck, and forced a carefree smile onto his face.

The lobby was no more or less crowded than usual for this time of night. Tresand headed for the front desk, and captured the clerk's gaze.

"Catherine Wellington is checking out. Her room is paid up?"

The tanned, sandy-haired man checked his computer, and nodded. "Yes, sir. Paid till tomorrow morning, actually."

Tresand nodded, then strode out the open glass doors. An elderly woman glanced at him curiously, then turned away, hiding a smile.

Tresand's expression never changed. But every person whom his glance had touched would swear to having heard the woman in his arms laugh playfully as he carried her from the lobby.

Centuries of existence had taught Tresand to control his emotions, to bar them even from himself. Yet that safety mechanism was failing. He drove faster than normal, faster than was prudent, desperate to reach the sanctuary of his home before the maelstrom of his emotions broke free.

Cailie was safe. She would awake whole in body, he had no doubt of that. The blood of his kind was renowned for its relentless power to survive.

He clenched his teeth until sharp pain shot up his jaw.

She had tried to kill herself, had nearly—God help them both—succeeded.

And she'd said not a word to him. Not a hint. Another few minutes, and she would have been gone. And he would have lost her yet again.

"Why, Cailie?" Tresand let his glance slide over to her, still too pale, but looking quietly asleep in the passenger seat. He shut his eyes for an instant, grasping for the control to draw vicious rein on his thoughts, his hands clenching the steering wheel.

He should have seen this coming. He should have recognized the odd discrepancies in her behavior, the underlying sadness that took hold of her at times, the nameless shadows in her eyes.

Gravel sprayed under the Jeep's tires as Tresand sent it skidding down the driveway to his house. He cut the engine even before the wheels came to a stop, then lifted Cailie out of the passenger seat. The sea breeze ruffled her golden hair against his neck as he carried her up the patio stairs, all the way into his bedroom. He pulled a fresh shirt from a drawer, and with shaky hands, dressed her in the white silk, then put her to bed.

Slowly awakening hunger uncurled restlessly in his blood. Not pain yet . . . Just a foreshadowing of need, awakened by the slight loss of blood. He suppressed it ruthlessly. Tomorrow night, Kimo would be back. He could wait that long.

Tresand banished his inner turmoil before it could raise its ugly head, kicked off his shoes, and carefully shifted onto the bed. Leaning back against the wooden headboard, he nestled the sleeping Cailie into his embrace and held her, in the silent darkness of the room, marking the hours as she traveled the path from the edge of death.

Chapter Nineteen

"A—Alec?"

"Gently, *mo chridhe*." Tresand's arms tightened around her, stilling her faint struggles, pulling her closer against him.

"Mocri . . . What?"

"I spent too many years speaking the Gaelic tongue, Cailie. Forgive me." His voice was too husky, too full of emotion, yet he could not hide it. She was awake, even if barely. She had survived her encounter with death. Yet for her too, the emotional storm was just beginning. God willing, they would ride it out together.

"How many languages do you speak?" Her words were slurred, her movements sluggish as she tried to turn toward him, to see him. Tresand reluctantly eased his hold and shifted her in his arms.

A Deeper Hunger

"I've lost count over the years, love. Are you always this talkative after trying to kill yourself?"

"I—I'm still alive?" A puzzled frown marred her sleepy features. Tresand smiled gently.

"Did you think I had followed you into the hereafter?"

"I . . . don't know." Cailie blinked slowly, still floating in some hazy realm just beyond the harshness of reality. "Where are we?"

"At my home."

"You came back . . ." Her frown deepened, and she fixed him with a befuddled yet accusing look. "You weren't supposed to, you know. Why did you?"

"*Why?*" Tresand made himself count to five, and forced the harshness from his features. "Because I am attuned to you to the point of pain, you damnably foolish creature! Did you think I'd not notice the draining away of your life?"

She shook her head faintly, appearing not at all fazed by the volume of his voice, which had risen despite his intentions.

"Now how could you notice a thing like that?"

Her childish disbelief stung, goaded him into speaking words better kept to himself. "I can sense blood very keenly, Cailie," he ground out harshly, his brows furrowed. "You might even call me an expert on the substance. You see, I am what mankind would call a vampire."

"Ha." Cailie looked at him, then dissolved into a sudden fit of giggles.

Sabine Kells

Tresand caught her gaze again and smiled, very slowly, very deliberately, revealing the tips of sharp, white canines much too long and delicate.

Cailie hiccupped, then yawned, and waved her hand at him sluggishly. "Nice try, Alec. But I've seen better caps at Halloween parties. One of the guys had ones that would even bite through a pop can."

"You do not believe me?" Tresand snapped his mouth shut, wavering between insult and incredulity. She was clearly not in control of all her faculties, not even half as awake as she looked, but still, he'd not expected her to *laugh*.

He shook his head, his features softening. She likely wasn't lucid enough yet to understand what she had seen.

"You must have a better explanation for my still being alive." She frowned, and yawned again. "I slit my wrists, you know. I should be dead."

"Why?"

Cailie said nothing, only shrugged and rubbed her eyes sleepily.

"Dammit, why would you do such a bloody—"

She dropped her hands, then smiled up at him too brightly. "Stupid thing?"

Tresand fought for another calming breath. "It wasn't quite the word I had in mind, but it'll do."

Cailie's eyes closed. After long seconds, she sighed. "It was the last part of my plan. And my time in paradise was more than I'd ever hoped for."

Her mouth curved into a serene smile; she looked like a sleeping angel. "Thank you."

Tresand stared down at her. It was far too early still for her to have awakened. He should have realized it.

Tightening his arms around her, he lightly kissed the crown of her head. "Go back to sleep, Cailie. We'll discuss this again later."

With a contented murmur, she burrowed deeper into his embrace, already drifting back into healing darkness.

The sun was nearing the zenith when Tresand sensed her rising toward consciousness once more, sensed the clarity of her mind that had not been there the last time. He lightly stroked her hair again, then shifted her onto the mattress and pillows and moved to the edge of the bed.

Her blue eyes opened, gradually cleared, until none of her earlier lethargy remained to dull her gaze. She stared up at him, frowning, puzzled, alarmed. Afraid almost. He wished, for a moment, he could not sense her emotions so keenly. He wished that she were not so very awake, alert, stronger than she should be after what had happened.

He wished too that she were stronger, so he could pull her into his arms and meld their bodies and souls into one, until the horror of the past night was but a faint shadow against the brilliant flame of love.

"Alec?"

He summoned a smile, one without bitterness. "Cailie."

She sat up, her frown deepening at her lack of weakness. "Alec, what happened?"

"Suppose you tell me first." His smile was still there, curving his lips, and only he knew what it took for him to banish his rage at her for what she had done. His rage, and fear. He had nearly been too late.

"Why, Cailie?"

She chewed her lip, her eyes growing huge in her still pale face. "I don't think I want to—"

"Talk to me, Cailie. Don't you dare keep this inside, or by God, I'll . . ." He shut his mouth, and sharply expelled the air in his lungs.

Cailie glanced away. "I planned to spend two weeks in paradise, and go out with a bang."

Her words were cold, defiant. Tresand forced a slow breath, forced utter control.

"It is possible to vacation in 'paradise,' as you call it, without killing yourself afterwards."

"I know." She looked at her hands, stared at them, at her wrists—her unmarred skin . . . Yet she made no comment on that, only shrugged halfheartedly. "And I didn't want to, really, not anymore. Not after I found out how . . . rich life could be. How it felt to be alive, really alive."

"Then why did you do it?"

She would not reply, only cocooned herself in silence. Tresand sighed, and tried once more. "Why didn't you just fly home?"

She shrugged again, still not meeting his eyes.

"There was nothing at home for me. I . . . left nothing behind . . . not that there was much to leave behind. I made a deal with myself, and I had to keep it."

For the first time she looked at him, pleading for understanding, though she would not speak the words that would let him understand. "I had to be true to myself, because there was no one else left."

Tresand squeezed his eyes shut, denying her absolution from the horrors behind her eyes. He shook his head, his breath rasping in a throat grown too tight, and forced himself to meet her gaze.

"You idiot." His voice was calm, soft, almost soothing. "Don't you know how precious life is?"

She didn't even flinch under his bright stare. With the tranquility of one who had seen death, she confessed quietly, "I didn't. Until I met you."

Every fiber of Tresand's body clenched, whipped steel-taut by that naked admission. He snapped to his feet, then stalked across the shadowed room, nearly staggering under the onslaught of too many memories of love, pain, and death inextricably intertwined.

Until I met you.

He wouldn't explore the underlying meaning of those words, didn't dare think of what they implied, what they would lead to in the future. He struck them from his mind, summoning control. Still, she had not answered his question.

When he could claim some semblance of composure again, he whirled around, then sank to his knees beside the bed.

"Why, Cailie? What in God's name could have driven you to this?"

She was silent for a long time, staring blindly ahead, her hands clenched in the covers. Finally, she met his gaze, her mouth twisted into a wistful smile.

"You want the truth? The real truth, deep down inside, after all the circumstances and twists of fate have been stripped away?" Her shoulders lifted helplessly. "I don't think you'd understand."

Tresand clenched his hands to keep from reaching out to her, taking her in his arms, and taking all the pain from her. But he had to hear the words from her lips, had to see her cleanse herself of this.

"Try me."

Cailie bit her lip. Finally, she nodded, though she would not meet his eyes when she spoke. She fixed her gaze on some spot of the comforter.

"I always knew that love existed. The kind of love—" Her voice broke, but a tenuous smile touched her lips. "The kind people die for. I dreamed of it, and . . . of other things, frightening things. Every night. Every night, I'd wake up screaming, or crying. But Mom always understood, helped me deal with them. And when she was killed—"

She broke off, and Tresand felt his own gut

clench in empathy as she struggled for breath, for control. She shook her head, the ghost of a movement.

"The dreams overwhelmed me. And—they—they became more worthwhile than life, because in real life I could never find that love. And so—and so I came here. To live the dream."

Tears flooded her eyes, but she lifted her gaze to meet his. "I wanted to die with that illusion, Alec. With the illusion of being loved. And you made it seem so very real."

With a hoarse sound of pain, Tresand pulled her into his arms, arms that were shaking because he was afraid of losing control, of crushing her in his embrace.

"God help me, Cailie, I . . . If I hadn't found you in time . . . I cannot go through that again. I cannot lose you again, *mo chridhe*. I have loved you for so very long . . ."

His voice became choked by the knot in his throat. His eyes closed, shutting in the pain, the soul-wrenching agony. Again, she had nearly died because of him—not because of his presence in her life but because of his absence. Because, somehow, her soul had remembered the love that would not die, had been calling out to him, but he'd not heard . . .

Tresand swallowed hard, let himself drown in the feel of her head nestled into his shoulder, of her body warm and pliant against him. All the answers he'd once had were gone, all the certainty that she'd be safe without him null and void.

"You never told me." Her breath whispered softly against his throat, a kiss without touching. The words tore a soft, broken sound from his soul.

"That I love you?" He shook his head sadly, still keeping his eyes tightly shut, still keeping her pressed against him. God, how often had he wanted to speak those words of love, paint them across her skin and sear them into her heart, until she'd never again doubt their truth. And how many other words he yet longed to speak, feared to speak . . . He shook his head again.

"Think about it, Cailie. You said it yourself. You hired me to make you feel cherished, loved. No matter what I said, you would not have believed it to be the truth. No words in the world could have convinced you that your illusion was reality."

She pulled back, until the space of a breath lay between them, until he relinquished the darkness of closed lids and met her gaze. There was something new in her eyes, something triumphant and yet fragile. Hope and fear to hope. A hunger for life and fear of living. Love and fear of falling.

"I am glad you found me in time."

"God." A shudder gripped Tresand, and his hands on her arms tightened again, crushing her against him once more, until he was afraid of injuring her with his strength and gentled the embrace. She burrowed close, and he found that she was trembling too, despite her level words. He held her, silent, motionless, until finally she moved away.

A Deeper Hunger

"Your turn, Alec. Why . . ." She bit her lip, then surged ahead. "Why am I not dead? Why—" Her breath broke as she raised her wrists for him to see. "Why are there not even *scars?*"

Tresand inhaled deeply, struggling to curb his dismay, his fear rising like bile in his thoughts at the prospect of revealing the truth to her.

He thought of the lies he might tell. That she'd not been too far gone, that she'd recovered from the blood loss on her own, that much more time had passed than she thought. She could not touch his mind yet. She had not awakened to the power, faint though it might be, lying dormant in her blood now. A slight smile curved his lips, wistful, bittersweet, as he met her tormented gaze.

"Because you are, in human terms, no longer quite human. No longer quite . . . mortal."

Her mouth tightened, scoffing. "You are joking."

Tresand stole a deep breath, almost a sigh.

"I am afraid not, *mo rún*. And it is only myself who is to blame. I . . . could not let you die."

"How could you stop . . ."

He rose from the bed, turned away, fleeing her logical, wounded, confused gaze fixed on him. This was his crime. In a flat, toneless voice, he made his confession.

"I gave you something . . . something that made you strong enough to recover from your blood loss."

"That's impossible. I didn't—didn't pass out until—"

Her voice broke on a wounded sound. Tresand spun to face her, saw her trembling fingers come to her mouth, as though to recapture the words already spoken. Harsh, dry sobs tore through her.

"Oh, God, Alec!"

He was beside her instantly, capturing the unsteady hands that reached out to him, holding her, taking the tremors wracking her into himself.

"Gently, Cailie. . . ."

"I was so afraid. I didn't want to die, not anymore, but it was too late, I couldn't hold on . . . dark, and so cold . . ."

"Hush, love." His arms tightened, rocking her gently, yet still her violent shaking would not subside.

"So afraid—afraid . . ."

Tresand's eyes shut. God, it had been so close, so close. A slight delay on his part, and he would have seen her die yet again.

He shuddered. Even his infinite strength would not have been able to bear that.

Chapter Twenty

He held her for time out of time, a heartbeat of eternity, before she finally quieted. Yet she spoke no more, simply stayed nestled against him, cocooned in the warmth and safety of his embrace. She slept like that, finally, and he held her still, giving and taking comfort in equal measure. The sun was near setting when she stirred faintly.

"Alec? You awake?"

His arms tightened briefly in reply to her whisper. "Aye, love."

Before she could say anything further, her stomach took the opportunity to complain of her recent lack of food.

"I'm starving."

Tresand raised his head to look down at her tenuous, somewhat sheepish smile, the faint blush staining her cheeks, and fell back onto the covers, laughing. A precarious instant later, Cailie joined him. Tears came too, tears of relief and joy, and he held her for long minutes yet before rising to find her something to eat.

The kitchen and living room were filled with the soft shadows of sunset. Tresand rummaged around cabinets and fridge, frowning.

He had long ago learned to blend in with mortals. There was always a bare-bones selection of groceries in the house—cans mostly, some frozen foods, crackers, cookies. Things that did not spoil or require frequent replacement.

"Poor love," he whispered to himself with a half smile, examining the scant, sadly dated selection. He had no need for human food—did not touch it, except when necessary to complete his disguise of a mortal man. Shaking his head, he went down the stairs into the front garden, shaded from the afternoon light by the house and its dense foliage.

When he returned minutes later, Cailie was standing by the large, ocean-facing dining room window, peering out between the fixed pale aqua blinds. She turned toward him as he strode into the kitchen.

"A coconut! Right off the tree?" She caught up to him by the sink, her appreciative gaze fixed on the object of her smile. Tresand's lips curved up slightly.

She looked far too right here in his house, her hair tousled, her face sleepy, her body scantily concealed by his shirt hanging down to mid-thigh, only half buttoned. Looked as though they'd spent the day loving, not battling the shadows of death.

The knife of ancient memories twisted in his gut yet again, taunting him with what he could not have, with the future that could never be.

Violent, defiant rage at the cruelty of fate rose in his soul. He finished stripping away the tough husk as though it were cotton candy, and met Cailie's eyes for an instant. Then he cracked the shell with his bare hands.

He saw her eyes widen, heard the soft intake of her breath, felt as his own the sudden quickening of her heart. He knew she was thinking of everything he'd told her, thinking and denying still, in that logical way of hers. Thinking the coconut had already been fractured, for what he had done was not acceptable to logic.

His face expressionless, he poured the opaque milk into a glass from the cupboard, then popped the succulent, fragrant meat from the pieces of shell.

Wordlessly, he handed her several chunks. Wordlessly, if with slightly unsteady hands, she took them.

"There is soup if you want," he offered, indicating the lower cupboards. "And not much else, I'm afraid."

Chewing, Cailie only shook her head. She swallowed and managed a smile.

"This is fine, thanks."

Tresand nodded, watching her drift back into the dining room, silently fighting his own demons. He should steal her memories now, before it was too late, before his strength gave way to his selfish need for her.

He glanced toward the bedroom, thought of the hours of anguish it had so recently witnessed, and knew he couldn't let her go. He couldn't condemn himself to endure the uncertainty of how she fared, where she was, with whom, the loneliness of existing without her. Their lives had been interwoven too often, too intricately.

"All right, Alec. I want the truth this time."

His own personal demon could not have chosen better words. Tresand's gaze snapped to Cailie's face, still pale, but with her chin determinedly raised.

"What did you give me? What in the world is there that's powerful enough to bring one back from the dead?"

Tresand crossed the short distance between them, and stopped so close to her that she had to tilt her head slightly up at him. But she met his eyes boldly, with a protective shell perilously close to anger. He had answered her before, yet the answers had not been satisfactory.

"You were not dead. Not"—he exhaled sharply—"quite."

Cailie backed away a half step, staring at him. He could almost see the wheels of memory turning in her head, replaying words he'd spoken earlier, words he probably should have kept to himself.

A Deeper Hunger

Her hand rose to her throat. "You've bitten me. Before . . ."

Tresand's body tightened at the mere thought of blood, burning in hunger. Yet he met her accusing gaze levelly.

"Yes."

"So I'm a vampire too, right? That's why I didn't die."

She didn't believe a word she'd spoken. A word he'd spoken. Tresand could feel it, could see it in her eyes, in her careful, testing smile. He sighed.

"No. It doesn't matter how many times I take blood from you, or anyone. Being a donor does not make someone a vampire, Cailie."

"Alec—"

Tresand avoided her exasperated glance. He turned from her to pace across the dining room and back, shutting out awareness of her thoughts, searching for the courage to face her.

"You were too close to death, *mo chridhe*. And I—" He stopped before the large window to the ocean, with its blinds nearly shut to block out the setting sun.

"I could not let you die. I gave you . . . of my blood. That is what kept you from death's reach."

Her soft gasp cut him as no blade could. He did not have the strength to look at her, to find revulsion—or worse yet, to find fear, the kind of horror that had sent her over a cliff to her death once before.

271

"You really expect me to buy that."

Tresand swiveled around on the balls of his feet. She was staring at him, her head tilted slightly to one side, her brows raised. She was choking back laughter.

Disbelief cut through him, quickly followed by anger at her stubbornness. Before, when she had been half delirious, he had understood. But she was wide awake now.

"Why the bloody hell would I make up something like this?"

She shrugged eloquently, her bottom lip caught between her white teeth.

Tresand shook his head as he ran a hand through his hair. She wasn't panicking, wasn't hysterical, wasn't any number of things he had expected. She was laughing. Silently, yes. But he could hear it.

He took a deep breath, and faced her squarely. In ages past, a man had but to whisper the word vampire and have a whole town in hysterics. This—this was not a natural reaction.

He shook his head again. "Precisely why, in your opinion, could I not be what I am?"

She smiled, her brows still arched, as though her answer were the most obvious thing in the world. "You're alive, you have a heartbeat. You're wide awake in the daytime. You eat real food. For starters."

So logical, so smug. Tresand rolled his eyes, and exhaled sharply.

"I also reflect in mirrors. And I don't rip out

my victims' throats, or grow claws when I feed, or sleep in a bloody coffin!"

Still she looked unimpressed.

"Vampires can't—" Cailie abruptly cut her own words off, flushing, staring at the floor. "Well, they're not supposed to be able to . . . you know."

He watched her squirm, and raised his brows inquisitively. "I don't think I do, *a rúin*. Would you care to enlighten me?"

She shook her head vigorously. "No. If you're a vampire, you should know these things."

She wasn't going to say it. He knew it, just as he knew that her mind was racing, frantically trying to backtrack her way out of this particular corner. He wondered what delightful shade of crimson she would turn if she knew just how open her thoughts could be to him.

With a perfectly straight face, Tresand gave a beleaguered sigh.

"First you accuse me of wearing caps on my teeth. Now you malign my virility. Pray tell, Cailie, just where do you get your information?"

She was blushing furiously now, closely examining the wood grain of the panelling on the dining room wall.

"B-books. I've read . . ."

"Ah." He nodded gravely. "Vampires, Cailie, are very misunderstood creatures, and very poorly known ones to begin with." He smiled grimly, showing his fangs. "But we do require blood to live."

She looked at him, her brows furrowing. She remembered the canines, he could see it. But she probably would have made that same crack about caps again, had he not shaken his head sharply, silencing her before she could form the words.

"You still don't believe me. What will it take, I wonder, to convince you? A little demonstration, perhaps?"

Cailie stared at the man she'd thought she had come to know so well, watched him clamp his mouth shut with an expression close to disgust.

He frowned at her an instant longer, then began pacing again, kitchen to dining room to kitchen and back. Cailie watched him with a mixture of puzzlement and worry. She had never seen him like this.

Good God, she'd never seen him at all before the last two weeks. What if he really was some sort of loony? Those insanities he'd been calmly trying to tell her certainly tended to favor that possibility.

Cailie found herself almost laughing aloud at the direction of her thoughts. Whatever he was, Alexander had saved her life! He'd given her more love than any man alive, love like only the phantom in her dreams had ever shown her. If that was madness, she'd happily spend her life with a lunatic!

She sobered abruptly. Despite his words of love, he'd never mentioned anything about sharing a life, and she was doubtlessly jumping to conclusions. Yet she could live now. Live her life alone, without the dreams, with only the memory of this love to carry her. Because it had been—it was—real. Not a lie, not an illusion. Real.

Alec didn't emerge from the kitchen after his latest round of pacing, but stayed there, clattering around out of sight, doing what she dared not ask.

"I cannot change into a bat, I'm sorry to say, and flutter in your face to show you the truth," he explained from the kitchen, his voice raised slightly to be heard. "Among all the abilities with which the literary vampire has been endowed, I'll admit shape-shifting is the one I envy most. Ah, how about this?"

He appeared around the corner to the dining room, holding something in his hand. Still overwhelmed by her realization about her future, Cailie smiled at him. In the shadows of the room, she couldn't make out what it was, at first, that he held. Then he turned toward her more fully, and she saw.

Cold fear blossomed into the pit of her stomach. In his hand was a knife. A sharp, wicked-looking thing with a point and a ten-inch blade.

Alec stopped directly before her, his features unreadable in the twilight. "Touch it, Cailie. It's real. Just as real as I am."

She nodded spasmodically, inching back. "I believe you." Her fear rose higher, nightmarish in its suddenness. "You don't—"

"Here." He held the knife out to her, grip first. "Take it."

She shook her head, and retreated another inconspicuous step. "I believe you." The words were catching in her throat, no more than a whisper.

"No, you don't. *Take the damn knife!*"

The crack of his voice stopped her retreat, and made her obey. Her fingers folded around the black plastic handle, unwillingly, gingerly. His hands closed around hers, warm and taut and impossibly reassuring.

"That's it. Look at me, Cailie."

She met his eyes, her insides clenching into such a tight knot she could not draw a deep breath.

"Now, let me start disabusing you of some of those literary notions you hold. We of the Blood are not demons, or devils, or Satan incarnate. As far as crosses go, an old friend of mine has been a priest—and a very good one, at that—for over nine centuries. Garlic holds no more revulsion for us than it does for any ordinary human with a keen sense of smell. We are difficult to kill . . . although decapitation, quartering, burning, all those time-proven methods of execution work as well on us as on the next guy. The 'wooden-stake-through-the-heart' routine, however, is not one of them."

Alec's eyes were burning into hers, and Cailie shivered violently. His hands had tightened around hers, until her fingers felt numb against the hilt of the knife.

"Unfortunately I do not have a wooden stake

276

handy—not even a wooden spoon that could be sharpened. But I assure you, this has basically the same effect." He was smiling as he spoke the words, while moving her hands upward, until the point of the knife hovered over his heart.

The taste of her fear changed suddenly, became fear for him, not of him. She tried to back away, pull free, and couldn't. His grip was immovable.

"Alec! God above, Alexander, I do believe you!"

He nodded curtly, holding her wide-eyed gaze with his intent, midnight eyes. "Yes, you will."

Before she could say another word, he jerked her hand forward violently.

"Alec!"

He bent double with a choked sound as the blade sank between his ribs into his chest. Cailie screamed his name again, struggling futilely to support his weight as he fell in slow motion to his knees.

"Jesus, Alec, you bloody idiot! No, don't!" Her hands flew up to his to stop the motion that would rip out the knife. "Just stay still, I'm calling an ambulance. For God's sake, don't pull that out, Alec, you'll bleed to death!"

Yet even now, his strength surpassed hers. With a hiss of breath, he tore the knife free, and it clattered to the floor. Cailie's hand pressed over his wound, to halt the deadly flow of blood from his chest.

He did not stop her, did not have to. It did not take her long to realize there wasn't nearly enough of the crimson fluid for such a severe wound.

"Look, Cailie. And believe." He was pulling open his bloodied white shirt, much too calm and composed for a man who should be dying.

"Holy God . . ."

Cailie's voice stuck in her throat. The wound had nearly stopped bleeding. It looked raw, painful, but by no means as deadly as it should. Even as she watched, the last trickle of blood from the cut slowed, congealed. She'd seen more blood when she'd sliced her hand in the kitchen.

"God, I'm afraid, has little to do with it."

The dry, sardonic remark brought Cailie's shocked gaze to his eyes. She sucked in a breath, and looked at the bloodstained knife on the parquet, then at her own hands, red with his blood.

He was nowhere near dying from what should have been a fatal wound.

She drew in another breath and held it. "You mean I could do that, and not die?"

The knife was in his hand before she could so much as blink. She'd never seen anyone move so quickly.

"No. Not . . . yet."

"But you said I—"

His gaze pinned her. "Nearly, Cailie. I said nearly immortal."

"Ah." She nodded, feeling suddenly giddy, repressing the urge to laugh hysterically. What she had seen was impossible. "So I am more immortal than the average Jane Doe, but not yet as immortal as you are?"

His lips twitched traitorously, for only an instant, before his expression grew somber. "Even I am not immortal."

"You could have fooled me."

"It seems a great many things can fool you. But don't feel bad. I've had centuries to perfect my disguise."

She made no reply to that, only refused to meet his gaze. He pulled himself to his feet as he held on to the dining room table, slowly, carefully, then shrugged out of his ruined shirt with a tight grimace of pain.

"You saw all that? Sure?"

He was using the shirt to dab at the blood on his chest. Cailie nodded, wide-eyed. "Yes."

"Good. Now, come with me. We're going to get this straight once and for all."

Cailie watched warily as he crossed into the kitchen, his walk only slightly unsteady. His shirt and the knife landed in the sink. Reluctantly, she followed him to the patio door.

Alec opened it, careful to avoid the rays of light that slanted in from the setting sun. His gaze traveled across the water, to the source of light, and his features tightened.

"I've not felt the sun on my skin for many years, Cailie. And I did not much enjoy it when I did."

Before she could reply, he held out his right arm, thrust it forward until his hand left the shade and was gilded by sunlight. His skin reddened, then blistered within seconds. Gasping, Cailie stared at his burning skin, at his face. His lips were pressed together, a bloodless line, but he made no sound.

"Stop this!" Horrified, she tugged on his arm. It was like pulling on a steel beam. Suddenly Alexander relaxed, shuddering. He let her pull his hand back into the shade, and the muscles in his arm spasmed.

Cailie stared at the blistered skin, and felt her stomach twist sickeningly. "Why isn't it healing?"

He drew a deep, unsteady breath, then exhaled slowly. His voice shook minutely. "With sunlight . . . it is different. But it will . . . heal. Just . . . takes a little longer."

Slowly, with deliberate motions, he backed away from the door. Cailie closed it, making sure the blinds barred the sunlight, almost as though she actually *believed* this madness. She shook her head.

"You know, Alec," she began, frowning at the blinds, "this is . . . Oh, my God, Alec!"

Cailie turned from the door just in time to see Alexander crumpling silently to the kitchen floor, like a marionette with its strings cut.

Chapter Twenty-one

"Alec! Jesus, now what?"

Cailie flew down beside him, turning him onto his back, her bloodstained hands helplessly fluttering over his still form. "Alec, come on, talk to me."

God, perhaps he *was* mad, perhaps he was dying now, belatedly, from that chest wound. But no, though it was still an ugly cut, it was no longer bleeding. It looked, as a matter of fact, as if it were some days old. . . .

Cailie swore softly, thoroughly, uncharacteristically. What he'd been trying to prove was ridiculous, of course.

"Alec! Dammit, wake up!"

"Tresand."

Cailie clutched his left hand in hers, her head falling forward in relief. "Oh, God, thank—"

"No. Tresand. My name is—"

"All right, Tresand." She was laughing now, laughing at his dogged muttering, laughing because she would cry if she didn't. "Would you please get up so I know you're all right?"

"But don't call me that when others are around. Even Kimo calls me Alec."

Cailie was nodding mindlessly, certain he was delirious. "Whatever you want." Still he hadn't moved. "Can you get up now? Please, get up?"

"Give me . . . a minute."

"All right." She remained on her knees beside him, watching his face, waiting for his eyes to open. Finally, after what seemed like hours, his thick black lashes fluttered up.

"Are you all right?"

The look he shot her silenced her. Alec—Tresand—pushed to his knees, then up to his feet with a low groan, clutching the edge of the counter for support. "Damn. The things I do for you."

Cailie scowled at him, saw him shudder and tighten his grip on the counter until his knuckles turned white. Her fear gave rise to protective anger.

"For me? I didn't ask you to do any of that idiotic stuff!"

"By God, woman, I don't need you railing at me now!" He glared at her, then nodded toward the hallway. "Just help me to bed."

"This had better not be some kind of trick," Cailie muttered under her breath as she slung his left arm around her shoulder.

He stiffened with a groan of pain. "What?"

"Nothing." Supporting a good deal of his weight, she steered him toward the bedroom. "What's wrong with you?"

He muttered something under his breath—curses, presumably. Then he said, "For someone who exhibited such alarm at my apparent demise, you show remarkably little sympathy."

"You're not dead."

A grin tugged at his lips. "I'm recovering. As I said, simple wounds or diseases can't kill my kind. They only disable us for a time. We are strong, stronger than humans."

She harrumphed, muttered under her breath, "So that's why you had no trouble carrying me." Ignoring his chuckle, she deposited him on the bed, watched as he settled back against the headboard with a tight grimace of pain, and utterly refused to feel any pity for him.

"If you're so perfect, why do you need contacts, huh? And don't try to deny it. I've seen them in your eyes!"

She stared at him, her chin tilted mutinously. He'd scared her half to death a number of times, and it felt good to lash out at him, even if only with words. But he only smiled, his blue-black eyes glinting. Then he turned away slightly, inclining his head, taking out the contacts.

Cailie was still glaring at him when he looked up again, focusing luminous, violet, *inhuman* eyes intently on her.

She shrank back with a choked breath, and came up hard against the wall behind her. Gooseflesh was rising on every square inch of her skin.

Unnatural, those eyes. Unnatural, like those of her phantom . . .

Slamming the door behind her, Cailie fled the room, the house, and did not stop until she reached the open beach. She stared out over the ocean drenched in blood-red light, breathing too fast and shuddering violently.

He'd finally done it. He had finally succeeded in terrifying her.

She fell on her knees in the cool sand, and buried her face in her hands, rocking gently, searching futilely for any trace of reality left in her world.

She did not leave, run away, though she finally, truly believed who—or rather *what*—he was.

It wasn't lack of money, or transportation, or any other mundane concern that held her there, on the darkening beach. She could have stolen the Jeep, and sneaked back into the house to retrieve the envelope with her money still sitting on the living room table.

But she did neither. The sun had set, and she sat on the cool sand in his silk shirt, shivering, wondering if he would come for her. If, perhaps, he would kill her. She wondered how she could possibly be afraid, when just yesterday she had nearly taken her own life.

A Deeper Hunger

But she didn't want to die. Not anymore, not for anything in the world. And though he could have killed her any number of times, he had not. Instead, he'd given her back precious life.

She ran her fingertips across her wrists. Not even scars left . . . For all the proof she had, the past day could have been no more than a nightmare. A dream.

Cailie stared out over the gently rolling, slate-gray ocean, and felt tears well in her eyes, tears of sorrow and joy as she realized, at last, that the haunting dreams of her phantom would not come again, not ever. Alec—Tresand—did not simply look like the man from her nightmares. He was that man.

And that was why the dreams had stopped. Not because of her change of scenery, the tropical paradise, or a multitude of other reasons she had conjectured. But because they had served their purpose—had brought her to him. She had found the love, the danger and fear and heartache. She had found the man who had haunted her all her life. And having found him, she could not leave him again. No matter what he was.

She walked into the sea, rinsed the dried blood off her hands, and washed her face. Then she waited, with the softly rushing waves, palm trees, and the scurrying ghost crabs for company.

The moon had risen over the ocean on a river of light when she sensed his presence. He'd made no sound, yet she knew he stood behind her, watching her, waiting for her to flee, perhaps.

"Why did you not leave?"

Her eyes did not waver from the moon-bright sea. "I never told you the whole truth about my dreams."

"Your dreams."

His voice was low, gruff, reminding her of endless nights and lonely days. She wished he would touch her, hold her. He did not move. She swallowed hard and nodded.

"That first night I met you—at the Café—I already knew you. Your face. For thirteen years, I saw you in my dreams. Only your eyes . . . Your eyes were different. But then, no man alive could have eyes like the phantom in my dreams . . . I thought."

She let out an unsteady breath. "They were beautiful dreams sometimes, full of the kind of love that exists only in fairy tales. But mostly, they were strange, frightening. I thought I was going mad . . ."

Tresand sank down beside her then, a controlled collapse as though all strength had drained from his limbs. With unsteady hands, he grasped hers, and brought them to his lips, his head bowed as if in prayer . . . or in shame. He smelled faintly of soap, and Cailie realized his hair was damp too. His inhuman eyes were shut tightly, hiding away some wrenching agony so great she could almost taste it.

"If only I had known . . ." He looked up and met her gaze. "We of the Blood cannot dream, Cailie.

286

We can only remember. I did not know you were w—" He stopped, then looked away.

"Were what?"

Wordlessly, he rose to his feet, drawing her with him. He led her up the beach, back to the house.

"Were what, Tresand?"

The sound of his name from her lips brought a tensing to his arm around her shoulders, yet still he did not reply.

"Tresand, tell me!"

He paused for an instant before opening the back door, and turned to gaze down on her with frightening intensity. "I will tell you. When the time is right."

With that unsatisfactory reply, he ushered her into the living room, sat her down on the crushed-velvet sofa, and turned on soft lights.

He'd cleaned away the bloodstains from the parquet, Cailie noted, and from the edge of the table. She looked up at him, and ended up staring at his bare chest . . . at the wound that should be there but wasn't.

"Yes. You believe now."

She nodded, still unable to tear her eyes away. The smooth, defined muscles of his torso were unmarred, as was the skin of his right hand. Not even a scar remained.

Just like her wrists.

We are strong, stronger than humans.

She remembered the words and shivered. She wished again that he would come and hold her. Yet he only stood, a few feet away, non-threatening, waiting for her to make the first move.

He was afraid, she finally realized, of frightening her away.

"You've taken my blood. When we . . . at night . . . And . . . in that dream."

"Yes."

Cailie could feel the self-condemnation in that single word, yet she held his gaze. "You did not hurt me."

He said nothing. Breath surged into her lungs, for even as she'd spoken those last words, clearer memories surfaced in her mind. She remembered the exquisite pleasure-pain as sharp teeth scored along her throat, a touch that left her body racked with fire and ice, her mind splintering into shards of light.

Her gaze changed, became filled with wonder. "Why . . . I don't understand . . . Why does it feel like that?"

Tresand shrugged, a pensive tilt softening the line of his mouth.

"It is the source of life for those of the Blood, *mo chridhe*. An affirmation of life, of damnation . . . Ah, I cannot explain to you why. But there is nothing to compare with it, in the world of the living or the dead."

"Is it . . . It's like a drug, that pleasure, isn't it?" Cailie shook her head, and spread her hands in the air. "God, if your victim can feel like that, what must you . . ."

A Deeper Hunger

Tresand stood before her in a heartbeat, catching her hands, his eyes deadly serious. "Do not misunderstand what is between us, Cailie. It is not always like this, for my kind and our . . . prey."

She frowned up at him. "What do you mean?"

He sighed as he squatted in front of her on the thick carpet, his face level with her own.

"Blood is necessary for us to live—blood from a living donor, at least at intervals, to keep us from going mad. Because blood alone—without strong emotion—is empty. There are those who would feed on terror, because it is easily aroused, easily taken. But there is a stronger emotion, a much rarer and more precious one, one which heals and sustains—and it cannot be taken, or forced."

He brought her hands up to his lips.

"That is what is between us, Cailie. What you have given me. Love. Pure, glorious, precious love. It is like living fire to me. When I touch the lifeblood within you, I touch the love. It is in every drop of your blood I've tasted, and I cannot help but return to you the ecstasy you give so freely."

Chapter Twenty-two

Cailie caught her breath at his husky confession. His violet eyes were intent on hers, and she was losing herself in the light that shone in them, the unearthly color, drowning in the emotion so tangible in him. Her blood pounded slow and heavy through her body as she slid off the forest-green sofa and came to her knees beside him. She could not recall ever being so aware of her own heartbeat. Her memory washed up images from endless nights of seductive pleasure, images shockingly vivid, rising higher with each throb of her heart, driving shivers down her spine.

"I . . . liked it . . . when you did . . . that."

He met her gaze with a mixture of alarm and stark hunger. "I know."

Tentatively, she reached out and touched his cheek. She traced the tendons standing out like tensile wires under the smooth, warm skin of his throat. "And do you . . . I mean, how soon . . ."

The breath exploded from his lungs. He caught her hand, his voice gruff.

"With each sharing of blood now, we are bound more closely. I do not dare take from you again, not after—"

"Why?" She shifted closer, tauntingly, hungrily. "What are you afraid of?"

"Afraid! What am *I* afraid of?" He shook his head, as thought disbelieving his ears. "You still don't get it, do you? You still don't understand that this is no game, no charade that can be forgotten when it is convenient!"

"I just don't see—"

"No, you *don't* see. And that is your problem, Cailie. You are courting a fate worse than death!"

She shot him a cool look, her passion fading. "Excuse me if I don't see it that way. I'm afraid from what you've shown me so far, being a vampire doesn't scare me off."

He stared at her as though she had lost her mind. Perhaps she had at that, discussing the pros and cons of vampirism with one who appeared to be of the persuasion.

"Do you know . . ." He exhaled sharply, shook his head, and frowned harshly at her. "Can you even begin to imagine what it is like to see everyone around you die, sometimes quickly, sometimes of old age? Do you know what it means to move, to change your name and disappear, time and again, before anyone can realize that you haven't aged a day while they've grown old and gray? It is not a life I'd wish on my worst enemy, Cailie!"

Tresand surged to his feet, and strode to the black mirror of the living room window whose aqua blinds were now open, letting in the night. Cailie could barely see his profile, a shadow in the darkness, hard and cold and bleak.

"One becomes tired of it. Tired of the cycles of life that pass by without pause. Do you know how often I've *yearned* . . ." He shut his eyes tightly as he drew in a halting, deep breath that steadied his voice. "Yearned to be mortal again? To find a woman to love, to see a son with my eyes, or a daughter with her face? To live a normal life, to grow old side by side, not to watch as time snatches yet another friend from me?"

He shook his head, his lips compressed into a thin line. Cailie felt herself dying under the heavy weight of his silence; quietly, she rose to her feet and walked across the beige carpet.

Though she wanted to, she dared not touch him. The face reflected brokenly in the window, with eyes of violet fire, was barely human.

"To many, immortality would not be a thing to shun."

A harsh sound escaped his throat, yet he remained motionless. "Oh, not for the first few hundred years, to be sure. But even we are not immortal. We age, however slowly." He turned to face her, reluctantly, it seemed, holding out one hand, palm down.

"This flesh and blood was not made to outlast the world, Cailie. I am not so old . . . I became one of the Blood in 879 A.D. At the time, I was eleven. Now . . . I could pass for thirty-five, perhaps older."

Cailie shrugged, then tilted her head, her brows raised pensively. "Even so, I'm sure many would choose it, if only for a few centuries. You could save thousands of lives. You could make millions selling immortality."

Tresand stared at her, astonishment and horror in his countenance that she could even conceive of such a notion. Then he turned away, showing only his profile to her again.

"I am wealthy enough to keep me in comfort for as long as I may choose to live." His voice was harsher than Cailie had ever heard it before, colder. "And we do not procreate randomly, Cailie. It is forbidden. A life for a life—that is the Law. For one of the Blood to be created, another must have died."

"Why? Isn't the goal of each species to increase its population? 'Go forth and multiply'?"

Tresand's gaze snapped to hers, a multitude of conflicting emotions struggling for dominance in his face. Odd, how she could ever have likened his features to a mask. Or perhaps it was only since he had saved her life that he no longer hid his emotions.

As if reading her mind, he turned away from her and crossed the room.

"The creation of one of the Blood is the original

sin of our kind, Cailie," he informed her, sinking down on the sofa as though he didn't have the strength to face her inconsiderate questions and remain standing at the same time. He leaned back, his eyes closing, his features smoothing into the mask Cailie had just happily considered a thing of the past.

"Let me give you a scrap of little-known history, love. Perhaps it will shed some light onto your extraordinary pragmatic view of our kind."

"But I thought—"

"Don't think. Just shut up. And listen. *Understand.*"

She frowned at him harshly, but his eyes were still closed. His words had been weary, quiet, not angry. Her lips pressed together, she plopped down in the armchair across from the sofa.

Tresand sighed, then drew another deep breath.

"Back in the dawn of time, the first one of our kind was stranded on Earth. She was the only one and she was alone, lonely through an eternity. And one day, in her weakness, she created another like her, another of the Blood, to share immortality with her. And so it went, through centuries, millennia—immortals giving eternity to beloved ones still bound to the cycle of death. Until it had to become forbidden to procreate, for the power of the Blood would spread like wildfire through humanity over time, and would eliminate the very source of life for our kind. We cannot live off the blood of each other, and only rarely take from another of the Blood.

"So the Law was laid down, and any transgressing faced destruction. The number of our kind could not be allowed to grow. Only for each death may there be another born, to ensure the survival of mankind and those of the Blood.

"But that was a long time ago, long before my time. The Law has not applied for centuries, for there are few of us left now, and fewer still who would condemn another living soul to this existence. We've grown tired of eternity, Cailie. Some of us wait for death, even pray for it, though it is impossible to take our own lives. We must call on the one who made us, or ask another's aid—"

"That old friend of yours!" Cailie stared at him, appalled, horrified. "Good God, he did come to . . ."

Tresand opened his eyes and nodded slowly, a vague smile tugging at the corners of his mouth. "Aramond? Aye, he did come to kill me. I asked him to."

He met her horrified gaze with his unearthly eyes. "To be successful, one must strike quickly and unexpectedly, for the power of the Blood is survival at all costs. It does not have a conscience, does not care about right and wrong. Imagine such a world, Cailie. A world of walking time bombs, waiting for the lash of hunger to set them off. Now do you understand?"

Dumbstruck, she only nodded. Of course. Eternity would have a price.

He gazed pensively at the rising terrain, the

distant hills silhouetted against the night outside the living room window.

"In times past, there have been those who would exploit the power of the Blood, who would wreak havoc and seek to rule with terror. They are not abided by my kind. They are destroyed, for through their acts they endanger all others of the Blood. We take care of our own, be it in aid or in judgment."

Cailie drew a deep breath and stared at the carpet beneath her feet. "Aramond cares for you. Very deeply. He . . . was glad that he failed." And he wasn't the only one who was glad. God, to think that he might have died, might have been killed in front of her eyes, taken from her just when she'd found him. She shuddered. It did not bear thinking about.

"He would be, I suppose."

Tresand was smiling. She could hear it in his voice, but did not look up.

"Aramond . . . made me and, as a result, took up the burden of destroying me, should I ask." He chuckled faintly. "And then, when I did, he was a century late, and botched the job to boot."

Cailie looked up at the genuine humor in his voice. She was astounded by the change it wrought in his face, softening the angles, easing the inhuman strain. "He made you."

Tresand sighed. "Aye. As I lay dying on the battlefield one night, he came to me, gave me of his blood. It was too late to keep me from death, yet I awoke in his sanctuary, to a different life."

The trickle of humor crept back into his voice. "I'd unwittingly saved his hide once before, from the fire of the sun. I'd let in an old man who was going from door to door an hour before sunrise, asking for lodging for the day. I'd had no idea what he was at the time. But he remembered me. Adopted me, in a way. I traveled with him for nearly a century, as a foster son and apprentice to the way of the Blood."

Cailie met his wistful eyes for a moment, then glanced at the bookshelves lining one of the walls, filled with titles in languages she couldn't even identify. Her gaze sank to the floor again. "You have—" Her voice broke off. She forced herself to look up at him, then shook her head slowly in awe. "The stories you must have to tell."

He chuckled faintly, without humor. "They would take a lifetime to tell."

Her body tensed, and she did not release his gaze. "Yes. I would like that."

Tresand seemed to freeze in the very act of breathing. Then, with great effort, he smiled. "I'm afraid I would bore you with centuries of history."

Cailie sucked in her lip. He had deliberately misunderstood. Damn him! And damn herself, for she did not know how to ask again.

So she stared at the carpet, irrationally angry and hurt, and found another tendril of fury. Her brows furrowed as she fixed him with a level stare. "You said you were wealthy."

Tresand shrugged, then nodded wordlessly. Cailie's frown deepened.

"So that ad for the escort service isn't for money."

"No." He rose, retrieved the white envelope from the table, and dropped it into her lap. "You can do whatever you wish with that."

She didn't even look at the envelope. Her brows almost met. "So that's how you get—how you get the blood you need? By playing gigolo to any woman who—who—"

Tresand actually laughed, waving off her accusation. "No need to get jealous, love."

But she was jealous. She thought of the things he had done to her while taking blood, the devastating intimacy, and her temper headed for the boiling point. She threw the envelope at him, venting her anger.

Yet she had not been here in years gone by. And he'd had to survive.

Still, she was miffed. "How many others have you been seeing?"

A corner of his mouth twitched as he snatched the envelope off the floor and dropped in onto the cushions of the sofa before sinking back down.

"I rarely hunt in the manner of my kind. No more than absolutely necessary. If you'd have looked at the date on that paper, you would know the last time I even ran the ad. It's easier, you know, to just pick up someone in a night club."

Cailie sucked in a deep breath, but before she could let fly with a fitting remark, he shook his head. "I would slowly go insane if I used only the blood Kimo brings me."

"Kimo!" This time the name rang a bell the size of Big Ben. "The guy from the hotel? Why, he's . . . He gave me . . ."

Tresand nodded. "He also works in a hospital. He supplies me with . . . bad blood. Blood that is contaminated for humans, that is rejected for use. I do not require much, you know. Only enough to control the hunger."

She stared at him. "Your eyes grow soulless when you say that."

He looked away, half hiding the sudden harsh tightening of his features. "You cannot conceive of the pain of hunger for one of the Blood. It is possible to master it only to a certain point. Then it controls you ruthlessly. It possesses your very soul, drives you to the edge of madness, then hurls you beyond."

He rose abruptly and stalked across the living room, toward the hallway. Cailie stared after him, suddenly conscious of the invisible tug pulling her toward him.

"You're hungry now."

He froze in mid-stride and shuddered. His hands were clenched into fists at his sides.

"Aren't you?" She swallowed and found a knot in her throat. "Tresand?"

He didn't reply. She pushed out of the chair and closed the distance between them, feeling as though she were floating on air.

"It's taken much of your strength to heal from those damned stupid tricks, and you need—"

"Get away from me, Cailie."

The barely leashed violence in his voice startled her. Yet she only shook her head, though he could not see it, facing away from her still.

"You need me. I can hear you calling . . ."

Slowly, so very slowly, he turned toward her. Cailie saw his face, and the breath caught in her throat. Violet fire burned in his eyes, mesmerizing, hypnotizing, luring her with the memory of ecstasy.

Tresand spun away and entered the bedroom. The click of the lock on his door was louder than a curse in the silence of the hall.

Chapter Twenty-three

2:26 A.M. Tresand squeezed his eyes shut, struggling to keep control of his hunger-lashed senses. The tendrils of need blossoming red-hot through his veins stripped away his conscience layer by layer, leaving only his driving hunger for blood.

And it was getting worse. Quickly. Much too quickly for the safety of the woman now peacefully asleep on the living room sofa.

He knew she was there. Even from here, he could feel the steady beat of her heart, the gentle rhythm of her breathing. He could sense the sweet rush of blood through her body, pure and intoxicating.

He cursed, snatched up again the note she would have left on the nightstand of her hotel room, and scanned it for the hundredth time.

" . . . cremated . . . ocean . . ." The two words

always stood out. He ground his fists into his eyes as he remembered their first night on the beach and her words of returning to the endless sea, completing the cycle of life.

He remembered that night on the moon-washed shore, where he'd covered her skin with the blue fire of fallen stars, glowing so brightly in the wet sand.

He remembered the desperate love of their last night together, when the future had seemed so cruelly inevitable, with no hope for either of them.

Remembered her body floating in crimsoned water . . .

He remembered it all, replaying every scene over and over in his mind, to retain the fragile shreds of control, to keep himself from slaking his raging need for blood on her—killing her. . . .

He stared at the clock again. 2:41. An hour since he'd last called. God, but Kimo should be back by now!

His hands were shaking. Badly. It took him three tries to get the number right.

"Yo."

The groggy, sleep-hoarse voice made Tresand want to weep with relief. He struggled for an even breath, for the control to speak.

"Get—over—here."

There was an instant of silence, followed by a gruff chuckle.

"Hey, Alec! You're starting to sound your age, *tutu kane*. Hard night?"

A Deeper Hunger

"Kimo—"

"All right, all right, so it won't keep till morning. I'll be up there in half an hour. Gonna last that long?"

Tresand closed his eyes and broke the connection.

Half an hour. Not so long. He could do it, would do it, because the alternative was not acceptable.

The hesitant knock on the bedroom door sent every muscle of his body into spasm.

"Tresand? Are you all right?"

He couldn't speak or even draw enough breath to have any left over for his voice.

The doorknob turned, then turned again. The lock held, of course. Still, Tresand stumbled to the door and leaned against it, as though to prevent it from opening with the weight of his body.

"Tresand? What's wrong?"

The wood was smooth, cool against his forehead. Though his eyes were closed, he could see her, in his shirt still, frowning at the other side of the door. He could almost feel the warmth of her skin, where her hand lingered against the wood. . . .

"Cailie."

The word was harsh, raspy, the last breath of a dying man. "Cailie, get out of the house."

The doorknob turned again, rattling.

"Tresand, let me in. Let me help you! If it's the hunger—"

"Get out!"

303

Silence met his roar. He panted softly for a moment. "If you come in here right now—Cailie, I'll—God help me, I might kill you. Just like the last time. So get the hell out of the house. Take the Jeep, get away . . . Just for an hour. Please, Cailie. Go."

"But if you need—"

Tresand slammed his fist against the door— clear through it. Wood splintered, slashed his skin. He sank to his knees, propped against the door, unable to halt the shudders that wracked his body at the thought of release from the pain of hunger so temptingly near.

He refused to open his eyes. Because if he looked up and saw her peering through the hole in the door, sleep-tousled, her eyes huge and full of compassion, offering herself, *again*, his control would snap.

"Run, Cailie. For the love of God, don't let this happen again!"

"But—"

"Christ, woman, don't argue about this now! Go!"

He sank further to the ground, seeking to curl in upon himself, to keep her presence beyond his senses. The power of his blood was lashing at him to rise, to capture and feed, but he stoically refused to move.

There was a chance that he wouldn't kill her, not now, not since her blood held a trace of power. But he knew better than to take that chance. It had been hard enough to stop before, when he'd not been ruled by the hunger, for the strength of her love, the rich emotion that permeated her very being, was as addictive as the sun was deadly.

Gradually, slowly, the realization that she'd left filtered through his pain-soddened mind. Gravel crunched beneath the Jeep's tires as it churned up the driveway and sped toward the road.

Tresand shuddered with relief. With a short prayer he reached up to unlock the door, and waited for Kimo to arrive.

Unspeakably weary, Tresand sat hunched over on the edge of the bed, his elbows on his knees, his head in his hands.

The dead blood had released him from the burning hunger, but it gave him little strength. Or perhaps it only seemed that way, after the luxury of Cailie's love.

Cailie's love. God, how he wished she were here, wished he could hold her, be held by her. He wished he knew how to solve the mess he'd gotten them both into, wished he didn't need to fear for her life, whenever she was near. . . .

"What the hell happened to you tonight? It's been years since you got it this bad."

Kimo plopped down on the chair by the dresser. Tresand could feel his stare, but only shook his head. The shadow of a smile crossed his features at the youth's habit of referring to his need for blood as something of an ailment.

"Long story, *keiki*." He glanced up at Kimo

briefly, tiredly. Even the mellow light of the bedside lamp hurt his eyes. "You look as bad as I feel. Why don't you help yourself to the sofa?"

Kimo rose wearily, rubbing his eyes. "Nah. I'd better make tracks, old chap. Besides, I left company at home, if you get my drift."

Tresand met the Hawaiian's eyes with somber intent. "Thank you."

"Hey, that's what friends are for."

Kimo stopped just inside the bedroom door, and ran a hand across the splintered hole. "I'll even bring a new door with me next time I come. Oh, and by the way, somebody made off with the rental Jeep. I saw it parked on the side of the highway, back toward Lahaina."

Tresand nodded. "She's borrowing it."

"She?" Kimo's brows rose. "I thought *she*'d left the other day?"

"She changed her mind."

With a hoot of laughter, Kimo headed out the door. "Let me know when I need to start bringing double rations, *tutu kane*," he said with a chuckle over his shoulder.

Tresand stared after him, cursing silently.

"Is it safe to come in now?"

Tresand nodded, without looking at her standing in the open doorframe. He hadn't moved since Kimo had left an hour earlier. But his thoughts . . .

God, he felt as though the rock slide he'd once been buried in had pounded through his brain.

Damn Kimo for that stupid crack. Damn him for seeing what Tresand himself did not dare even imagine, for seeing a future that could never be.

Realizing that Cailie still stood there waiting, for an explanation if not an apology, Tresand raised his head and met her level stare.

"I am sorry you had to see this."

Cailie shrugged. She was watching him with a carefully blank expression. "You did warn me before."

"Some things must be learned firsthand." He sighed, wearily lying back onto the bed to stare at the ceiling. Was she afraid again? For once, he could not tell. But she would be, if she had any sense at all.

"It is not usually this severe. Only after an injury, or a long sleep." Tresand groaned. "God, I should have known better."

He shook his head, finding a smile for her sake, trying for a lighter tone. "You affect my rational thinking in the damnedest way, Cailie. It's not often I try to reveal my curse, and no one has ever disbelieved my words on the matter."

"It's not often someone tries to tell me monsters are real."

Tresand froze to the core of his soul. Slowly, he sat up and stared at her, dumbstruck.

God, but he should have known.

Chapter Twenty-four

"Why are you staring at me like that?" Cailie raised her brows at Tresand's suddenly ashen features. He still didn't seem fully recovered.

Shaking her head, she crossed to the bed and plopped down beside him with a sigh. He shrank away.

"Cailie—"

"Look, I'm sorry if I insulted you. I really didn't mean that the way it came out."

She inclined her head to send him a sideways glance, wishing she hadn't put her foot in her mouth yet again. But that defensive streak in her cropped up without warning, especially when she was dead tired and stressed out. She smiled brightly, hoping to put him at ease.

"Besides, I've always had a thing for monsters. Even as a kid, I loved those old vampire and werewolf movies, and I really wanted to go to Scotland some day to see if Nessie is real, and—"

"Cailie—"

"You're from England, right? Have you ever been to Loch Ness? Maybe you know—"

"Cailie!"

She caught her lower lip between her teeth, worrying at it like a small child caught red-handed at some minor mischief.

Tresand shook his head. "You are . . . impossible."

His voice was hoarse, yet one corner of his mouth had inched up in an obviously reluctant grin. Cailie released her bottom lip and gave an uneasy smile of her own.

"Does that mean you're not mad at me anymore?"

Tresand seemed about to reply, then caught himself. After a moment, his mouth quirked into what could almost pass for a real smile. "That depends."

"On what?" A thin frown line appeared between her brows.

Sighing, he let himself fall back onto the covers, his eyes closing, something akin to peace smoothing his features.

"On how much longer you're going to sit there staring at me, instead of getting where you belong."

She stiffened, suddenly filled with the horrible certainty that he was about to kick her out, send her away, because she knew his secret. Hot, helpless tears welled in her eyes.

"I—"

Tresand reached across the bedside table and pulled the plug on the lamp. Darkness was utter and instant.

"You are tired."

Cailie swallowed hard, mute. They'd never talked of the future, *their* future. Perhaps there had simply been no opportunity. Perhaps there could be no future for them.

"I—" she tried again.

"Come here, Cailie."

Gentle hands pulled her down beside him, into the haven of his arms. A choked sob escaped her throat as she struggled to accept the suddenly looming threat of a good-bye.

"Ah, *mo chridhe*, my heart. My poor love."

He was touching his lips to her brow, drawing her tightly against the heat and power of his body. "Don't you know that this is where you belong? Right here, with me?"

Cailie sniffled, opened her teary eyes to stare at him blindly in the darkness. "You mean . . . you're not going to tell me to leave?"

He buried his face in her hair, his breath harsh. "How could I, Cailie?" He cursed softly, in a language she didn't understand, tightening his arms around her until she thought her ribs would crack. But she didn't complain.

A tremor shook him, fracturing his voice. "How

can I ever find the strength to send you from me again?"

Cailie woke in paradise. She had no clue what time it was. She only knew that the blinds of the bedroom window were luminous with sunshine. Tresand still held her in a light, possessive embrace, a dark stubble of beard shadowing his cheeks and jaw, looking for all the world like a buccaneer of days gone by.

Smiling, she nestled closer, watched him come awake . . . and smile, softly, peacefully, as he saw her.

"I do believe this is the first time I've had the pleasure of wishing you a good morning."

Cailie met his lips in silent reply. His smile was a tiny miracle to her. The hidden pain that had marred his features on that last night of their contract seemed almost gone.

Perhaps it was only hidden more deeply within.

Pillowing her head again on his shoulder, Cailie sighed and ran her fingertips across his chest, tracing the indentations of muscle and bone.

"Tell me something. If I were to go out onto that nice, sunny beach out there, would I turn into a bag of charred bones?"

She watched his profile and saw him flinch minutely at her words. Then he met her gaze. "No."

A bright smile radiated across her face. "Good! Because that beach is exactly where I'm going as soon as I get up."

A shadow rose silently in Tresand's violet eyes, but he said nothing. He closed his eyes again, for a moment, then gathered her into his arms and touched her with such heartbreaking tenderness that she cried even as they loved.

It was past three by the time Cailie finally made it out onto the beach, but the four hours till sunset gave her more than enough time to think. She realized, without a doubt in her mind, that Tresand had spoken an infallible truth last night.

This was where she belonged. With him. No matter what. She only needed to convince him of the truth of his own words, to fight against the shadows that lingered in his soul, and the pain that had caused tears in his eyes just hours ago.

She had found paradise, and the phantom from her dreams. And she was terribly afraid that she was going to lose him to his fear for her, because he did not trust himself.

In the end, there would be few options . . . if any.

Cailie rose from the cooling sand, pulling his white shirt more tightly around her as the sun dipped quickly toward the horizon.

She would miss that—the sun. But it was not nearly so precious to her as Tresand. Tresand, who was her very soul.

The violet reflection of the dying light on silver wavelets was a mirror of his eyes; the murmur of the waves, his voice, rich and deep and seductive.

A Deeper Hunger

The brush of the shifting breeze was like his softest touch, the trace of sea wind on her lips like the faint salty taste of his skin.

Cailie watched the burning disk sink behind the hazy islands and the high clouds catch fire. She felt his presence behind her as soon as the beach lay in shadow, but did not turn.

"Tresand." His hand came to her shoulder even as she spoke, a touch as light and warm as the wind. Then his fingers tightened.

"Only so few hours apart, *a rúin*, and already I have missed you."

Cailie smiled, though he could not see it, standing behind her. But it was a bittersweet smile, because his voice, so rich with emotion, spoke eloquently of the things he kept from her, of the pain yet to come.

She shifted her weight back, and his arms folded around her to draw her against his bare chest. She felt the light, hot touch of his mouth against her neck, her shoulder, and trembled. Yet he did no more, simply held her, and she was content.

Together, they watched night fall, until the last colors faded into black and brilliant stars appeared in the velvet sky.

It was Tresand who took the first step toward the house.

"Come, let's get dressed. We need to get you some dinner."

Cailie nodded and walked up the beach beside him, fitting against his side every step of the way.

She did not want to relinquish this closeness, no matter how much her stomach complained about missed meals. She did not want to go back to the real world outside of this house, the world she had so recently left behind.

But Tresand was probably right, and she would likely feel better about going out once she was on her way.

In his bedroom, Tresand hauled her carry-on bag out of the closet.

"Your things are in here. I'm afraid the dresses will be a bit rumpled by now. I did not unpack the bag."

Cailie met his gaze, smiling. "You took care of what mattered." She saw the shared memory of that darkest day in his eyes, and felt her throat go dry. "I never did thank you—"

"Here." He shoved the bag at her. "Better get dressed."

Without another word he disappeared down the hall again.

Cailie sighed, then trundled into the washroom with her carry-on in her arms. The first thing that spilled out of it was the white shell, entangled with the aqua sun dress and the pareu. It landed on the counter with a crack, its spine tips snapping off.

With a soft cry of dismay, Cailie snatched up the shell before it could tumble off the counter and fall to the floor.

A violent tremor stole over her as she recalled only too vividly the last time she'd held that

314

shell, but she did not drop it back into the bag. Instead, she placed it in front of the mirror by the sink and stood off to one side a bit, tracing its multiplied reflections in the two opposing mirrors into infinity.

With a somewhat hollow smile, she picked up the crumpled green pareu, painstakingly banishing the many shades of horror that touched her even as her fingertips caressed the rich silk. It was a task easier than she would have thought; the memories of Alexander and a night of loving were stronger than the nightmarish memories of blood.

Slowly, she folded the length of silk. It needed ironing, badly. If not for that, she would have worn it tonight.

Smiling tentatively, she stripped out of Alec's shirt and stepped into the shower.

Half an hour later, wearing the cheerful flower-print dress, she strode into the living room and settled down on the sofa to wait for Tresand. Beside her, on the cushions, was the white envelope with close to ten thousand dollars in cash.

Before she could do more than stare at it, Tresand came in from the patio. Cailie surged to her feet in surprise, unaware that he'd left the house. He stopped in front of her, impeccably dressed as ever, and tucked a plumeria blossom behind her ear.

"Ready to go?"

She nodded. He'd put the contact lenses in again, veiling those mesmerizing eyes, hiding

315

their luminous color—hiding part of himself from her, it seemed. Or perhaps only hiding it from the world. They were going out, after all.

Turning from those thoughts, Cailie cleared her throat and gestured at the envelope. "I . . . You should probably put that away somewhere."

Tresand glanced at the money, then shook his head. "It is not mine to put away."

"But it's your—"

The sudden cold narrowing of his eyes cut her off. "Don't say it, Cailie. Not ever."

She frowned at him. The contact lenses could not hide his emotions as well as before.

"But you spent a lot of money the last two—"

He started down the hall. "Forget it."

Cailie collected the white envelope from the sofa and followed him into his bedroom. "Well, I think you should take it."

Tresand snatched the envelope out of her hand without a word, and pulled the cash from it. Then he took another wad of bills from the envelope on the bedside table, casting aside a crumpled piece of paper Cailie recognized, blanching.

Yet he did not comment on her note. He lifted her hand, placed the money in it, and very gently, very firmly, closed her fingers over it, until the gold band of her ring dug into her flesh.

"But—"

She saw his eyes, the set of his features, and for once, wisely decided against arguing. She put the money into the bottom drawer of the nightstand. "I'll go to the bank tomorrow."

Tresand did not argue. "Come on, then. Let's get going."

Cailie nodded halfheartedly. Tresand put his arm around her shoulders, and drew her down the hall with him. She stopped to dig her old, fat purse out of the beach bag, then sighed.

"Good Lord, I drove without my license last night."

"Don't worry about it."

She hesitated, and Tresand turned to face her, taking her hands in his. Slowly, he brought each wrist to his lips, then covered her mouth with a lingering kiss that started as an apology and quickly grew into fire. Cailie sighed with the pleasure of his touch and slid her hands up his shirtfront, around the warm column of his neck, into his raven hair, holding on to him, wanting never to let go.

Yet he pulled back all too soon, a strangely pensive light shining in his midnight eyes.

"You are beautiful, Cailie. You are in my soul."

She believed the truth, this time. And for the first time, she dared speak it.

"I love you." They were a mere whisper, these words she had never spoken in her life. She traced the smooth-shaven line of his cheek, jaw, brushed her fingertips across his lips. He kissed them lightly, his eyes oddly bright, then drew her toward the patio door.

"Come on, or else you won't get a meal tonight. You have the keys?"

Slightly dazed, Cailie automatically started digging through her purse. "Just a minute." She actually fished out a metallic glimmer before the realization hit her.

"I didn't have my purse last night." Stricken, she looked up at Tresand, then at the key in her hand. It was the spare for the white Probe, the one she should have left in the rental car.

Plopping her purse down on the counter, Cailie frantically looked around the kitchen, scanning countertops, then strode into the dining room, then the living room.

"I know I took them out of the Jeep." She shook her head in exasperation, flushing. "Good God, I can't believe I did this again! I've never lost car keys before coming here."

Of course, she hadn't had access to a car since moving to Seattle after her family's deaths, but she'd never lost Dad's car keys either. And house keys were almost the same thing, and she'd never lost those.

Before she could search herself into a frenzy, Tresand's arms came around her from behind, strong and warm, pulling her back against him.

"They'll turn up, Cailie. Probably somewhere between the Jeep and the terrace."

"Right." Cailie started forward, intending to search outside, but Tresand wasn't letting go. He only turned her, holding on to her hands until she faced him.

"But I thought—"

"And I wasn't." He shook his head curtly.

"Thinking. We don't have to go out, Cailie. Hell, we can order something in if you're hungry." A corner of his mouth quirked up. "Even pizza."

"And stay home?" She tried to keep her voice neutral.

"Stay home," he echoed, slowly, nodding, still watching her closely. Cailie suddenly felt guilty for thinking of his house as home. She was no more than a guest here, a stranger.

Uncertainty assaulted her. She looked down. "All right."

"Or we can look for the car keys." Releasing her, Tresand stepped away. His voice was brusque, almost angry.

Cailie's head came up. "No. I'd like pizza. Really. But I know you don't, so it doesn't matter what . . ." She let her voice trail off, and sucked in her lip.

Tresand saw the gesture and closed his eyes, then fixed her with an intent stare.

"This isn't about dinner, Cailie."

She blinked. "It isn't?"

He shook his head with a harsh mien and turned away.

"Wait! Tresand, I can't read your mind! What—"

"The future, Cailie," he ground out, spinning to face her. "That is what's on my mind. Remember what I told you that night, at La Perouse? This is the dark side of that glory. I've seen the present become ancient past, seen the shape of the past replayed by the future too often. What will happen next week, next year, next century? Where will you be a hundred years from now, Cailie?"

Taken aback, Cailie answered promptly. "Dead, I presume."

Tresand's features were stark as he nodded. "Yes. And where will I be?"

Cailie shrugged. "I—"

"Alive! Looking a year or two older. Living under another name, in another town. Alone. After having watched you die yet again!"

"What does—" She broke off and shook her head, frowning. "Again? Tresand, what do you—"

He whirled away from her, ignoring her words. A second later he faced her once more, his countenance sculpted by inhuman pain. "Do you think I want to go through that?"

Cailie stared at the floor, then slowly looked up at him, her eyes huge. "Do you think I do?"

Part 3

– AWAKENING –

Chapter Twenty-five

Tresand froze, then spun away, letting loose with a string of multilingual curses. Cailie understood only snatches, but those were enough to make her cheeks flame.

He caught himself just short of punching the wall. Cailie had no doubt that his fist would have gone straight through it, as it had through the bedroom door.

"What in the world would you have me do, Cailie?" he rasped out hoarsely, his back to her. "I cannot stop the hands of time, cannot stop the sun from rising . . ." A harsh breath broke his voice. "Cannot change what I am . . ."

Her heart in her throat, Cailie closed the space between them. She stopped just behind him, close enough to feel the warmth of his body, to sense the violence flowing just beneath the surface, barely leashed. The adrenaline pumping into her blood made her voice shaky, but her resolve was as solid as the muscles delineated under Tresand's turquoise shirt.

"Then change what I am."

She heard the catch of his breath that was almost a sound of pain and saw the tremor that gripped him.

"You . . . cannot know what you ask of me."

Cailie swallowed hard, bit her lip at the despair so evident in his words, turning that soft, rich voice into something cold and desolate. But she would not relent.

"I believe you have told me most of what matters already."

A choked sound broke from his throat. "Have you not had enough of death, Cailie?" He turned slowly, facing her with a face alien to her—harsh, bitter, so full of anguish.

Her brows drew together in puzzlement. Tresand strode past her to the sofa and sank down on it, his face in his hands. "Don't you know that you must die to awaken to the Blood?"

Cailie stared at him, then closed her eyes. She drew an unsteady breath, struggling to control her voice. "I can handle that."

Tresand erupted into curses again. When he looked up at her, the colored contacts were missing from his eyes, leaving violet fire to burn her with each glance. He shook his head slowly.

"You have no idea what you're doing to me, Cailie. I would give my worthless existence to keep you by my side, but I cannot condemn you to—"

"Why not?" Cailie cried, falling to her knees before him, grasping his hands beseechingly. "Why will you not give us a chance for happiness together? You promised me. You promised!" She drew breath and quoted him with shattering accuracy. " 'Whatever you wish—any thing, everything,' you said. 'If it is in my power to give it, you shall have your heart's desire.' I want this, Tresand! With all my heart!"

His eyes grew half-lidded with pain. "Ah, Cailie, how can I make you see?"

He brought her hands to his lips, in that now-familiar gesture that brought the sting of tears to her eyes. Then he released her, his voice growing cold. "Perhaps I should fill you in on some of the more unsavory aspects of living in the power of the Blood." He snapped to his feet and started pacing, his countenance coldly set.

"Do you know the most merciful quality of the human mind, Cailie?" he rasped, staring ahead into space. "It allows you to forget. It quietly files away many small, ugly memories in some dark corner of your brain, where they might remain hidden for the rest of your life. Aside from great tragedies, you remember the good things, the happy times.

"Our memory does not fail, Cailie. It will not let us forget. *Ever.*" Tresand stopped as he met her gaze, a glint of madness and despair in his eyes.

"Ask me what Cromwell wore when he stormed

Drogheda with his troops, and gave the city and its people to his men in an orgy of slaughter lasting days. It was over three centuries ago, but I can see it as though it happened yesterday."

Cailie drew an unsteady breath, remembering Mom and Dad joking about the weather, and Beth radiant in her wedding dress. She remembered pain and twisted metal and fire and smoke, and the bleeding, crushed bodies of her family, and a wedding dress dyed crimson. "I can deal with that."

He stared at her for an instant, undoubtedly hearing the quaver in her voice, the reluctance . . . and perhaps, too, the determination. Then he spun away and resumed pacing.

"Can you now? Can you deal with remembering, in perfect detail, each mistake you've ever made? And how about murder? How well could you deal with that?"

Her brows furrowed, her eyes widening. "Murder!"

"Yes, murder!" He whirled around and dropped to his knees in front of her. "How will you feel when you've killed someone, Cailie?"

She opened her mouth, then closed it again. "I—I wouldn't—"

Tresand shook his head, laughing, a cold, grating sound.

"Vampires kill, Cailie. It happens, especially to those new to the Blood, those who have not yet learned to control the hunger. The thrill of the kill is older than time, older than the barbaric ritual of eating an enemy's heart to gain his strength and courage. When a vampire kills in taking blood, he gains the power and vitality of his victim. It is not easy to forgo that rush, Cailie. It is something we condemn, yet sometimes the power of the Blood will overwhelm you. And then, when you regain your senses and find yourself lying beside a corpse, how will you feel?"

Cailie stared blindly at the floor, battling the fear and horror and doubts whipped to life with each of his angrily spoken words. She tried to remember the gentleness of his touch, the light in his eyes when he loved her.

"Have you . . . killed?" She forced out the question in a painful whisper.

He did not reply, and finally she brought her gaze up from the floor and looked at him. She had never seen his skin so pale, his eyes so bleak.

Meeting her gaze, he nodded. "Aye. I have killed. Only a hundred years ago, I took a human life. Your . . . life."

He surged to his feet and strode across the room to stare out the window. Cailie stared at his back, dumbstruck. "My . . ."

He shook his head, a short, angry motion, as if to rid himself of visions in his mind. "You know that I am old. Yet you . . . your soul . . . 'Tis as ancient as mine. You have only forgotten."

"Tresand . . ."

He pivoted, crossed the room again in measured steps, and sank to his knees before her, his eyes hauntingly luminous as his gaze sought hers. He touched the blossom behind her ear with trembling fingers.

"I can remember the first time we met, as clearly as though it were but a day ago. I can still smell the blooming heather, and the wildflowers crowning your hair, see the—" He broke off as he ran his hands through his hair and across his face, struggling to breathe.

"Is that why you write history? Without . . ." She smiled crookedly, remembering the solitary computer in his office with no stacks of history texts. "Without needing research notes and books?"

"Aye." He met her eyes, visibly grateful for the moment of distraction. Then he sighed resignedly.

"It helps me keep my sanity, in a way. Keeps me busy too. Sometimes, I sleep during the hours of light, because it gives me reprieve from the memories. But mostly, I write." He smiled thinly. "Besides, who better to tell of history than one who has lived it?"

Cailie nodded. "I've always loved the past, you know," she reminded him solemnly. "I could get lost in it sometimes. Often did. Back in high school and college, they'd have to kick me out of the library at closing time. And even when I worked there, later . . ." She shrugged.

Tresand caught her gaze again, held it, searchingly. She felt as though those violet eyes were penetrating to the depths of her soul, touching, waking *something*, bringing it to life.

Then his gaze was gone and the sensation vanished. His expression darkened and he rose, stalked away again, his fists clenched and his voice rough with tenuous control.

"I cannot do this, Cailie. Can't—can't even damn you to remember . . ."

Disoriented from the sudden loss of his gaze, Cailie shook her head, frowning. "Remember? As—as you remember?" She pushed to her feet and stopped before him, her heart pounding with the gradual understanding of what was in his power to give.

"Don't shut me out, Tresand, please don't. Let me share—"

"The blood? The pain, Cailie?" His eyes were wild, inhuman. "There is so little worth sharing in the past times we have come together. Each time—*each time*, Cailie, you died because of *me!*"

She saw the long, slow shudder that tortured his body, caught at him as he stumbled forward to lean heavily against the paneled wall, his eyes closed tightly, his face a mask of pain. Gently, she stroked his hair, the tautly drawn line of his back.

"If I loved you in the past as I do now, I would not have wanted to be without you, no matter the price."

He laughed harshly, bitterly. "You don't know what you're saying."

"No, I don't!" she was quick to agree. "Because I don't know what's missing! I don't know what memories you see when your eyes cloud with pain."

She caught his face in her hands and met his gaze beseechingly. One step at a time, she would bridge the chasm between them.

"Help me, Tresand. Let me in. Let me see . . ."

It was as though her plea had drained the last of his strength. He sank to his knees in slow motion, and she followed him down to the carpet, never letting go. His gaze was locked onto hers, his features twisted into terrible despair and love.

"Cailie . . ."

His eyes changed then, imperceptibly. Cailie had not known of the constant guard he kept, the wall that shut away the true power of his unearthly eyes. Now that shield dropped away, leaving her breathless with the wonder of her discovery. Then his gaze was penetrating into her mind like living fire, brightly burning. Nerveless, her hands fell from his face.

It was as though a dam had been opened in her mind, blasted away by the touch of his gaze. Images tumbled through her head like scenes of a movie seen in childhood, distant and remote and all but forgotten, then gathering momentum, until they were like a waterfall pouring into her mind. They were like the dreams that had haunted her all her life, only now they weren't disjointed, disturbing fragments anymore, but a seamless tapestry of lives lived and lost in the passage of time.

There was hunger and misery, struggle and

violence and death. But there was also
and tranquility for a few short moments . . . And
there was love, a love so pure and indomitable it
outlasted death again and again.

Cailie's eyes fluttered closed.

God, no wonder her dreams had haunted her
so. For two souls to intertwine so many times, so
closely, then be sundered . . .

The world spun dizzyingly around her, too
many memories, too many pictures all at once,
too much remembrance. She felt herself reeling,
felt strong hands catch her and pull her into
warmth and safety. A gentle touch smoothed her
hair, caressed her cheek, her throat, while the
deep, rich sound of that beloved voice surrounded
her with peace.

Slowly, she opened her eyes. Tresand was
holding her, watching her, sharp lines of concern
etched into his features.

Tresand. She had known him for so long, had
loved him and feared him and . . . and died for
him. Because of him. He had told her before—
and now she knew, from those ancient memories
new in her mind.

She suddenly felt very old.

"I have always been a danger to you."

Cailie met his gaze. The words had been so soft,
she wasn't sure she'd really heard them, but the
remorse and grief in his voice cut her to the core.
With trembling hands, she sought his.

"I know," she replied gently. "You . . . on the
mountain . . ."

"Aye. That is what happens when the hunger takes control." He lowered his gaze, his voice. "You could have run from me that night, and I would have died." Closing his eyes, he turned his face down, away from her. "God, you should have."

"No! No," she repeated more softly, touching his cheek, her fingers like the brush of a butterfly's wing. "I cannot think of a more worthy reason to die, Tresand, than to save another life. Especially the life of one I love."

He sighed deeply, and with reluctance faced her and met her gaze, almost pleadingly. "But you understand now, don't you?"

She nodded. Yes, she understood, because now she knew. And the knowledge strengthened her resolve to walk by his side, become like him, a creature of man's darkest dreams. For so long, her old soul had waited for this chance. . . .

"My answer has not changed, Tresand." She reached out to him again, smiling, feeling radiant with the joy that blossomed through her, the knowledge that they had come full circle at last. "Remember that night, in the darkness beyond the village gates? I swore that I would find you again, no matter where you went. And I did."

"No!"

He flew to his feet, cursing again. Cailie stared at him blankly. The sickening sensation of falling slowly rose in her.

"Not that!" His hands were fists, bloodless, trembling. "Why won't you understand that we cannot—*must not*—remain together? The past repeats itself, Cailie, and it has done so too often already. If you stay, you will die!"

"But you—you can't—" She gasped for breath, choked by suddenly welling tears. "Can't mean that you've given me all this, the memories, and now . . . You can't send me away—not when I've been waiting for you all my life! *Waiting*, damn you! You knew, didn't you, the other night, on the beach? You knew when I explained to you about the dreams, and you were too cowardly to tell me!"

Tresand turned away, ignoring her outburst. "I should not have shown you the past. I thought you would understand."

Blinded by tears, Cailie pushed to her feet, her determination fueled by despair. "But you did show me, and you can't just take . . ."

Her voice died as Tresand faced her stonily.

"Yes, I can. And I will. I have to!"

"No," Cailie whispered, swiping tears away, her eyes growing huge as she backed away. "No, you can't!"

"'Tis best for you, Cailie. 'Tis what I should have done the morning you awoke here. Take your memory of me, of all this, even of your dreams, your phantom. Then you can go back to a normal life, a safe life, far away from me, with only the memory of a vacation in paradise . . ."

Tresand closed the distance between them so quickly she did not see him move. Hands frighteningly strong gripped her shoulders, held her captive as eyes of violet fire burned into the core of her soul. . . .

Chapter Twenty-six

"No!" Cailie jerked her gaze away from his, panting.

Tresand's eyes widened in surprise, then narrowed in determination. She was stronger, already, than any mere mortal. She'd broken the hypnotic power of his gaze, had resisted the gentle intrusion into her mind, had shoved him out when she should not have had that power.

He inhaled sharply, struggling to keep hold of the resolve that would let him banish her from his existence again. He need only think back a few hours, when he had seen her lying out in the warm sun, playing in the surf, living in the gentle light of day.

That was where she belonged. He could not condemn her to an eternity of shadows, an existence in darkness, by his side. It was a future that could not be.

"Please, Tresand, don't do this! Why won't you remember the love that is between us? It can be different this time, *a ghráidh*. We can make our own future—" She broke off, startled into daring a quick glance up at him.

Tresand cursed silently, his hands clenching on her shoulders. She'd felt the sudden tension in his body, but wasn't even aware of what she'd said—or what language she'd spoken in.

A ghráidh.

The truth hit Tresand harder even than the memories interwoven with that Gaelic endearment he'd taught her so long ago. This wasn't just Cailie anymore, battling him for the chance of a mutual future. This was a soul as old as his own, even if it would be some time yet before her memories became fully integrated.

Did I 'ear a smidgen o' that lovely old Gaelic? It 'as been ages, I swear.

Tresand stiffened at the intrusion as much as at the accent. He released Cailie and stepped back from her. Damn Aramond and his atrocious timing!

"What?" She glanced up at him again, obviously still wary of his intentions, of the power of his gaze.

"Aramond."

Her brows rose. "Is he back?"

Tresand grunted in reply.

'Tis no way to greet someone, with curses! If 'tis

interrupting I am, ye might simply say so.

You are interrupting!

There was a brief silence of thought, shadowed with something very much like laughter. *I thought as much.*

Tresand dropped a quick kiss on Cailie's brow, and with a sigh turned toward the kitchen. "He's out on the terrace."

"Oh." There was wariness still in that word, and a shade of disappointment. "Are you having another private conversation?"

He shook his head and summoned a smile. "Most definitely not. You're welcome to join us."

Tresand held out his hand. Her ready acceptance, without the hesitation that was so much Cailie's, set another knife twisting inside his chest.

"Is he staying on Maui then?"

There was something hidden in her voice, something devious . . . something that fanned to life wariness in Tresand. Shrugging in reply to Cailie's question, he led her out onto the terrace.

Aramond, leaning against the railing, utterly ignored him. Instead, he bowed to Cailie, then met her eyes, grinning. "In a bit of a temper, isn't 'e?"

Cailie nodded, sharing Aramond's glance at him, her eyes filled with new knowledge, old memories. "He'll come around soon, I'm sure."

Tresand stared at her, then at Aramond. Curse them both! Cailie had found an ally, and she knew it. Vexed, he flicked the hapless palm-sized cane spider crawling up the house wall off into the bushes around the terrace.

He should have known this would happen. With her newfound memories, Cailie doubtlessly remembered Aramond. Perhaps she even recalled the time she and the old man had ganged up on him before, in that seraglio in Constantinople.

But Aramond should know better now. Their escape with her had been by the skin of their teeth that time, and disaster had found them then too. Yet he'd had five years with her, five glorious years. . . .

"Dare I 'ope ye've forgiven me for that wee misunderstanding then?" Aramond was saying, all attention on Cailie.

She smiled back magnanimously. "Oh, certainly. Actually, I—"

"Well, old friend," Tresand butted in, smiling somewhat viciously. "What brings you here at this hour? Any important news?"

"Not really, no," Aramond replied without a trace of the accent. "My life is not nearly as exciting as yours, you know." He rested his elbows on the railing of the terrace, and took in the view. "But they've started construction on a beautiful house up Hana way, with all those fancy blinds and such. Daria had the plans for it drawn up before the words had left my mouth."

"You always did like the rain," Tresand retorted, clinging to his anger. "But to each his own."

Listen to what ye're saying, Tresand. 'Tis bloody

good advice. "Always. They think me mad, to have a house built at my age."

Aramond laughed, lightly slapping his hand on the railing, while Tresand frowned at the unspoken words twined so casually with what Cailie could hear.

"In any case, I have the gold, and they've too much of a liking for it to speak their minds." *And some 'ave the gold, and no mind to keep it.*

"So you'll be staying on the island?" Cailie piped up.

"Surely will, lassie." Aramond winked at her, blithely ignoring the barrage of Tresand's silent curses.

"I do hope you'll visit often. You and—the wife?" Cailie smiled back at Aramond, leaving no doubt in Tresand's mind that she had full access to centuries of dirty tricks. The timid, shy Cailie he had greeted only two weeks ago would never, ever have had the nerve to pull something like this.

But then, she hadn't known what she was battling for.

"Aye, we'd love to. Anytime you'll have us over." *At least someone 'as their wits about them.*

Tresand shot Aramond a warning look from narrowed eyes, but the crafty old rogue was busy taking leave from Cailie, bowing over her hand. The sound of another vehicle coming down the driveway made Tresand want to throw his hands up in defeat and run for cover.

He didn't, of course. He couldn't take the

chance of Cailie finding out she had yet another ally in her cause.

"Hey, Alec, guess what! I've brought your wheels back! Bet you—" Kimo stopped dead in his tracks halfway up the stairs, gaping at the two unexpected visitors on the terrace with Tresand.

"You!" Cailie was the first to recover her voice.

"Oh, man!" Kimo managed to look extremely uncomfortable and nonchalant all at the same time. He met Tresand's hard look with a crooked grin. "Sorry, old chap. If I'd known you had company, I would've called first."

"That might be something to keep in mind for the future, *keiki*."

Cailie glared at Tresand. "Don't swear at that nice man! I'd never have found you if not for him."

Kimo laughed at her quick defense of him and climbed the stairs. "You'll know it when he's cursing, lady. And he doesn't, ever, in Hawaiian. We have this agreement, you see. He gets to call me a child so long as I get to call him old man. Grandfather."

Kimo was staring at Aramond as he spoke those last words. Tresand sighed.

"Kimo, meet Charles Dar—ville." He showed his teeth in a chilly grin and heard Aramond's laughter echo through his mind. "Charles, this is my friend, Kimo Travis. A highly valued connection, so be nice to him."

"Hi, Chuck." Kimo glanced from Aramond to Cailie, cracked a smile, then quickly faced Tresand again to hand him a set of keys.

"Truck's back, and a copy of the bill inside. It's got a new door for your bedroom in the back seat too. If you get me the keys, I'll take the Jeep down for you."

Tresand nodded, turned on his heels, and immediately turned again. Cailie was looking at him with huge, guilty eyes that weren't quite hiding her amusement.

"The keys are"—he exhaled sharply—"somewhere between here and the Jeep."

Aramond cleared his throat. "I shall go look for them," he announced officially, before turning toward the stairs and adding in a mutter, "Seems to me I saw a glimmer of light back there somewhere."

"I'd better help, seeing how I lost—"

"No." Tresand caught hold of Cailie's arm before she could follow Aramond down the stairs. "Kimo can help him. And when he has the keys, he can return the Jeep."

"But I meant to ask him—"

"Cailie . . . !"

"—if he knows a good pizza place," she continued right over his growl, smiling at Kimo. "Do you?"

Kimo's brows shot up for an instant before he recovered his cool. "Well, there's—"

"Never mind!" Tresand glowered at the Hawaiian. "Kimo—"

"All right, all right, I'm gone."

Before Kimo could reach the bottom of the stairs, Aramond's shout of "Eureka!" wrought a sigh from Tresand. Beside him, Cailie choked back giggles.

"That's closer to his time than the theory of evolution, I'd guess."

Before Tresand could reply, Kimo appeared at the bottom of the stairs again.

"I'm giving your—ah—relative a ride to his place, okay?" he called up with a grin.

Tresand closed his eyes in silent prayer. "Please do."

Seconds later, the Jeep's tires ground over the gravel of the driveway.

Sure wouldn't mind if this here family were to grow by another generation, laddie. Daria'd be delighted to have a daughter in the Blood. . . .

Tresand groaned at the less than subtle hint trailing off in his mind. Damn Aramond!

"I like your friends." Cailie smiled brightly, nudging him in the ribs. "They're so—"

"Don't say it. Please."

She met his gaze, grinning. She was winning, and not the least bit humble about it.

"Tell me, Tresand. How old is he really? Aramond, I mean?"

He gave her a crooked grin, grateful for the momentary change of topic. At least she showed some mercy . . . occasionally.

"You wouldn't believe me if I told you. Hell, I'm not so sure *I* believe him about that."

"Come on. Try me. I'll believe anything, remember? Or perhaps we could resume our previous conversation?"

Tresand frowned down on her, then shook his head. He knew when he was beaten. But in this case, to the loser went the spoils. He caught her against him with one arm.

"First, we're going to get you fed." He dangled the truck keys in front of her nose, plucked the slipping plumeria blossom out of her hair, and tossed it over the railing.

"And since we're already dressed, we might as well go out. During dinner, perhaps I'll tell you Aramond's version of the fall of Atlantis." The corners of his mouth turned up at her incredulous stare. "And after we come home—"

"No," Cailie cut in, shaking her head, a stubborn tilt to her chin. "Before we come home, I'm going to climb the banyan tree."

The smile he'd been holding at bay escaped. "My mistake," he corrected somberly. "After dinner, with a full stomach, you're going to play monkey in the banyan tree. Then we're going to come home . . . and spend the night as we did this last week. *Then*—"

"Oh, *a ghráidh*." Her arms came around his neck, but he held her back, to frown down at her and finish his sentence.

"Then, tomorrow morning, after we have talked, we will see further. That is all I promise."

Her smile was as radiant as the sun. "It is enough."

With that, she came into his embrace, her body supple against his, her lips softly parted, telling him without words of the love that drove her to battle even him.

Tresand held her, thinking of the future, and prayed.

This time, it would be different. It had to be.

Chapter Twenty-seven

The sun had almost crested the mountains. Tresand stood before the eastern window of the living room, staring at the blinds half aglow with the radiance they shut out. His bearing was stiff, his face inscrutable as he turned to look at her.

"My mortal ancestors worshipped the sun, Cailie. It was the source of life, the god of light. And I am cursed never to touch its rays again."

He looked at her, long and hard, where she sat curled up on the sofa, in her white gecko T-shirt.

"You can see that beautiful sun, Cailie. See it from the sanctuary of the shadows. But you'll never feel its warmth on your skin again. Ever."

Cailie stared at the edge of light gradually creeping downward along the blinds as the sun rose. She wanted to go out, bathe in that golden radiance one last time. Instead, she rose, crossed to Tresand, and very deliberately turned her back to the light.

"I won't need the sun if I have you."

Her voice, rough with emotion, snapped his gaze to her eyes. She saw his uncertainty, the hope buried under centuries of despair, his love for her.

Wordlessly, he shrugged out of his shirt, stood before her, motionless, a half-naked statue of white gold. She could sense the heat of his skin, the familiar musk of his body, could smell the faint perfume of the hibiscus blossoms opening with the dawn.

"You must be certain, Cailie," he entreated softly, urgently. "Very, very certain. There is no going back after this."

His voice sent a shiver over her. She bit her lip, then released it. "I am sure."

"You are afraid."

She did not deny it. Fear of living, fear of dying—they seemed as one. She could not distinguish between the nuances of her fears. But she would not dwell on them. "Aren't you?"

The whispered words snapped Tresand's composure and control. Breath rushed from his lungs, and his eyes squeezed closed as though in agony. He reached for her and pulled her against him so tightly she could not breathe.

Then his hands caught her shoulders, putting a measure of distance and sanity between them.

Still, she could hear the rasp of his breath as he struggled for control, his eyes blazing.

"Aye, *mo chridhe*. I am afraid. Of losing you again, because I have always lost you. Have always k—" He pulled away, drawing himself up straight. He would not meet her gaze. "I have always been alone, in the end."

Cailie reached up and touched his cheek, until he would look down at her. "You won't be anymore. Not if I can help it."

He shook his head, his eyes beseeching. "You are sure, Cailie? Truly, truly sure?"

Her smile was genuine, filled with gentle laughter at his repetitive question, and with achingly tender love for this extraordinary man.

"Yes, yes, and yes. In that order."

He laughed softly, his hands coming up to cup her face. "You are a delight, Cailie. Eternity with you would not be enough," he whispered softly, but drew back. "There is one more . . . consequence of this action that I've not told you yet."

She placed her fingertips against his lips, shaking her head. "It doesn't matter."

He grabbed her hand, kissed it, and nodded somberly in contradiction.

"It does matter. Remember your concern about the possibility of a babe."

Cailie stiffened, then closed her eyes and sighed.

"Yes, I remember." She met his gaze. "But you said—"

His hands came to her shoulders, tightened, halting her words.

"Because of our blood and what we are, we have near immortality, but we cannot father or conceive children." He hesitated, then released her. "It is not too late for you to change your mind."

Cailie took his hands in hers, shaking her head. "I said it doesn't matter, and I meant it. I want to be with you, to stay with you—if you will have me. That has not and will not change."

At his doubtful expression, she added with a crooked smile, "Besides, we could always adopt . . ."

She thought she saw pain in Tresand's eyes just before they closed. "Oh, Cailie!"

His arms enfolded her tightly, held her for a long, timeless moment. Then he found his voice again, found another consequence to tell her. "And you must destroy all pictures of yourself. Never have another one taken."

Cailie laid her head against his shoulder, hiding her amusement. "I thought you said you reflect in mirrors."

"I do. The danger of pictures is not that you don't show up but that you do, looking fairly much the same over several centuries."

She considered that. "Well, I didn't leave any behind, so you can rest assured."

Still, he wasn't done stalling. He set her at arm's length and eyed her warily.

"And I must tell you about food. Real food."

"Yes?" She was all ears, beaming up at him. They still hadn't had breakfast.

"Our bodies cannot metabolize it. We do not need it, have no use for it."

She smiled brilliantly. "So that's why you didn't gain any weight! Heck, Weight Watchers, move over! Here comes the new diet of the twenty-first century!"

Tresand frowned down at her soberly, not at all touched by her amusement. "It's actually a very old diet, Cailie. The Romans perfected it. Whatever you eat, you have to . . . regurgitate."

She snapped a full step away from him. "Throw up?"

"Yes."

Cailie scowled at him. No matter how ill she ever got, nausea was the worst. She absolutely *abhorred* vomiting.

God, to think of all those dinners *he* had shared with her . . .

Tears suddenly threatened to rise in her eyes, and she banned them. There had been enough tears shed. Instead, she straightened her shoulders huffily.

"You could have told me about this earlier, you know, before we went through all this fuss. I don't know what made you think that I'd be willing to forfeit all those wonderful dinners . . ." Tresand's dismay at her words was almost comical. But it served him right, for his persistence in trying to push her away from him. " . . . for a measly eternity with the man I love more than life."

"Cailie—"

She put her hand over his mouth and shook her head. "Now, if you're just about finished, perhaps we can continue where we left off when you started trying to change my mind?"

All the jittery humor drained out of her at Tresand's bleak look. Then his eyes changed, slowly, mirroring acceptance perhaps, or surrender. He took her hands in his and kissed them. Then he sank to his knees on the thick carpet, taking her with him, and in soft words, painted the path into eternal darkness.

She listened, silently, then looked up at him. "I have to—"

"Aye. 'Twill not be distasteful to you for long, I can assure you." The hint of a rueful smile played around the corners of his mouth. Cailie remembered the devastating pleasure of his touch, and believed him.

Tresand squeezed her hands once more, then rose and disappeared into the kitchen. A moment later, he returned. Cailie recognized the knife in his hand and shrank back. Were he mortal, that blade would have taken his life before.

"'Tis the sharpest," Tresand offered somewhat apologetically as he dropped to his knees before her, and put the knife aside. "'Tis not too late to change your mind, Cailie."

She shook her head. After all her brave, convincing words, she couldn't very well ask for time out to get used to this. And she was more afraid that any hesitation on her part would change his mind again. "I'm ready."

"Very well."

His luminous, violet eyes allowed no retreat. He kept his gaze locked to hers as he leaned closer and raised her chin with his hand.

Her eyes drifted shut as Tresand's mouth descended on hers, softly, lingering. It was like that first night on the beach, only this time, he did not stop. Twining her arms around his neck, she let her rising passion shut out her uncertainty and fear of what was to come, and gave herself over to the flood of fire shivering along her nerves. He trailed tiny love bites along her throat, gentle reminders of another touch, and she arched her neck, her breath breaking under the splinters of sensation.

Then he abruptly shifted away. Cailie struggled for a deep breath and opened her eyes, seeing the knife in his hand, and unspeakable anguish in his eyes.

This was the edge of the precipice.

Tendrils of fear uncurled coldly in her stomach, but she didn't care. All she knew was that she didn't want him to leave her and make her forget again, ever. And this was the one way to be sure.

She watched in still fascination as he made a small, deep cut at the base of his throat, then discarded the knife. Blood welled, bright crimson. His eyes never strayed from hers, watched every nuance of her emotions.

"Your choice," he offered quietly.

Shivering, she moved against him, tentatively. She kissed his jaw, his throat, then touched her mouth to the bleeding cut. She heard him catch his breath sharply and felt his hands clench on her back, urging her closer.

She remembered what she had felt in those nights of dreams. . . .

It did not taste like blood at all, she realized hazily. Not the coppery, cloying taste she knew. It was like—life.

His arms closed more tightly around her, holding her as she drew his life into herself. A drugging liquid heat flooded through her body, and she relaxed against him, dizzy.

The cut at his throat healed even as she watched. Cailie touched it in wonder and felt only the strong, steady throb of his pulse beneath her fingertips.

Her eyes closing, she clung to him.

"This is but the beginning, Cailie. And already, there is no turning back."

She said nothing, only nestled against his comforting strength, trusting him to take care of her, to do what must be done. To take her mortal life, so that she could awake into another.

"You would leave me with that burden," he mused softly after a moment, as though having read her thoughts. Gently he set her away to rise.

Bemusedly, Cailie watched him disappear into the shadows of the hallway, then, after a few moments, cross into the kitchen. Without him in her vision, keeping her eyes open was not worth it. She retreated into darkness, curiously lightheaded. Her body felt odd, on edge, as though it were a vessel to some violent current, resonant, vibrating.

Tresand returned long minutes later, carrying a cup with steam rising from its contents. He sank down beside her, leaned against the sofa, and shifted her into his embrace.

"Tea?" She glanced at him, then at the dark liquid.

He met her eyes and nodded solemnly. "'Tis poisoned. Quick, painless."

Cailie's breath caught, her body stiffened. Then she realized she was shaking, shaking too badly to put her hands around the cup Tresand was holding.

"Gently," he whispered into her hair, setting down the cup. He wrapped his arms around her, and simply held her close for a silent, endless moment, until she had calmed.

Then she nodded spasmodically.

Tresand grabbed her chin with his hand and turned her head toward him. He brushed her lips with his, softly, gently, so longingly that tears sprang to her eyes. Then he took up the cup again.

"'Tis an ancient path, Cailie. Socrates traveled it."

Her hands went around his, holding so tightly her knuckles turned white. The tea was cooler than she had thought. Sweet, and strong. She almost choked on it, but at last Tresand set the empty cup aside, and cradled her against him once more.

"Rest easy, Cailie. You will feel no pain, I promise you."

"Talk to me," she pleaded softly, trembling, her head nestled against his shoulder. His arms tightened around her.

"About what?"

She smiled shakily. "History. Your . . . parents?"

"Ah, yes." He sighed deeply, stroked her hair and back, soothing her while his velvety voice surrounded her.

"It was a brutal, glorious time, Cailie. My mortal father was one of the so-called pagan invaders, who came in 867 and took Eoforwic from the Northumbrians. They renamed it Yorvik, made it a Viking capital, and from it ruled for half a century.

"My father was a jarl, and it seems he took first pick of the captured local beauties, a girl with raven hair and dark eyes. I was born nine months after the eve of victory, or so it was said."

A faint smile touched his voice. "I owe him my height, if nothing more. Else I'd be sadly stunted by today's standards."

"I don't think you'd be stunted," Cailie protested faintly.

He chuckled softly. "That's because you're barely five foot four yourself."

She smiled tremulously up at him, brushed back errant strands of silken black hair that had fallen across his eyes, and traced his lips with her fingertips. "You have your mother's coloring, then. And . . . her beauty."

"Ah, Cailie, you flatter me."

She laid her head against his shoulder again and closed her eyes, comforted by the rhythmic rise and fall of his chest, the steady beat of his heart. Cold was slowly creeping up her legs toward her chest, a growing numbness that claimed more and more of her limbs.

Stark, naked fear struck her with blinding speed. She twisted in the arms that cradled her, barely moving because of the paralysis claiming her body.

"I don't want to die, Tresand!" Her voice was a hoarse whisper, more breath than sound, more panic than reason. It was all just a dream, the promise of eternal life by his side. It was a nightmare, a delusion, and she was going to die!

Tresand's arms closed more tightly around her, holding her with the strength of steel beneath his silken touch. The heat of his body blazed like a furnace against her chilled flesh.

"Hush. Don't be afraid, Cailie. I'm here. I won't let you go."

"Tresand!" An obsidian abyss was rising up to swallow her, too quickly, stealing away all sensation. Suddenly she could no longer feel his arms around her, could no longer see his beloved features because her eyes had closed and would not open again. She was paralyzed, deaf, trapped in an icy realm of darkness.

I am with you, Cailie, even here. Trust in me. And go gently, mo chridhe. *You need not fear this.*

His voice was in her head, her heart, her soul, a benediction laying to rest the fear. Then the void was complete, and her world disappeared.

Cailie had no concept of time. She floated in an ocean of night, gently rocking amidst warm waves. Dawn was an eternity away, until a gentle call drew her forward, out of the darkness.

She blinked and saw a smooth, muscled chest pillowing her head.

Her vision wasn't much different—only keener, as all her senses seemed to be. She could hear a faint pulsing of blood, and realized that it was the sound of Tresand's heart.

"Bright eyes," he greeted her softly in his beautiful, rough velvet voice. And she knew, without seeing her reflection, that her eyes were no longer sky blue, but like his now. Unearthly.

"Am I . . ." She leaned back, tilting her head up at him. Her gaze fixed on the column of his throat, on the artery pulsing just beneath his skin, and never made it to his face.

It was like she'd been struck by lightning. A hunger, a soul-deep burning, ravaged her body with sensations too close to pain. The blazing fire grew, threatening her sanity, until a sob tore from her throat.

"Gently, *mo rún*—"

She twisted frantically in his suddenly confining hold, raking his chest with her short nails. Blood welled in thin streaks. The sight of it froze her instantly and utterly, like the soul of a damned being offered salvation.

Then she began to shake in the grip of that unspeakable need, that unholy hunger. She'd not understood Tresand's words before, had come nowhere close to realizing what he'd meant when he'd spoken of the pain of hunger.

Still, she did not understand, for understanding would have required conscious thought, and she was far beyond that.

"Tresand—"

"'Tis all right, Cailie. For this first time, 'tis all right. And for sharing love. That much we of the Blood can give each other."

She stared at his chest, at the quickly drying streaks of blood, and felt her gaze drawn back to the artery in his throat. Fear gripped her as the hunger lashed her, urged her to taste the lifeblood in him until the need was quenched, until the pain had been drowned in the source of life.

How will you feel when you've killed someone, Cailie?

The memory of his words roused sheer terror in her—of losing control, of letting the hunger take her, of injuring him—*killing*.

"Don't—God, Tresand, can you stop me? I—I can't—" Her voice drowned in ragged breaths that were close to sobs.

Tresand captured her face in his hands and

brushed his lips against her open mouth. "I am stronger than you, Cailie. I won't let you go too far."

He kissed her again, aggressively, demanding a response that left no room for thought. Her hands clutched at him frantically. And still, the hunger grew mindlessly, tearing her apart.

Tresand pulled back suddenly. Cailie stared at him, dazed. She realized there was blood trickling from the corner of his mouth, and she knew, even as her own tongue made the discovery, that something had happened to her canines.

"'Tis done, Cailie." Tresand closed his eyes and slowly drew her against him, shuddering as her mouth found the pulsing life in his throat.

"God help us both, but 'tis done."

Bright eyes.
Cailie blinked sleepily in response to the soft, calling touch deep in her thoughts. She was on Tresand's bed, in his embrace, skin to silken skin, one with him, utterly at peace.

For a moment, she wondered that they should be together while the sun was bright against the shut bedroom blinds. Then it all returned, the last few hours, the years, centuries.

Her hand clenched on Tresand's chest. Her tongue worried at her canines, which were no different than ever.

"Is . . . Did it really happen?" She couldn't meet his eyes because she knew, even as she spoke the words, that the memory of the past few hours was not a dream. It was something she would never forget.

"'Tis time for you to choose a new name, if you wish," Tresand broke into her thoughts. "Many do, when they become of the Blood."

She glanced at him sideways, grateful for the sound of his gruff voice. "What was yours when you were mortal?"

He chuckled, then shook his head. "I'm not telling."

"Don't you like Cailie?" she challenged with a tenuous smile.

He met her eyes with gentle humor. "It is for *you* to choose, not me."

"I'm good at choosing names, you know," she mused, trailing her fingers across his chest. "When I was eight, I trashed Catherine Linette and only kept Cailie."

"I know."

She frowned. He grinned, even as she understood the depth of communion between them, and felt the heat rise in her cheeks.

"You have still much to learn, Cailie. And I shall delight in teaching you."

She sent him a defiant smile and flexed her hand, her nails lightly scoring the smooth skin of his chest. Then she pushed up and touched her lips to the faint marks. She paused and met his flaming gaze.

"Call me Rubie."

Rubie.

His approval was clear, in thoughts and voice,

and in the slow dawn of a smile on his lips as he pulled her down across his chest. She wriggled against him provocatively, and watched with purely feminine satisfaction as his features tightened in naked hunger.

Growling something unintelligible under his breath, Tresand hauled her against him and rolled on top of her, capturing her hands and her mouth, and she laughed even as she met his lips.

She was *Rubie*. No longer the bashful, timid creature who had searched so desperately, so valiantly for a love she thought she could never have. The memories of other lives, of love, gave her a strength Cailie had never possessed, a burning desire to live to the fullest, with all her heart and soul, each moment of her existence.

But the magic Tresand was weaving through her body left no breath for words, no will to explain to him that wondrous revelation. Instead, glorying in the dawn of this new future, she arched against him hungrily, eagerly, twining her body with his.

Love me, Tresand.

And in her mind, more intimately than any touch of their bodies could be, came the exultant promise:

I do, mo chridhe. *And I will. Into eternity.*

Epilogue

Rubie stood at the border of grass and sand, looking out over an ocean still luminous beneath a fading twilight sky. The sultry breeze tousled her hair and whispered gently against her skin, bare beneath the caressing silk of the pareu.

She felt the presence behind her and briefly closed her eyes, filled with a serenity she had never, as a mortal, dreamed possible.

But then, she no longer felt quite so human. She felt ancient, as if the world lay at her feet. Felt precious. Cherished. Loved.

The light touch of Tresand's hands on her bare shoulders guided her back against him. His arms circled her, enfolding her in the silken heat of his skin, in inhuman strength carefully controlled. His mouth brushed the juncture of her shoulder and throat, a pale shiver of fire.

You are loved, mo chridhe.

With a contented sigh, she leaned into him, folding her own arms over his. Holding him close, she was at home in his embrace while the last traces of light faded from the horizon and darkness claimed the sea.

She thought of all the sunsets, and starry, moonlit nights to come. She felt his arms tighten around her in response to her thoughts, and smiled.

Such a beautiful place to spend eternity.

TIMESWEPT ROMANCE

TIME OF THE ROSE
By Bonita Clifton

When the silver-haired cowboy brings Madison Calloway to his run-down ranch, she thinks for sure he is senile. Certain he'll bring harm to himself, Madison follows the man into a thunderstorm and back to the wild days of his youth in the Old West.

The dread of all his enemies and the desire of all the ladies, Colton Chase does not stand a chance against the spunky beauty who has tracked him through time. And after one passion-drenched night, Colt is ready to surrender his heart to the most tempting spitfire anywhere in time.

_51922-4 $4.99 US/$5.99 CAN

A FUTURISTIC ROMANCE

AWAKENINGS
By Saranne Dawson

Fearless and bold, Justan rules his domain with an iron hand, but nothing short of the Dammai's magic will bring his warring people peace. He claims he needs Rozlynd—a bewitching beauty and the last of the Dammai—for her sorcery alone, yet inside him stirs an unexpected yearning to savor the temptress's charms, to sample her sweet innocence. And as her silken spell ensnares him, Justan battles to vanquish a power whose like he has never encountered—the power of Rozlynd's love.

_51921-6 $4.99 US/$5.99 CAN

FROM LOVE SPELL
FUTURISTIC ROMANCE
NO OTHER LOVE
Flora Speer
Bestselling Author of *A Time To Love Again*

Only Herne sees the woman. To the other explorers of the ruined city she remains unseen, unknown. But after an illicit joining she is gone, and Herne finds he cannot forget his beautiful seductress, or ignore her uncanny resemblance to another member of the exploration party. Determined to unravel the puzzle, Herne begins a seduction of his own—one that will unleash a whirlwind of danger and desire.

_51916-X $4.99 US/$5.99 CAN

TIMESWEPT ROMANCE
LOVE'S TIMELESS DANCE
Vivian Knight-Jenkins

Although the pressure from her company's upcoming show is driving Leeanne Sullivan crazy, she refuses to believe she can be dancing in her studio one minute—and with a seventeenth-century Highlander the next. A liberated woman like Leeanne will have no problem teaching virile Iain MacBride a new step or two, and soon she'll have him begging for lessons in love.

_51917-8 $4.99 US/$5.99 CAN

LOVE SPELL
ATTN: Order Department
Dorchester Publishing Company, Inc.
276 5th Avenue, New York, NY 10001

Please add $1.50 for shipping and handling for the first book and $.35 for each book thereafter. PA., N.Y.S. and N.Y.C. residents, please add appropriate sales tax. No cash, stamps, or C.O.D.s. All orders shipped within 6 weeks via postal service book rate. Canadian orders require $2.00 extra postage and must be paid in U.S. dollars through a U.S. banking facility.

Name _____

Address _____

City _____ State _____ Zip _____

I have enclosed $_____ in payment for the checked book(s).

Payment **must** accompany all orders.□ Please send a free catalog.

FROM LOVE SPELL
HISTORICAL ROMANCE
THE PASSIONATE REBEL
Helene Lehr

A beautiful American patriot, Gillian Winthrop is horrified to learn that her grandmother means her to wed a traitor to the American Revolution. Her body yearns for Philip Meredith's masterful touch, but she is determined not to give her hand—or any other part of herself—to the handsome Tory, until he convinces her that he too is a passionate rebel.

_51918-6 $4.99 US/$5.99 CAN

CONTEMPORARY ROMANCE
THE TAWNY GOLD MAN
Amii Lorin

Bestselling Author Of More Than 5 Million Books In Print!

Long ago, in a moment of wild, rioting ecstasy, Jud Cammeron vowed to love her always. Now, as Anne Moore looks at her stepbrother, she sees a total stranger, a man who plans to take control of his father's estate and everyone on it. Anne knows things are different—she is a grown woman with a fiance—but something tells her she still belongs to the tawny gold man.

_51919-4 $4.99 US/$5.99 CAN

LOVE SPELL
ATTN: Order Department
Dorchester Publishing Company, Inc.
276 5th Avenue, New York, NY 10001

Please add $1.50 for shipping and handling for the first book and $.35 for each book thereafter. PA., N.Y.S. and N.Y.C. residents, please add appropriate sales tax. No cash, stamps, or C.O.D.s. All orders shipped within 6 weeks via postal service book rate. Canadian orders require $2.00 extra postage and must be paid in U.S. dollars through a U.S. banking facility.

Name_____
Address_____
City _____ State_____ Zip_____
I have enclosed $_____in payment for the checked book(s).
Payment <u>must</u> accompany all orders.☐ Please send a free catalog.